CH00685633

DEATH COMES IN THREES

Also by Michael Jecks

The Art of Murder series

PORTRAIT OF A MURDER *
LANDSCAPE OF MURDER *

The Bloody Mary mysteries

REBELLION'S MESSAGE *
A MURDER TOO SOON *
A MISSED MURDER *
THE DEAD DON'T WAIT *
DEATH COMES HOT *
THE MOORLAND MURDERERS *
THE MERCHANT MURDERERS *
MURDERING THE MESSENGER *

The Templar mysteries

NO LAW IN THE LAND
THE BISHOP MUST DIE
THE OATH
KING'S GOLD
CITY OF FIENDS
TEMPLAR'S ACRE

Vintener trilogy

FIELDS OF GLORY
BLOOD ON THE SAND
BLOOD OF THE INNOCENTS

Shanghailanders series

ONE LAST DANCE BEFORE I DIE

* *available from Severn House*

Visit www.michaeljecks.co.uk for a full list of titles

DEATH COMES IN THREES

Michael Jecks

**SEVERN
HOUSE**

First world edition published in Great Britain and the USA in 2025
by Severn House, an imprint of Canongate Books Ltd,
14 High Street, Edinburgh EH1 1TE.

severnhouse.com

British Library Cataloguing-in-Publication Data
A CIP catalogue record for this title is available from the British Library.

ISBN-13: 978-1-4483-1380-8 (cased)
ISBN-13: 978-1-4483-1381-5 (e-book)

All Severn House titles are printed on acid-free paper.

MIX
Paper | Supporting
responsible forestry
FSC
www.fsc.org   FSC® C013056

Typeset by Palimpsest Book Production Ltd., Falkirk,
Stirlingshire, Scotland.
Printed and bound in Great Britain by TJ Books,
Padstow, Cornwall.

Praise for the Bloody Mary Tudor mysteries

"Full of period details, bawdy behavior . . . and clever deductions"
Booklist on *Murdering the Messenger*

"Fans of the series will enjoy Blackjack's familiar quick wit and appealing joie de vivre"
Booklist on *Murdering the Messenger*

"The comical hero provides an amusing instrument for exploring the mores and history of the period"
Kirkus Reviews on *The Merchant Murderers*

"An amusing mystery replete with historical tidbits and fascinating local descriptions"
Kirkus Reviews on *The Moorland Murderers*

"Plenty of historical detail, loads of twists and turns, and a hilarious tale of criminal ineptitude"
Kirkus Reviews on *Death Comes Hot*

"Steeped in the rich, bawdy background of 16th-century London . . . Enough suspects and red herrings to keep mystery fans intrigued"
Booklist on *The Dead Don't Wait*

"An enjoyable jaunt through mid-16th century England . . . The novel's energetic pace never flags"
Publishers Weekly on *The Dead Don't Wait*

About the author

Michael Jecks is the author of fifty novels, including the acclaimed Last Templar medieval mystery series, modern spy thriller *Act of Vengeance*, and eight previous Bloody Mary mysteries. A former Chairman of the Crime Writers' Association, and founder of Medieval Murderers, he lives in northern Dartmoor.

www.michaeljecks.co.uk

This book is for John and Sue
With much love

PART ONE

Jack Blackjack's Tale

ONE

Tuesday 9th August, 1558

I suppose many people will just say, 'Oh, it's his own fault. He deserved everything he got.' But that's hardly fair, is it? I did nothing wrong. Not on purpose, I mean.

What if I was with Mistress Susan Appleby? It is not against the law to be friendly with a neighbour, after all. No, we are all encouraged to be neighbourly, to act as friends in the community, as companions within our parishes. And if she and I grew a little over-amicable, well, maybe that was the result of an abundance of enthusiasm for our Christian duties.

Admittedly, she was no longer my neighbour by that time.

Mistress Appleby was the wife of Saul, who lived opposite me until I moved away. It was in part to remove myself from the risk of gossip and embarrassment that I had taken a new house a short distance away in another parish. That, of course, did not work out, as I was to discover when I took up residence and was soon accused by the interfering bully, my master John Blount, of murdering one of his agents. But I will not go into that here. That affair is still somewhat raw in my memory.

In any event, it was a catalogue of errors, as far as I was concerned. And, consequently, it was me, the unwitting innocent, who was blamed and forced to suffer the indignities and trials of being an assumed perpetrator, rather than the unwitting victim.

How did it all begin? I suppose it was when I arranged a purely friendly meeting with my old neighbour. Susan Appleby is one of those women who is difficult to miss. She has a face that calls for a man's attention, a figure that brings beds and pillows to mind, and a wayward eye that tempts and challenges all at once. In short, she is a life-enhancing bundle of joyous lust.

As I had already discovered, the woman was not entirely satisfied with her husband for a few reasons – and being a wench with a keen interest in pursuing her own interests and pleasures, she was not slow to take advantage, let us say, of satisfying herself when opportunities arose. She would occasionally become more than a little friendly with other men. I was one of her more popular distractions, I think it's fair to say and, of course, when I was available she would have no interest in other diversions. There is no doubt that I could eclipse her other amusements.

My association with her had got me into trouble before, and I was wary of further involvement after the matter of Rachel Nailour's murder, but time was heavy on my hands that summer, since there was little, apparently, for me to do; my master did not maintain regular contact with me. He was spending much time away from the city with Lady Elizabeth, half-sister to the queen, while I spent much of my waking hours in the stews, my favourite gambling dens and taverns. But after some while the temptations of the bawds in the whorehouses palled, and even the best brandy started to taste sour. Familiarity leads to tedium. I need novelty and freshness. Thus it was that, when I happened to meet with Susan one afternoon – entirely accidentally, I must add – it was a delightful event.

'Mistress Appleby,' I said, 'I hope I see you well? You look as sweet and pert as a fresh rose.'

I have always been gifted in the manner of speech with women, as you can tell.

'Master Blackjack, is that a new suit of clothing?'

She could hardly avoid noticing my new garments: a rather impressive deep-blue jack and hosen, with red piping, and pale silken lining in a fresh, apricot tone. It was, I have to confess, extremely striking. But a man of my situation requires clothing that matches his importance. I discovered some while ago that my position in Lady Elizabeth's circle made suitable display important.

So, I struck a pose, bowing low with the elegance I had learned before my current profession, when I was concentrating more on an occupation as a dipper, taking men's purses to see what they held. I had a natural skill at the art, which was what originally led, by a circuitous route, to my present career.

There were always moments of anxiety in those days, of course. I knew many times of extreme concern. I do not refer to the concomitant issues which redound upon a man of my profession, but rather the terrors that arose from the dire political situation. 1558 was a year of significant turmoil from the very outset, because of the war.

After meeting with my delightful companion and arranging for a mutually satisfying assignation the following week – at a location in Clerkenwell far enough away from both of our houses to be safe from unwanted witnesses – we parted. I confess it was a happy Jack who strode along the lane to my house, the threats and tribulations of politics left behind. I was contented with the prospect of a good mattress-walloping with Mistress Appleby.

It was hard in those days, you will recall. All over London there was a winding sheet hanging over all, a sense of grim trepidation. I would not say fear, exactly, but definitely concern. The queen's health was a cause for perturbation – how could it not be? She was living without her husband, for King Philip had trudged back to Spain after involving England in one of his regular squabbles with the French, and that war cost England dear.

For those who have read my past chronicles, there will be an understanding of my military competence. Of course, for others, it may surprise you to learn that I have been, in reality, a soldier, and I look on military affairs with the clear sight and understanding of a man who has been in battle. Admittedly, I have never commanded soldiers, but I have stood with others and defended our city. It is experience of that nature that marks a warrior, and naturally I can comprehend warfare better than the average fellow.

So, I can tell you that the war with France was a disaster. It cost a lot of money, led to the distress of many London merchants and others, and finally broke the poor queen's heart, because in January it led to the loss of England's proudest possession, Calais, by those perfidious and treacherous French.

That they should steal away the principal jewel in the queen's realm was no less of a shock to Queen Mary than to the rest of the people. Of course, with English skill and martial prowess, we would soon win it back, but nonetheless it was a blow, and one felt all the more keenly by the queen herself.

Owing to my unique position and knowledge of the court, I was aware of other matters that did not immediately come to the attention of less well-connected subjects. First and foremost was the health of the queen. She had been determined that her marriage would be fruitful, owing to her religious devotion, and must have enticed her husband to her bed for a little pillow-pummelling whenever he appeared in her realm. Some months ago, when he arrived to persuade the queen's advisers and members of the House of Lords that he required England to join Spain in the war against France, she had wearied herself (and him, I have little doubt) in the honourable task of providing her kingdom with an heir to the throne. Indeed, I was to hear that she was so convinced of the success of this latest sheet-tangling that she had made a new will.

There are some people who, no matter how often they are confronted with reality, continue to believe that one more attempt, involving the same efforts, will this time produce, as if miraculously, an alternative result. Thus it was with Queen Mary. She had endured numerous pregnancies, according to her own perceptions – one of which, the first, lasted for more than ten months – and each time she was forced sorrowfully to accept her error. This time, however, she was persuaded it would be different. This time, she was convinced, she had been fertile, and was holding a babe in her womb.

For her, it must have been some compensation for the grim loss of her continental territories, to feel that she bore a child. It was not the feeling about the rest of the country. For most, it was difficult to continue to earn enough to put food on a plate. Not that I had that sort of problem, of course. I was fortunate enough to be a respected citizen with a high income in my chosen profession. Not that I had chosen it for myself, precisely. It was more a role I fell into.

Or was pushed into.

In any case, that day I met with Susan because I was on my way to my old accommodation, a rather large hall opposite her home. This house was a good-sized, two-storey building with a large jettied second floor that overlooked Susan's bedchamber – which was how I had first grown aware of her. When a fellow wakes and is presented with a view of a comely woman in the chamber opposite in a state of undress, it is difficult not to pay her attention.

Especially when the woman concerned is built in the manner of Mistress Susan: on the lines of a warship, if you know what I mean – all billowing cloth and firm upper castles.

But I digress.

That day I was returning to my old haunts because I had not sold my old house. Rather, I had taken the advice of a friend, and was renting it out to a passably wealthy young fellow.

His name was Geoffrey Vanderstilt, and he had recently set up in business as a merchant in London. He came from somewhere called Amsterdam, and naturally I was reluctant at first to take him in as my tenant, because who can tell how reliable a foreigner might be as a tenant? But he persuaded me that he was moderate in temperament, that his living was sufficient to pay the high charge I demanded, and since he was of a clean-looking, well-mannered form, I believed him to be a worthy guest in my house – especially when he passed me a purse with coins that rattled most fetchingly as proof of his value.

However, that was some weeks ago, and recently I had heard nothing from him – not to mention that the coins had not been appearing as regularly as I wished. Thus, today I was making my way to my old home to confront him and ensure he was not a scoundrel who took me for a fool.

I knocked firmly on the familiar door, and soon was shown into my rooms by Vanderstilt's gaunt bottler. He was a scruffy soul and spoke with an incomprehensible accent. Vanderstilt, I knew, had a similar, thick tone. I have heard men from Saxony and other outlandish places, and this sounded similar, but even harsher. Lots of glottal expectoration and other noises that emanated from the back of his throat, all of which made conversation more than a slight trial.

The Dutch, I have often noticed, do not have the dress sense of their English counterparts. I was unsurprised to see that the same could be said of their servants. This man was clad in dark, but faded clothing, with stains of food on his breast, and breeches that looked as if he had been kneeling in mud. He was the only servant, I believe, so perhaps he had a number of duties that involved fetching salads and vegetables from my garden. That was a thought, too. I had not given permission for my garden to be raided. I must add that to the monthly fee.

He was one of those people who seemed to scowl at the world. A fellow with the grim outlook of a suspicious gaoler, I thought, as if he suspected me of being a felon, damn his eyes! It was tempting to pass a comment and advise the man to watch his manners, but he had a knife at his belt, and although my courage is second to none, I had no wish to be censured for brawling with the lower classes. It was better to ignore him.

In any case, I took myself to the chamber and waited. Presently, I heard steps on the flags, and Geoffrey Vanderstilt soon appeared, calling for his bottler, Peter. After a few moments, the bottler arrived and was instructed to fetch wine. He returned bearing a tray holding a pewter jug and two goblets. When we had been served, he set the tray on a sideboard, standing inconspicuously, like any good steward, while his master and I chatted about inconsequential matters. At last, I came to the point.

'I am persuaded, Master Vanderstilt, that you are late with my fee for the tenancy of this house.'

'It is a matter of enormous shame,' he replied, smiling but with a show of sadness in his eyes. 'I find I am from a little embarrassment suffering. It is a short-term affair, you understand, but it does mean that I have this month difficulty.'

'That is a great shame,' I said, and toyed with my goblet, scowling. You must know, if you know my chronicles at all, that I always attempt to be accommodating, and dislike confrontational disputes. However, this was a matter that was close to my purse, you might say, and I was not prepared to wait for *his* monetary embarrassments to be cured. I had my own expenses to cover – I had not yet paid for this new suit of clothes, after all. 'You will understand that I am very happy to help . . . and yet I have my own priorities, as you will appreciate. I cannot leave my property in your hands without compensation.'

He paled. Master Geoffrey Vanderstilt was a man of perhaps six-and-twenty years, with thinning fair hair and complexion of a pale form. On a woman, I would have found his effeminate appearance appealing, but I have to confess that on a man I found it less so. He had the look of moderate feebleness, and that was to me a surprise, because most merchants I have known have been larger-than-life, full-bodied men with the appetites of gluttons. Their epicurean tastes could only be satisfied with the most expensive food and drink, and with an ostentatious display of gaudy wealth, yet when I looked around me at the parlour, all I could see was evidence of an ascetic economy. Even his clothing was as austere as a priest's – one of Henry's odious new priests, I mean: not a man like the local catholic vicar. The new rash of young priests were more likely to clothe themselves in pure gold, if it were possible.

'I do understand, Master Blackjack,' he said, and there was a certain trepidation in his manner as he motioned to Peter to replenish our goblets. 'Perhaps, if I were to pay a little more per week until my business improves?'

'How much more?'

He looked blank, so I quickly suggested another fifth, and continued before he could protest, 'How much longer before your business improves?'

He still had a shocked look on his face, and was so flummoxed he took a few moments to register my question. 'How long? Er, it is all dependent on the vagaries of politics in my country. I believe my ship is in port held because of the Spanish administration. This happens sometimes when the officials have reason to suspect that some of the items on board might be heading to an unfriendly state – and the war with France has led to great confusion about exports. All my goods should very soon be here, but actually *when*, I am fear I do not know . . . A *fifth*?'

His mood was all too plain now, as he snapped at his servant to hurry with the wine. The old fellow moved sluggishly, and I was less than impressed by his demeanour. He all but tipped wine over my lap. From his expression, I could tell he was not happy to hear about his master's finances. Perhaps the fellow was concerned he might soon lose the roof over his own head?

'You cannot tell me when I am to be paid?' I am a fair man, as all who know me can assert, and now I saw that a compromise was required. 'Very well, then. I will accept two fifths extra for the last month and all months until your ship arrives and you can settle the full debt. And then the rent of my house will remain at one fifth above our past arrangement. I cannot be expected to sit and wait and merely hope that your ship will appear. What if it has sunk?'

If he was shocked before, now he was appalled. '*Two* fifths? Surely one should be sufficient.'

'Two. You have left me waiting for my money for too long. If you had but come to explain that there was a delay, in preference to making me come here and learn for myself, I could have been lenient, but you did not. You chose to force me to come and discover the facts for myself. Do you have no spare money? When you came to negotiate the tenancy, you had a full purse of gold.'

'Alas, that has been much depleted since I had to purchase goods to be sold on the next shipment,' he said, and he did look quite mournful.

'You mean you have nothing with which to compensate me now?'

It was a ridiculous situation. I had expenses of my own to be repaid, as I explained irritably and at length.

'I can only offer my apologies,' he said. 'The war means trade is disrupted, and there are always other merchants seeking to disturb my business. Only the other day, I heard that another merchant had sought to halt my ship. I wonder me whether he has paid an official to delay my ship so he can benefit.'

He went on about merchants and the deep skullduggery that they employed to prevent other mercantile vessels from leaving ports, so that they could complete their own orders knowing that prices were higher since they possessed a monopoly. Such acts were illegal in England, of course, but these foreigners had no compunction in fleecing poor Englishmen. They would corner a market, if they could, and the lack of competition would mean rising prices, and then, when Vanderstilt managed to dock his own ship, the prices would tumble because the market had already paid for the inflated prices of the other merchants. However, he also suspected that enemies of his, competitors in business, were learning of his ships and their cargoes, and were paying officers in the ports to hold his ships back, so that his profits would reduce, perhaps even putting him out of business.

It did make me wonder whether I could take a share, were Vanderstilt to corner his market – but it was a fleeting thought. First I needed to be reassured that he could pay me what he already owed.

When I asked who this other trader was, of course, I learned it was yet another foreigner.

'He is Lewan de Beaulieu, an older fellow. He also is from Amsterdam come. He is a man with few morals, little hesitation about violence and deceit, I fear. I had thought him a friend, a companion of my father, but now . . .'

That was all one to me, I considered as I took up my stick and walked to the door. His bottler was standing at the wall, glaring at me, and I threw him a black scowl of my own as I reached my door. It was in part his lack of attention that annoyed me so much, leaving me, a guest in the house, to open the damned door, but as I pulled it wide, I could not help but turn, after stepping through the doorway, and vent my anger.

'This may be how you conduct business in your own country, but here in the queen's realm we rely on honourable men paying their dues when they are set to be paid, not telling their creditors that they *may* pay at some time in the future! I expect that extra money quickly. And in case I see nothing, I will advise people that this house is available for rent once more.'

'But, Master Blackjack!'

'I will hear no more! You have left me disappointed, and I must make remedy as best I can. That must mean my recovering your debt to me by any means I can.'

'Master Blackjack, I am sure that—'

'Nay, master. My money.'

'I shall see whether I can borrow the sum, but you have to give me a day or two.'

'I will expect it in two, then. With the added two fifths.'

'But—'

'Not another word! I should never have trusted a foreigner. I expect money, Master Vanderstilt. Money! If I do not receive it, you will leave my house or I will have your hide!'

Not exactly the worst threat in the world, obviously. You can tell that I was out of sorts from the way that I lost my temper, and you see, I did have good reason.

My master, John Blount, had been less and less keen to speak with me for the last months, ever since his mission sending a female agent to the continent had failed. Another had caused that project to be closed, but he yet suspected, I think, that I might have had some involvement in the subsequent death. Of course, it was nothing to do with me, but Master Blount was nothing if not committed to his singular interpretation of other men and their motives and actions.

In my case, he had firmly persuaded himself that I was in fact a keen slayer of other men and women. I was hired on that express understanding, all owing to an unfortunate experience I had had during Wyatt's revolt. I was seen in the presence of a dead man, and Blount formed an entirely mistaken opinion about my responsibility for the death.

Erroneous though his conclusion had been, there were benefits to his impression. First there was the new suit of clothing every year; then there was the property in which I had just harangued the Dutchman, God burn his ballocks; and the regular bonus each time I fulfilled his requirement of removing some poor soul from this vale of tears and misery. He was delighted with my expertise, and I was more than happy with the money. It meant that I could afford to hire a thoroughly competent killer on my own behalf, and then ensure that I was many miles away from any murders when they were committed, causing Blount on several occasions to look at me askance, as though wondering how on earth I had managed both to be in the presence of a corpse, while also being witnessed in a tavern, entertaining a wench, or playing dice in an alehouse. As a consequence, he grew more and more impressed with my abilities.

However, that all changed when his chosen agent was murdered, and no matter how I swore that I had nothing to do with it, my protestations only served to convince him that I must have been responsible. It is a hard cross to bear, this matter of supposed infallibility, when on occasion it leaves others to wonder whether I had in truth been the man involved. But I was not!

He did send messages to me indicating that the queen's half-sister, our mistress Lady Elizabeth, was taking up much of his time. That, I was sure, was an excuse, and not a particularly good one. After all, she had been forced to keep her head down after the queen's husband had tried to force her to marry a man she did not wish to, and since then, so I had heard, she and her sister were barely on speaking terms. Elizabeth had returned to the countryside, and Mary remained here in London, nursing her sisterly hatred. No doubt she was missing her husband. He had come to stay with her in the last year, but only for some three months. As soon as it became clear that his plans to wed Elizabeth to a friend of his had come to naught, and once he had agreement of the English parliament to join the war against France, he meandered back to his home country. England took the decision to join the war reluctantly, although it was aided by the ridiculous invasion of Sir Thomas Stafford, who took Scarborough with two ships of English and French mercenaries.

I mean, why *Scarborough*? Surely they could have thought of a better, more propitious landing? Anyway, the fools were caught and Stafford executed in short order. However, after all that excitement, the king left for Europe and Mary was forced to await his return while praying and hoping for the security of her child. Elizabeth, from all I had learned of her, was meanwhile politicking from her manor some leagues from London, and that suited me well. The farther from me she was, the safer I felt. She was undoubtedly a beauty – but the carvings on my handgun were also elegant and beautiful. It did not change the fact that the gun was still deadly.

So, my master was spending time away from London. Perhaps that was a reason for my isolation from him.

Perhaps. But I knew Master Blount to be a man who would bear a grudge, and that was a cause for concern, for if he were to decide to cancel our arrangement, I would be without income or a master, and that, for a man in the year fifteen hundred and fifty eight, was a fearsome prospect.

TWO

Only two days later, Raphe, my incompetent and troublesome servant, grumblingly went to the door when a visitor knocked. He stood there a few moments, and I could hear him rudely accosting whoever the visitor was, and then the door closed and I could hear his steps making their way towards me in my parlour.

'Some scruffy old foreign git wants to see you,' he announced.

'Where is he?'

'He's not English. I left him outside,' he said.

After the usual remonstrations and telling the fool to bring in the stranger, I was soon confronted by Peter, Vanderstilt's servant. 'Master said this for you,' he said, dropping a leather bag on my table.

I had, at the time, been involved in trying to work my way through my expenditure and coming to the worrisome conclusion that, were I not to find some money soon, I might be forced to leave London for a period before some of my creditors came to visit. One or two of these were not the type of men to accept a simple response of *I don't have it right now, but if you come back in a week.* They were more likely to take a hand or a foot in part payment.

Inside the leather pouch was the money to pay for all the debt so far, and more for the subsequent month.

'His ship has finally arrived,' the steward said. He peered about my chamber with every sign of disgust. Perhaps he was another protestant. He did not appear to like my choice of decoration. I like bright colours and had gilt painted on my carved seats and panels, and he seemed to shy away from my silken tapestries.

'Good,' I said, waving him away, and weighed the purse in my hand before counting the coins. With his cash, I could at last look to paying off my debts without risking hands, feet, broken limbs or other impediments to enjoyment of London's life. Satisfied, I pushed many of the coins into the bag and happily took my key to my strongbox. I carefully stowed the money in the chest and struck a stern pose. 'Raphe, under no circumstances mention to your friends that this money has come in, understand? Not even your wench in the kitchen.'

'Why?'

'It is not for you to question my decisions,' I said loftily. The simple fact was, I knew several of Raphe's friends, and they were the type to take an inordinate amount of interest in any man's wealth. And as for the hussy who acted as cook for our household, I had no great impression of her either. She had materialized from the street, and while she was moderately comely, she was a terrible God-bothering young draggle-tail. She could recite the Gospels whenever it suited her, so it seemed, and yet was content to go and rattle her bubbies with Raphe every night without bothering the vicar with legalizing their marital bed. She had skill with a pan and copper, I admit, but as to whether she was genuinely loyal, I was yet unconvinced.

'My affairs are my own,' I said. 'You will keep them from others. Nothing you hear in this house is to be shared with your drinking companions or others.'

There would soon come a time when I would regret that firm command to Raphe.

But I was unaware of that as I relocked my chest, took my pleasantly weighty purse in hand and fitted it to my belt, and then, whistling, left the house and entered the street.

It was a busy day. I saw several loitering vagrants who stood languidly leaning against walls and trees, and ignored them as a man of quality must. I thought nothing of them, in reality. Beggars and knaves were commonplace. Such rogues were a cause of concern to most men of degree. New laws were constantly being created to try to control such feckless individuals. I was aware of some of these fellows watching me, and I have to confess, I hurried my steps somewhat. Not that I was scared, you understand, but it is best not to tarry.

My road in St Helen's parish was just off Bishopsgate, and I walked up to the Vine, a pleasant inn not far before the city's gate. I was looking forward to an assignation with a delightful young maid called Alice, whom I had met some weeks before, and with whom I had begun to enjoy a weekly tussle. She no doubt saw me as a route out of her life of drudgery, and were I not quite such an important man, she may well have succeeded in convincing me, mainly because of her inventiveness and enthusiasm for bedchamber battles. Sadly, she was not of my station in life. No one could accuse me of elitism, but she was of a lower class. She would have to continue working as housemaid to her master, a rather superior man called George Loughgren, who fancied, so she said, that he was a great politician, and man of enormous authority. There were many who fooled themselves into such beliefs. I assumed he had a minor role as alderman, or perhaps worked with the mayor – wiping his arse for him, no doubt.

It was while on my way to the inn that I was accosted by a young man of perhaps two-and-twenty years, who looked me up and down with a sneering gaze. I returned it with condescension. I doubted he was of the same quality as a gentleman of my standing.

A man of my position has to become accustomed to the puerile insults of the less fortunate. And when I say less fortunate, I mean the lazy and the good-for-nothings who frequent the cheaper gaming houses, of course. There are so many vagabonds and Egyptians about London nowadays, all attempting to cozen poor gulls into parting with their money, that this one barely merited more than a glance. However, to my surprise, he fell into step at my side.

'I knows you, master.'

'How fortunate you are.'

'You was at your old house two days since.'

'I have visited my house often,' I said. Then I realized what he had said. 'What of it? Are you following me, fellow?'

Usually that sort of accusation would make a scoundrel retreat. They know that a gentleman of my status and importance would be prepared to defend himself and his honour by beating a vagabond unmercifully, and with good reason. Some of these fellows have no idea how to behave in the presence of their betters. I used to see it when I was living roughly on the streets, in my past when I was a pocket-dipper, and others would treat those with money as mere fools and knaves, even when they were severely beaten.

Now, of course, I was one of the wealthy, and this was a piece of human garbage.

'Begone!' I commanded him, and struck a pose, chin in the air, hand near the hilt of my rapier. 'Go, before I teach you manners at the point of my sword! I am not interested in your vapid maunderings.'

'Oh, you will be,' he said, and there was a nasty look in his eye.

I strode on, choosing to ignore him, and it was as I passed through the alley towards the Vine that I glanced to my side and saw that the churl was still there.

'It is good to see that you can walk about the city a free man still,' he said, seeing my gaze.

'How *dare* you! I am a gentleman!'

'Oho! A *gentleman*, eh? I knows all about you, *Master* Blackjack. I knows how you used to earn your living, all about you and the others living by the river. And about that house you rent to the Dutchie now.'

'What of it?' What did he mean, *all about me*? Did he mean he knew I was an assassin?

'It would be a shame if people was to hear that you had been threatening the man, wouldn't it? Master Vanderstilt, I mean. People might come wondering how serious you was. Might think, "What sort of a man makes threats like that?"'

I gaped. After all, this was two days after my interview with my tenant, and I swear I had all but forgotten the threat I had given. In truth, it was some moments before I realized what he was talking about.

'You was seen and heard,' he mentioned again. 'It'd be sad, was news of your arguing over money to come to the hearing of those what distrust you.'

That was enough. I grasped the hilt of my sword and drew the first foot free.

My companion was not the sort to show fear, sadly. He twisted his lips and shook his head. 'You think to scare me? Not a good choice, master. I think you'd do better thinking how to cut your

losses, not seeking to make enemies. You show your blade in
public and you'll be arrested. That would delay your dalliance
with the maid, wou'n't it?'

'What do you want?' I rasped.

'I just want to give you peace of mind. Why should you be
afeard? Us wants a chat, that's all.'

I could only gaze at him with bemusement and confusion.
Although I am noted for my quick mind and ability to think my
way out of problems, this man seemed to speak in riddles. I had
no idea what he was actually saying. 'A chat about what?'

'Give me a little of your time,' he said again, and this time
his voice held authority. 'Or news may spread of how you earned
your money.'

We were at the time still in the alley that led to the Vine, and
there were several men about us. Seeing a narrow way, I strode
inside, the rascal behind me. As I went, I felt his hand on my
shoulder.

It was enough to raise the natural, instinctive anger of a gentleman.
I span, starting to draw my rapier, but on turning, I stopped. 'Come!
What is this all for? There is no need to fight,' I said.

What had curbed my martial spirit? The sight of the two brutes
who now stood with him, one tapping the palm of his hand thoughtfully with a heavy blackthorn club, while the other took to glowering
at me with a face so broken and brutal, I could only assume he
had been involved in more fights than the bears at the Surrey pits.

'Now, Master Blackjack, we'd like to speak to you,' my first
interlocutor said with a vile smile. And yes, his accent and tone
had changed. He stood a little taller, as if he had been play-acting
the part of a rogue. Somehow he reminded me of an adder
confronting a chick.

I studied him more closely. He stood some five feet six inches
tall, and was as thin as a whip. It was obvious that he was no
match for me, but of course he was not alone, and the other two
bullies with him were more than capable of overcoming any
defence I might attempt.

In past chronicles I have spoken of the grim, grey, damp, foul
and bleak tin-mining moors of Dartmoor. On those moors there
are certain moorstone outcrops which the locals call 'tors'. Some

appear to have been hewn into fantastical shapes, such as the faces of men, or of enormous creatures lying atop their hills like dragons hoarding gold. These two men were formed from a similar mould as those stones. Their speed of thought may have been as slow as a rock's, but they were able to give the impression of strength and resilience. I swiftly decided I did not wish to test my sword on their hides. From the look of them I would blunt my blade. Or snap it.

Instead I spoke sharply, with a degree of hauteur. 'What do you want with me?'

'Don't squeak, little mouse,' the first said snidely, and the two moorstone figures sniggered. 'If you'd listened, you would have quickly understood. I am called Bagnall. Perkin Bagnall.'

He looked as though that should have impressed me. It did not. Well, not as much as his companions. A name doesn't hurt you. The two trolls at his beck and call may well do.

He continued: 'We knows a lot about you, Master Blackjack. Such as, you was at your house to demand money from your tenant, and you made threats against him, didn't you? A man should be more careful. There are people might hear such threats and speak out.'

Yes, this fellow was warning me of blackmail, it was plain. He wore a nasty smirk as he said all this, while I imagine I was wearing a frown of concentration. He must have thought it was a glare of growing rage, because he actually took a half pace back, and hastily continued, 'Don't try nothin' foolish. It's pointless.'

If only he had known the truth – I was in no manner capable of attacking him and his companions. A large block of ice had settled itself in my bowels.

As for the suggestion that some may wish to speak out – what did he mean? The obvious inference was that he knew of those I was thought to have murdered in my capacity as an assassin – and that was the conclusion I swiftly reached, that he was threatening my exposure. That gave me pause for thought. I had been convinced that my profession would remain secret, but this rogue was apparently aware of it. Who could have let that slip? My master? Unlikely. My servant? He wouldn't dare. Who else knew?

However, whoever it was, the main concern I had just now

was the fact that this fellow seemed to know. It was deeply troubling. And for the moment I was unsure how to proceed. The leader was gazing at me with sublime confidence, clearly thinking that they had me by the curly hairs; however, I have always been bold. This was only a temporary setback. I would learn how he had discovered me.

'I don't know what you mean,' I bluffed.

I also have a very honest face. It has been my saviour on many previous occasions. Today, though, it seemed to carry little weight with the rogue.

'Not only your house, neither. We've followed you other places, master, ain't we, boys?'

'A boring occupation, no doubt,' I said.

'To Master Loughgren's often enough, ain't we? You like his house, do you? Or him?'

Loughgren, as I think I have mentioned, was the man who employed Alice. And suddenly I realized – these men were seeking to threaten me not about my supposed career as an assassin, but with exposure! If Loughgren were to learn I had been bedroom-bouncing with his maid, I might receive a drubbing at the hands of his other servants. No doubt this trio wanted payment.

The relief was overwhelming. And if they thought they could threaten me in that manner, they were mistaken.

So, I smiled at the ruffians, and was relieved to see that their concerns were assuaged. It was there in the eyes of the man before me, even if it wasn't in those of the two tors behind him. But then, you don't expect stone eyes to register any kind of emotion. They were probably just waiting for someone to give them a command they could comprehend. From the look of them, that could be a very long time.

Seeing that, I made use of my usual courageous approach. I thrust the rapier back sharply into the sheath, removed my hand from the hilt, and then suddenly kicked with all my strength at the codpiece of their leader.

It was deeply satisfying to see how his eyes widened, and then his hands reached for his injured plums, while his body arched as if trying to prevent them flying past his backside.

I was disinclined to remain and enjoy the sight. Already there was a loud graunching sound, and I was sure it would be the two tors beginning to move towards me. Rather than wait to see how fast moorstone could move, I chose to demonstrate how quickly an anxious assassin could run. I took to my heels, pelting down the narrow alley.

There was a sharp right turn, and I thundered into the wall ahead and pushed myself away without slowing my pace. My feet moved as quickly as a galloping horse's. At another little alley I turned right again. That meant, by my reckoning, that I was now pointing straight at the Vine, and beyond a slight dogleg I could see the welcoming sight of the inn's yard ahead of me. I was safe.

I ran on, glancing behind me occasionally, but there was no sign of my pursuers, and I slowed slightly, panting with exertion. I was concerned that the trio might reappear at any moment, and the idea of confronting them again just now was deeply unappealing.

It has often been said that I have the senses of a cat. My agility, speed and quick perception of dangers have always impressed people, and just now, while I was unable to see the three, I had the firm conviction that they were there, just out of sight. It was alarming, but I turned and traipsed over the last few yards to the inn. I would have to explain my tiredness – I was not exactly spent, but I was weary. However, my innate genius came to my rescue. After all, I reflected, no woman can resist a tale of her man's heroism, and were I to tell her that I had been set upon, and had bested three or four . . . or possibly five vagabonds who had attempted to steal my purse . . . or knock me on the pate, to take my suit of clothing and my purse, perhaps – it was all one. The six tried to rob me, but with my rapier in hand, dagger in the other, I beat them off. I injured three, and their four companions instantly fled. Or knocked two down, and injured the other six? I glanced down at my sheathed sword. Oh, yes, I cleaned the blade on the shirt of their leader.

With that story firmly fixed in my mind, I sauntered inside.

I am, of course, a gentleman, so I will not go into the details of my entanglements with Alice. Suffice it to say that my courage inspired her to greater enthusiasm and excitement than I had known her to display before.

She was a fresh little thing, Alice. And she loved to chatter after her first exertions. Now she tried to make me jealous, telling me of other men who had tried to entice her into their beds, men in the street who attempted to grab her and force her to kiss them, or who offered her money – as if I would be jealous of them, when I was myself enjoying all her best favours already!

It was a weary and worn Jack who left the chamber some hours later, while Alice remained in the bed, ravished and languishing from our joint exertions. It has been said many times by my past lovers that I am most competent, and I knew I had acquitted myself well. A last glance behind me as I closed the door showed her to best effect: a slender figure, with fair hair tumbled all about her shoulders, one breast peeping from the sheets. Ah, she was a sight to spur a man to ever greater demonstrations of adoration – but she was, I must admit, tiring.

The staircase from that upper chamber was a little slippery and took me straight down into the inn's bar area. In a comfortable parlour, I ordered a large cup of wine to refresh myself after my efforts, and was enjoying my drink when I heard a cry from outside. When I went to the door, I saw that there was an altercation in the yard near the gates leading to Bishopsgate. A small group of men was brawling. It was nothing to do with me, however, and I returned to my seat, finished my drink, and beat a retreat, before Alice could appear and demand a return match of which I felt less than capable just now.

Instead, I took up my hat, which I had set aside, threw down a few coins for the innkeeper for the wine and the room, and made my way outside. I no longer had the impression of being followed, and I strode on with vigour, but the crowd effectively blocked my route, and rather than try to pass through them, I returned by the alley through which I had entered. It struck me that the group of rogues were hardly likely to have waited all this while. Rather, they would have made their way elsewhere in the hours between our encounter and my return.

And so it proved. I soon found myself on Bishopsgate, where the crush of other people was enough to reassure me. After all, no one would attempt to injure a fellow in broad daylight with many witnesses, unless they wanted to be caught and held captive in a gaol or slaughtered out of hand. The London mob is a terrifying sight when roused, and a man committing a murder before them will invariably force a response. Yes, some would watch and admire the purpose of a man, his elegance, his economy of effort, perhaps, or the speed with which he struck. But others would be more keen to clobber him over the head with a mallet, since the murder would mean locals paying dearly in taxes for the infringement of the queen's peace.

My walk home was slower than usual. In part, yes, it was the effect of the strenuous exercise at the altar of lovely Alice's body, which necessarily had an impact on my pace and speed, but there was also the matter of the three brutes to consider. I was mentally invigorated after my mattress duels, and my mind could return to the three waylayers and their demand.

It was blackmail, of course. They had almost said as much; they wanted payment to secure my secret, else they would broadcast my liaison. It was notable that the fellow had two brutes with him – were they his usual companions, or were they hired as his bodyguards in case I should turn to a simpler, cheaper remedy than acquiescing to his demands? Hirelings, I concluded. He looked so little like a gentleman who could afford to maintain a household, these two must be paid by the hour.

Which meant I really only had the one man to contend with. That scrawny bag of bones who dared to threaten me was the only one with a brain, I felt sure.

Well, I had no desire to meet the man again. I doubted that he would take my parting shot with any form of gratitude. If he was like me, he would deprecate that kick and wish for an opportunity to return the favour. I was keen not to give him an opportunity.

I had no need to travel abroad until my assignation with Susan Appleby, so I chose to remain indoors for a few days. Having instructed my more than deficient servant, Raphe, to keep an eye on anyone who could be watching the house, I retreated to my parlour with a flagon of wine, and rested.

After my efforts with Alice, I felt the need of it.

THREE

I t was late morning the following Saturday that I was due to meet with Susan Appleby. I had sent a message to Alice, but there was no reply. It was not surprising; the maid would have to bide her time, since she was fully engaged as a working servant in her household, but it was annoying to be ignored, or so I felt. Perhaps her master, Loughgren, had resented her afternoon with me. It was not as if maids were granted afternoons away from their households. It was irritating, especially since I was keen to arrange our next assignation. However, I determined that on the Friday it was impossible for me to leave the house in case Bagnall and his two vagabonds were outside. So I waited patiently, and by Saturday I felt secure enough. Besides, I was full of excitement for the bouts to come. Susan is an excellent bedfellow, and I was looking forward to a mutually wearying encounter, as I instructed Raphe to step to the door and ensure that no one was waiting outside. I had already loaded and set my handgun in my belt, where I could quickly bring it to bear.

On hearing his confirmation that all looked well, I slipped out, past the great church of St Helen's, and back to Bishopsgate, where I procured a horse from a stable I knew, and trotted off, out of the city and up into the countryside. It had rained the previous weekend, and the waterways and ditches were full, the sun sparkling off the water. In such glorious weather, the journey was most pleasant, with pedestrians and riders alike smiling and cheerful in the bright sunshine. For my part, I was in a mood to be tolerant of all. I had my money from Geoffrey Vanderstilt, and while I had heard nothing from Alice, there was still the strumpet Susan to entertain me.

On reaching the inn, I soon saw her sitting decorously in a corner. Two patrons of the bar were attempting to engage her in conversation, but she was more than capable of fending them off, I knew, so I went and haggled over the price of a room for the afternoon, and had soon engaged a good-sized bedchamber over the front of the establishment. As soon as I had the key, I walked over to Susan, and gave the two suitors a cool glance as she took my hand and followed me, all meekness and sobriety, to the stairs. I had not climbed halfway before she was panting in my ear and yanking at my codpiece.

'Woman! Wait till we are installed in our room,' I pleaded, but she only chuckled throatily, and thrust her little hand inside, almost making me collapse there and then.

Somehow I managed to escape, and hurried up the staircase to the room allocated, where I entered, pulled her inside, and locked the door before she attacked me again.

This time I was prepared, and cast off my hauberk, sword, belt, jack and codpiece. She rocked back on her heels, already clad only in her chemise, and then we were grappling on the bed, and – well, as a sophisticated gentleman, I shall leave us there.

Suffice it to say that two hours later, I was exhausted, and Susan rose and prepared to leave me and return home. We parted on contented terms, she with a demure kiss and a prayer that we might meet again very soon. Standing there in the doorway, she looked as chaste as a nun. No one could tell what a ferocious vixen she was in bed from looking at her.

'It was a shame, wasn't it?' she said as she pulled on gloves.

'What?'

'Your tenant. His disappearance.'

I gaped. 'Disappearance?'

'Yes.' She glanced at me. 'Didn't you know? He went out two days ago and never came back.'

'I had no idea. What happened?'

'Last Thursday he went to a friend's house for a meal, but did not return. His servant hasn't seen him since. He was supposed to visit another merchant in the city, and he visited that house, but by all accounts, he left there in plenty of time to get home. Geoffrey disappeared between his house and yours.'

'But that is terrible!' I blurted. I was dependent upon the money from my tenant. Without it, I had a hole in my finances until I was instructed and paid for a fresh assassination. But, as

I have explained, I had received little by way of encouragement that I could expect further commissions. It was a horrible situation in which to find myself. 'Where can the fool have gone? I hope the constable is aware and searching for him?'

'Of course. But there is no indication of foul play. Nobody saw him, and no one has discovered his body, so it's thought that he must have run away. Everyone knows he owed you money for the house, for it's said you were overheard threatening him. Others were owed too.'

'No, he paid me,' I said absently.

'He didn't pay his other debts. I know he kept saying that the money was coming shortly, but perhaps he thought it wouldn't come soon enough, and he chose to run back to Holland. That was where he came from, I think.'

'And this was Thursday?'

'Yes.'

I cast my mind back. Of course, that was the evening after I had been happily rattling Alice at the inn. But although Vanderstilt had paid his original debt, I was depending on his regular payments. Susan slipped through the door, blissfully unaware of the horrible revelation she had imparted. I had debts of my own, in God's name. If this poltroon of a foreigner had simply grabbed his things and run, what was I to do?

The first thing I must do was find out what had happened. I gathered myself, dressed, and rode back quickly to the stables, where I deposited my mount, and then hurried over to my old abode.

It was a house apparently in mourning. When I hammered upon the door, it opened slowly to display the features of the old bottler, Peter.

'Where is he?' I demanded.

The old man's greying features were twisted and he exhibited every sign of distress. If he had only been a little younger, I could have been sympathetic. Younger men tend to be faster to resort to their fists. Since this fellow was so ancient and feeble, I felt secure in my ability to overawe him.

'Where is your master?'

'I do not know,' he said, gazing at me from eyes bleary with age.

I knew how to deal with such recalcitrance. I kicked at the closed door. 'Don't give me that, churl! Has he taken his clothes? His money? His belongings? No? Then he must mean to return! Where has he gone?'

'He went out to visit a customer, but he never returned.'

'Which customer?'

The old man gave me the sort of look a gardener would cast at a slug. Eventually I learned that his fool of a master had gone to see a certain Sir Edmund de Vere to discuss business, but that he had not returned.

'You must have some idea – did you not ask Sir Edmund's household whether they knew what had happened?'

Of course not. The bovine fool could not imagine such a presumptuous course. I continued, trying to restrain my rising frustration, 'Where is his office? Where does he work?'

The old man led me up to the room that had been my own strongroom. There he took a key from the ring at his belt and opened the door.

I studied the lock with interest, and then I took the key from him. He tried to hold it back, but I was stronger, and jerked it free. His head lowered, as I thought, in submission or acceptance of his subservient position, and I looked at the keys.

'This lock has been changed!'

'Perhaps my master did not trust that another key was held by someone.'

'Only I had another key,' I pointed out. Then I realized his insult. 'You mean to suggest that I might break in and burgle the house? *My own damned house?* Yet he trusted *you* with all his keys? Why would he do that?'

'Mayhap he felt I was with his keys and money safer than others might be.'

'You villain! You dare insult a man of my standing?'

He said nothing to that. Obviously being confronted by a gentleman was unnerving for him. I tossed the keys back to him and stepped into my strongroom.

Little had changed. There was a new table, with a chest behind it. On the table sat a pair of quills and ink, while a pot with a spoon in it held sand for drying wet ink. After a show of reluctance, the servant shuffled forward and opened the chest. Inside there was no money, only a selection of papers that spoke of the wealth Geoffrey Vanderstilt was bringing in with his ships. There were also a number of notes itemizing his personal debts, with money owed to merchants, tradesmen, a master of defence, and a number of ship's chandlers and other fellows of that sort. I riffled through a few. Most were to moneylenders, some to Lewan de Beaulieu and other merchants, some to his vintner – which was a shocking sum. The man must have had the belly of an elephant from the look of the wine he consumed!

'Where is his money?' I demanded, aghast. The money he had sent the previous week, I had thought, meant his ship had docked, and that he had money. Had he spent it all? It had not occurred to me that there would be no money here in his strongbox.

'I do not know, but wherever it might be, it is his.'

'I need my rental money for the month.'

'He paid you for last month and this when I brought the money to you last Thursday,' he asserted accurately enough, damn his eyes!

'Yes, but there are other expenses, and if he wants to be able to return here, I will need the next month booked and paid for,' I said. A listener might have said I sounded unconvincing, perhaps that I blustered a little, but the fact was, I was obviously in the right of it, and was due more money.

He disagreed. Perhaps he thought I sounded unconvinced. It is certainly true that I was a little unsure of my position. But it was my house, and I was within my rights to demand payment in advance. Especially if the house's tenant had picked up his bags and fled. True, he had left behind a strongbox with proof of all his debts – but most men would be happy to leave all their debts behind.

'He will be halfway to Holland by now,' I said glumly. 'He has taken his money and fled. You will have to clear off out of my house while I seek a new tenant. I'll sell his goods to try to recoup some of my losses.'

'He will return.'

'Really? Where is he, then? I think he has run away. Did he have problems? Women? He certainly had enough debts.' Unconsciously my eyes turned as though I could see through the walls to Susan's house opposite. Had the harpy Susan taken a fresh lover from my old house? It would not surprise me if she had. She was ever eager for a romp.

'No, he had no problems of that sort.'

'Right, well, give me those keys. I will need to see what has been taken.'

'No, master. These are his, and I will hold them,' he said.

'I think you will find I have the right to demand them,' I said, and I squared up to him, fixing a stern glower to my features. I have been told that my stern looks can terrify even hardened warriors.

Not, apparently, in this case. The man, unperturbed, hooked the keys back on to his belt. 'No.'

I snatched at them, and to my astonishment the old man moved like a snake. In terms of speed, I mean, because his arm came down and blocked my grasping hand, and he turned his left side to me, both fists raised in the unmistakable stance of a professional fighter. 'I said *no!*'

Seeing he was determined, I gave him a conciliatory smile and stepped back a pace. 'Friend, I did not mean to insult you,' I said, rubbing my forearm where he had struck it. 'But this is my house. I have to ask for the keys. If a door is locked, I must have access. You say your master will return. That is all well, but if he was knocked on the head on Saturday and his body dropped into the river, what then? Do you expect to be permitted to live here rent free until his body is discovered? It may never be. Too many men have been dropped into the Thames and never seen again. He may be one such.'

'You seem to know much about murder.'

'Me? No! No more than any other man,' I protested. 'Now, the keys.'

A little while later I left.

It was apparent to me that it was more diplomatic to allow the old fellow to keep the keys. He clearly felt a loyalty to his foreign master, and was most reluctant to pass them to me. That was all well, I felt. Besides, he looked as though he could best me even when I was armed with a sword and he had no weapon.

So I departed my house empty-handed, and as I did, glancing up the street, I saw a familiar face. It was that of the tor who had not possessed a club when the two moorstone blockheads accosted me with their master.

Seeing him, I was instantly convinced that it was time I was on my way, and even as he lumbered upright from his leaning position, I turned and took to my heels at the fastest rate I could go.

These fellows were infuriating. They must have known that I would return to my old haunts, and were prepared to leave a guard outside my house until that moment. But what did they want from me? A simple matter of blackmail, is how it had appeared to me then, but now a more thoughtful Jack was reconsidering. They had known I had been back to my house; they knew to watch for me. The question was *why*?

In the absence of my master, John Blount, there was only one man I felt I could speak to.

But first, I had to dislodge my persistent pursuer. I hurried to the river, and managed to gain the attention of a wherryman who took me over the water to the Surrey side, and then, by dint of hurrying down a series of alleys to London Bridge, I took a second wherry to near the Tower, where there was a landing stage.

From there, I managed to make my way home, a thoughtful Jack, wondering what on earth could have tempted these fools to follow me. They wanted to blackmail me as an assassin, so perhaps they were following in the hope of catching me in the act?

All I knew was I needed advice and help.

FOUR

Sunday 14th August

Next morning, as soon as I had attended Mass, and received a filthy look from the priest for my irregular appearances, I made my way to Rose Lane and knocked at the familiar door.

'What do you want?'

I have spoken before of Mark Thomasson. He was one of those fellows who is the living proof that a man of intelligence has no need to satisfy other men's visions of fashion. As a philosopher he cared nothing for any conventions of dress or conduct. His hair was awry, his gown had stains from experiments, or perhaps soup and gravy, all down the front. There was a significant burn hole at the breast, surrounded by a spattering of smaller ones. He told me he had been divining the best mixture of saltpetre, charcoal and brimstone to make explosive powder, when something had gone rather wrong.

His expression was ever charmingly baffled, like a schoolboy presented with a theory of . . . something difficult. His constant companion was a huge, drooling hound called Peterkin, whose rumbling growl made the plates on the sideboard rattle when I entered his chamber.

As always it was filled with the sort of rubbish that belonged in a midden. A helm with a bullet hole at the temple, a series of bones from some creature, a huge telescope on a tripod, bows, guns, a crossbow, harness, a breastplate with two holes punched through, a second helm, this time with a vast dint in it . . . I have seen frippers' stalls more orderly. Somewhere beneath all the accumulated items were tables and chairs, I believe, although I had to take that on faith. None was visible.

'Jonah! Fetch wine.'

His irascible old servant snarled something and was off, returning as slowly as only a geriatric like him could manage.

When Mark was seated, and I was perched on the corner of a desk which he had cleared for me, he nodded to me encouragingly. 'How may I serve you?'

Jonah came back while I was speaking about the three men. 'Do you know of any reason why they might be following me? I thought it was just money they wanted, but now . . . surely after two days they would have gone in search of an easier gull to blackmail. If they are still after me, I wonder whether there is more to this.'

He agreed. 'Yes, it hardly seems likely that they would be pursuing you for swiving a maid.'

'What other reason could they have had?' I scoffed – and then gaped as the obvious struck me: the man Bagnall had hinted at knowing much about me. Could he have learned of my position for John Blount as remover of obstacles to Lady Elizabeth? I was her assassin, and if they knew that, their silence might be worth a lot to me.

How they could have come to know my position under John Blount was unimportant. The clear fact was, that my position did not scare them or cause them alarm. I mean to say, most would consider carefully before attempting to threaten a known assassin, after all. He might well view their demands for ransom as a matter to be easily dealt with by a simple remedy, such as steel to the breast, or a swift garrotte in a dark alley.

It was enough to make me swallow with a cold, clammy sensation of impending disaster. 'Perhaps their interest was due to politics, or some other intrigue.'

I have known Mark Thomasson for many years now. His was the brilliant mind behind the solving of the cipher when I was in the unfortunate position of being suspected of murdering an important messenger. More recently he has helped with other matters, but this, I felt sure, would test him to the full.

He frowned. 'Politics? Hmm. There are rumours that our queen is unwell. She announced her pregnancy last August, I think. A twelvemonth since. In March people began to talk about her pregnancy, saying that it was no more authentic than her previous assertions, and I have heard that physicians are whispering about her health. I know that there are rumours that she has written a new will.'

I had heard that too. My master, John Blount, was a member of Lady Elizabeth's inner circle of advisers, and over the spring and summer he had regularly disappeared from the city to go and visit Elizabeth wherever she may be at the time, whether to Hatfield or Brocket Hall, or to travel as far as Longleat to meet with her cofferer, Thomas Parry. I never liked him. The Welshman was too smug and self-satisfied for his own good, and I was fully aware that he would not hesitate to see me executed. He would stand at the gallows cracking nuts while I died, I expect, and call for more wine. That was the sort of man he was. Having said that, he was utterly devoted to Lady Elizabeth, and would have crawled over red-hot coals to protect her. Or, rather, he would have been willing to sacrifice any number of others to try to keep her safe. John Blount was the kind of fellow who would always be certain that only his brain was agile enough to see how to do so, and perhaps he was right.

Matters were coming to a head for the queen. She was unwell, as all could see, and she was, I believe, aware that something was amiss. Perhaps she was growing to understand that her reign would not last much longer.

Mark frowned. 'What might she have put into her will? Could she be foolish enough to try to rule from the grave? Perhaps she might consider a stern injunction upon her subjects to obey Philip, her husband. Perhaps a similar instruction that all must continue in the Catholic faith, no matter what. Or even move to ensure that Lady Elizabeth might never take the throne? It would be most instructive to see what was in that will.'

'What does that have to do with me?'

'Oh, possibly nothing. Nothing. So, these men came to you and you think they know you are an assassin for Lady Elizabeth, when such knowledge is only granted to a few. And if they did know, they could easily inform the queen, and see you arrested and taken to the Tower. But they have not yet sold you to the queen's questioners; that must mean that they are not necessarily her agents. Nor, necessarily, that they know your position as assassin. You may have misconstrued their desire to see you.'

'Which means?'

He shrugged. 'Well, it may mean you will live a little longer than if they were agents for the queen or her husband.'

I felt that slab of ice in my bowels once more.

'The question really is,' he continued thoughtfully, 'what do they want from you? Other than money, of course. Perhaps you should go and speak with them?'

'*Speak* with them?'

Admittedly, I had not in fact mentioned the fact that my boot had connected with the man's cods, but even so, the mere fact that this Bagnall was threatening to blackmail me was a bit of a clue, I thought, to the fact that it might be hazardous for me to try to speak with him and his companions. After all, it was plain enough to me that they were threatening to expose me to Alice's master. She would lose her place, but I might get a whipping.

His words did give me pause for thought, though. Was that their meaning? I had rushed to assume that they considered me a dangerous opponent. Was it possible that they had some other form of blackmail in mind? Or did they simply mean to rob me? They had known I had visited my old home – perhaps they knew that Vanderstilt's money had come in, and they sought to take a portion of my rent? But no – if they were that assured, they would have knocked the bottler on the head. He would be an easier foe than me. At least, at first sight he would be. As I had discovered, he was less a bottler than a master of arms. Possibly the leading member of the trio had tried to take the purse from the old man, but had soon found himself bested, so in preference he sought me out to take my money from me instead. Did it matter? They were prepared to assault me in the street – or an alleyway – to demand money by menacing me. And whatever it was that made them think they could take my money, my going to them and speaking with them was hardly likely to end in a favourable result for me, so far as I could see.

'It would give you an opportunity to discuss the affair with them,' Mark said, nodding to himself. 'Then, at least, you will be better informed to know how to proceed.'

I gave an indeterminate sound, which led to a loud and alarming rumble from beneath my legs. When I glanced down, I saw the enormous head of Peterkin below me, jaws open and a little trace of drool falling on the floor. His teeth were very white, I noticed. I resolved not to make any unnecessary movements or noises.

'Perhaps such an opportunity would not be too dangerous,' I managed after some moments.

'It is always best to understand the motives and desires of others,' he admonished. 'How else can a conversation be fruitful? If you only have one side of an argument, you have a declaration. With both sides discussing, you have rational debate.'

He was, as I have mentioned, a philosopher. I was not persuaded. 'If their sole desire is to rob or injure me, it will be difficult to hold a rational debate with them,' I pointed out.

'Ah, you will find everything can be resolved using logic,' he said, waving a hand airily.

It was, I felt, easy for him to say that.

'What if they decide against logic? They may not be philosophers.'

He looked troubled to hear that. 'Ah, true.'

'And my tenant has disappeared,' I said, and explained about Vanderstilt.

'That is interesting,' he mused, his chin on his fist.

'What should I do?'

'I would suggest you speak with your tenant's friends and business associates. Perhaps one of them could help.'

After talking it through with him for a little longer, I left with the matter unresolved. Mark's only suggestion was that I should speak to Vanderstilt's friends – perhaps also the man Lewan de Beaulieu, whom my tenant's servant had mentioned – and go to the three wayfarers and ask what they wanted from me. But the three were the issue that absorbed me as I walked homewards. If I were to do as he suggested, I had no doubt that I would be robbed, and beaten, and blackmailed as well. It made no sense for them to be demanding money unless they knew about my job as an assassin, and if they knew that, they held my life in their hands.

I didn't want to be beaten, I didn't want to be robbed, and I didn't want to live knowing that the three held my life and safety in their hands, for if they were determined to blackmail me, they were money-farmers. A farmer would always come back to the same cow for more milk, day after day, and in the same way, surely these three would return to me demanding more money every week until I was entirely spent – and then what? Likely they would sell me to a thief-catcher or constable for their final payment.

No, it was not to be supported.

Making my way towards Ludgate, I became aware of a prickling at the hairs on my neck. There was nothing I could see that merited concern when I looked about me, but there was some kind of nervous sense that I was in danger. I am a man with experience of such sensations, and it felt to me that I was being followed, but when I glanced about me, there was no sign of a familiar face tracking my steps.

I don't know whether you have experienced that kind of thing, when there is nothing obvious, but you are sure that your instincts are correct. Of course, some four years ago, I had been here, and the rebellion against Queen Mary's marriage to Philip of Spain had come to the gates of the city itself. And this was where I had been when Wyatt's mob were finally forced to admit defeat. At the gates of the city, when he strode to the gates and asked the citizens of London to join him, he was met with jeers. He lost his head – literally – when the queen caught him.

Perhaps this anxiety was merely a remembrance of that day, and the end of the poor Kentish fools who followed young Wyatt? But that made little sense. I had been up this road many times since that day, and never had the slightest intimation that there was anything amiss.

On a whim, I turned into a side street heading towards the river. I have always felt that the Thames was a soothing sight – perhaps because it carried so much effluent, detritus and corpses that a brief glimpse of the foul, muddy waters was enough to make the rest of the world seem a brighter, cleaner place.

That feeling would not leave me. Worse, as I stood staring across the river, the sense of something dangerous approaching would not leave me. Rather, it grew even as the sound of footsteps grew louder.

'Master Blackjack. Kind of you to come down here.'

I turned, so scared I could not even make a squeak of protect. The voice belonged to the enormous moorstone block whom I had seen standing outside my old house. He now stood over me, peering down like a . . . well, like a giant peering at an ant to squash.

His fist rose.

I ran.

I have been an expert in running for most of my life. My slim figure, my practice since my youth, and the fleetness of foot earned from years of escaping constables and bailiffs, all merged to make me as swift as a terrified hart. I sprang away, and could almost hear the swoosh of his fist as it missed my face, but then I was head-down and flying across the beach, avoiding the darker patches of mud in which, I knew, I could become mired. Up ahead there was a rickety bridge of planks over a gutter which brought much of the ordure from St Paul's to the river. The stench from it was so foul it made me blench, which just goes to show that even the most religious types still shit like any other men. I have always said that if a fellow is alarmed by a man of authority in a position of power, one need only bring to mind a vision of that fellow on the privy. He sits with his hosen about his ankles just like any other, and the product of his squatting is as noisome. Thinking of that always makes even the most intimidating man seem less frightful.

Be that as it may, I was over those rotten planks like a bolt of lightning. They were green and slimy, as you would expect of planks washed daily by the tidal flow of the river, but when I reached the other side, I realized my error. I was in an entirely walled space, and to escape from here I must either climb the wall, or swim. I cannot swim. And the wall's stones and pilings were as filthy and slippery as the planks of the bridge. I turned in time to see the tor stepping up onto the planks.

Have you ever been in an accident? If you have, say, been thrown from a horse, or fallen from a great height, or suddenly been accosted by a vagabond with a cudgel, you will know what I mean.

Here I was, standing in a small area of only a quarter acre or so. Even if I attempted to run to the water, to escape by rounding the wall, it would mean galumphing over Thames mud. I would barely make five yards before my pursuer had caught me – and if he was even slower and failed, it was likely that we should both become enveloped in mud and held there until we drowned with the rising waters. If I tried to clamber up the wall itself, I would undoubtedly be caught.

When such situations strike, I have always found that the event leaves an imprint forever on the mind. It is burned there, like a brand seared into wood. Time itself is halted, so that every moment of exquisite horror must be relived for as long as a man must live. Not that it would last long, were this walking rock to catch me. I was firmly convinced of that.

'Stop, Master Blackjack! Perkin wants to talk to you, that's all.'

I had no idea who this fellow was, and was not of a mood to listen in any case. I was too petrified. Instead I attempted to find an escape.

He stepped onto the plank, which squeaked in protest. I could see it bend. With a bleat of terror, I pulled my sword free. I wished I had had the foresight to bring my handgun with me, but that was far away in my house. Why hadn't I brought it today! Pointing my blade at him, I tried to enunciate the words 'God's pains, I will fight!' but the only sound came out as a sort of strangled rasp. Even I was not sure what I said.

The moorstone's face cracked and I could distinctly see two teeth. Others were missing. He took another step, and I bleated again, with less optimism than before. And then his smile sort of flickered. It was there one moment, and then consternation overwhelmed the levity. He looked down, just as I heard it. A distinct cracking sound, not harsh and sharp like a dry twig; this was more like a bone breaking. I have heard enough of them in my time, and there is a sort of sogginess to such a noise, which is horribly unpleasant.

A broken arm or leg is without a doubt deeply unpleasant. It means a man will be in pain for months, and probably crippled for life. This, however, was worse. Recalling other unpleasant events that appeared to happen very slowly, I once was left hanging to the walls of a midden, with the stench of a tavern's excrement overwhelming me as a man attempted to make me fall and drown in it. There can be few more terrible ways to die than that.

As he was about to learn.

*   *   *

The man tried to leap for it, but too late. Or perhaps his attempt was enough to shatter the last splinters which bound the plank together. Whatever the reason, his legs bent to jump, but when he straightened them in his last effort, the planks snapped with a dull sound like a stone slapping a pond, and his eyes widened in horror. I could swear he hovered there for a moment, like a hawk. Time paused, as though he was hanging between Heaven and Hell – and then he disappeared.

As I mentioned, this sewer came from St Paul's. It was a fast-flowing brook, full of the contents of the privies at St Paul's. However, it was also fed by an offshoot of the River Fleet, which flowed past the privies and took the unwanted waste away from the cathedral and out to the Thames. So this bridge collapse left my opponent falling some five feet or so into a river of foulness. His arms flailed, and for a moment I was transfixed by the sight of his eyes, round as pennies with horror, as he gripped the edge of the wall about the sewer, but then his feet slipped and slid on a century of shit, and his eyes reflected a kind of desperate realization that his life had always been shit, and now it was to end in shit. His eyes begged me to rescue him, but even as I considered reaching down and reluctantly gripping his wrist, two considerations struck me. First, were he to live, there was no assurance that he would not attempt to kill me again. Second, he was covered in sewage. I hastily withdrew my hand and watched as he was washed away into the Thames. Which was, I suppose, some relief, since at least those waters were, in relative terms, more pleasant as a final resting place.

He splashed and wailed, his head appearing and then sinking several times, but the flow of the river soon took him away, and just before he passed from sight, I saw his body become still, his back to the sky.

That was when I realized that I was still in an area that was enclosed, and now there was no bridge.

It was some while later that I heard voices and, by shouting, managed finally to enlist the aid of two student lawyers who were passing through the gardens above the wall.

They had lunched well, from the evidence.

It was some little time before I could get them to look over the wall and talk to me. They had been staring, I assume, all about them, wondering where my voice came from, until one suggested that I might be in the river.

Peering over the wall, they were intrigued by my appearance, demanding to know why I had reached that specific area of riverbank. One, the drunker of the two, was convinced that I had been dropped there by a wherry. His companion, a ginger-haired lanky type, was more interested in what had tempted me there, no matter how I had arrived.

After at last getting through their fog of wine or beer, one of them caught on and went to fetch a man with a ladder or rope, and soon thereafter I was on the top of the wall, knocking the worst of the mud and slime from my new suit. It was enough to make me despondent. After only a short while, my suit was already marked. I would have to hope that my maid, Cecily, was as efficient at cleaning cloth as she was at cooking.

At last I could leave and I made my way past St Paul's Cross to the tavern just beyond. Here, I knew, Humfrie would often stop for a whet when he was not busy.

Humfrie – how does a fellow describe Humfrie? He is an almost invisible man. I don't mean that he is literally hidden from the naked eye, but he is one of those fellows who is easily ignored. A man who could stand in the midst of a large crowd, and yet still be unobserved by all about him, a figure a little taller than me, but hunched. Nobody would notice him at a small gathering. He was as unobtrusive as any servant, just a mere figure standing quietly, and not worthy of attention. It was one of his greatest skills, this fading into the background, because Humfrie was my associate.

Yes. As an assassin, I suffer from two faults. One is the intense dislike of pain, most of all that inflicted on me. However, I also have a revulsion at the thought of killing people. I can do it. I have done so, probably, when fighting to protect London from the rebels, but that was at distance, not close to, not up close. That was why the tor had terrified me, even though I had a sword and he no weapon other than his hands. I would possibly have died at his hands. He was one of those brutes who seems specifically created to injure others, whereas I am designed not to harm any creature. This is a failing in a supposed assassin.

For these reasons, I was tempted to refuse the offer of a position when John Blount originally proposed it to me. If he had not threatened me at the time, I would not have accepted. And then, when I realized the value of my contract – a house, annual suit of clothes, access to money, to women, to society – well, by then it was hard to admit to the truth, that I could not murder on command. Instead, I hired Humfrie, who was father to a maid I was seeing at the time, and he agreed to take on the dirtier side of the business for a share of my fee. Since those early days, we had been jointly responsible for a number of deaths, but I was careful always to ensure that I was far from the actual murders, and with many other people, so that I always had a firm alibi.

Humfrie now peered at me over the top of his leathern tankard with a frown. He had the sort of face that was like a roadway map that has been used too often. There were creases within creases, and wrinkles that flourished like branches and twigs on a tree. Just now his expression was bleak, and he set his drink on the table and leaned back, the candlelight throwing his face into shadow. Only the glint of his eyes flashed occasionally.

'Describe them again,' he said.

'The two brutes were cast from the same mould. Both tall, about five feet eight or nine, with faces like statues. Their arms were strongly muscled, and they had short brown hair, caps, jacks and threadbare hosen. The other was their leader, I think. He was skinnier, but with strength, you know? Like a blacksmith. He said he was called Perkin Bagnall.'

He shook his head, indicating the name was unknown to him.

'Hair colour?'

'I don't know. Mousy, I suppose. He had a thin face, sort of like a man who's not enjoyed the very best of food all his life.'

'Describes half the scrotes in the city,' he said pensively. 'Did he have a scar or birthmark? Anything to distinguish him?'

'Not that I remember. But his eyes – they were very keen. Fierce, even. He scared me.'

'And you kicked him hard?'

'Oh, yes. He won't forget that in a hurry.'

'You should stay at home a while.'

'Which home?'

'Either. They know where you live, don't they? They can keep an eye on both houses with ease, and go after you wherever you try to hide from them.'

'What should I do? I can't just sit in the house and wait for them to come and kill me!'

'I can come and help you,' he said consolingly, but with a certain edge, as if he thought I was being unreasonable. I thought my panic perfectly reasonable.

'You'll come and guard me?'

'I will come by and see that you are safe, and remove any of those who seek to hurt you.'

And beyond that, he would say no more. It did not calm my concerns.

This was not ideal. I confess, I would have preferred to think that I had ten or fifteen men to come and guard me at all hours, rather than one who would appear occasionally, when there was nothing better for him to do. A full-time guard was preferable.

Yet Humfrie was different. He was a professional in every way, a cool, collected assassin who would take infinite efforts to remove those whose continued presence was thought unnecessary, but with the minimum of fuss and as little pain as possible. His intention was to bring his victims to their end, ideally without their even realizing they had died. In addition, I knew him to be as effective as a guard. He has protected me before, you see.

So I left the tavern with a little more of a spring in my step. I felt considerably happier to know that Humfrie was to be on hand, were I to need him. I suppose it was that which made me feel confident enough to change my mind. After all, the man who had followed me the day before had been washed away with all the other garbage in the Thames. I was presumably safe for a while.

Mark had suggested talking to the three men. Now there were two, but I didn't feel it would be sensible to visit them and attempt to explain how the third would not return to them. He had also suggested talking to Lewan de Beaulieu, and other competitors to Vanderstilt. He could have a point there. But how should I introduce myself? It would take some thought to consider how best to conduct an enquiry there. And so, I considered it preferable to wander up to where Alice lived and see if she was prepared to arrange another assignation. I had a need for her young body again.

However, first I returned to my own house. The giant who had followed me was gone, and it would be a while before his comrades realized he had disappeared, but I saw no advantage in being quite so prominent and obvious. I went to my closet and clad myself in poorer, meaner clothing.

With a cowl over my head, and rough, workmanlike shirt and hosen, I was sure no one would recognize me. It was embarrassing to be clad in such demeaning garb, but these were troublesome times, and it was better not to be clothed in a higher-quality suit.

The house where Alice lived was north of mine, and I walked up Bishopsgate with a spring in my step in hope of a pleasant afternoon in store. She was a succulent little strumpet and, with her sweetly innocent expression and boundless enthusiasm, she was just what I needed.

Walking with my head bowed like an old man, hooded and thus concealed, I felt safe. Certainly, no one took the trouble to glance at me a second time.

Alice's house was just along the city's wall from the gate itself.

Now, believe me or not, I had not actually thought much about whether she might be free for an assignation. After all, she was a working servant, and it was possible that her master, George Loughgren, might deprecate her disappearance for the afternoon. Still, I felt it was worth a try. I leaned against a tree just inside the wall, and gazed at the house, wondering what might be the best approach to get to her. In the end I decided that the best route for me would be to wander to the rear door, where the kitchen should be, and enquire after her there.

The door was a half-and-half stable type, with the top open, the bottom closed. I stood there with my cowl over my head and knocked respectfully.

A maid came to the door. 'Yes?'

She was not terribly pretty, with a face rather round and a dumpy figure, but she did have an appealing expression, and I gave her one of my special smiles that never fails to win over a maiden's heart. 'I'm here to see Alice. I haven't heard from her, and thought I should drop by and make sure she was well.'

My winning smile was not working. Hers fled like sticks washed away downriver. 'Alice?'

'Yes. She told me she lived here. Is she busy?'

'I . . . Alice is your friend?'

'She and I have an understanding,' I said, with one of my milder leers, the sort to indicate that I knew I was a bit of a rogue, but had a heart of gold and meant to marry her. You know the sort of look. 'She may have mentioned me – I am Jack Blackjack.'

To my distress her face crumpled like her ragged apron, and she began to bawl.

'Hush! Hush! What have I said? What is it? Is she not here?'

'Alice is dead! She was murdered in the roadway only this last week!'

There have been times when I have been lost for words, and this, I would say, was about the worst of them. It did not seem credible that Alice, lovely Alice, could be no more. I shook my head with a fixed grin of consternation on my face, but I was unable to make a sound as she wept and wailed. Soon a stern-faced old knave appeared and pushed himself between us, glaring at me. 'What is this? Buckle your mouth, child. You – what have you said to distress Marge? Who are you?'

'He was Alice's swain, sir! He was asking after her because he's heard nothing from her since she – since . . .'

That heralded the next onset of misery, and her steward flapped at Marge to shoo her away like a goose. 'Begone, child. I will deal with this. You go and dry your eyes and make yourself presentable. In God's name, go!'

He returned to me. I was standing somewhat glassily, the smile still fixed to my mouth, but I know that my features displayed my utter confusion at this ghastly turn of events.

'Master,' he said, 'I suppose you were keen on young Alice? My condolences. She was taken this Thursday past, and I do not suppose there is anything I can say that will make your loss any the easier. Certainly, she was a pretty little thing, and a good worker. I do not know that we shall be able to replace her with any girl as willing and eager.'

I almost responded that I doubted whether I could either, but reconsidered. It might have been considered in bad taste. Besides, I still had Susan. I nodded and grunted in agreement.

'If it is any help, she was not . . . ruined before death. I . . . well, whoever did it was cruel, but the coroner was convinced that she was not spoiled in . . . that way. Very sad, but I'm sure it's a consolation to know she wasn't . . . um . . .' he trailed off, plainly unsure whether I was relieved or not. In any case, he put aside my feelings for the nonce and began to bustle. 'So, you will need to be about your business. I am sorry not to be able to help you, but her death has left us all with a lot more work.'

'But who could have . . .?'

'I am sorry. My master is returning,' the man said, jerking his chin to point at a large fellow clad in expensive-looking clothes who was now approaching. 'I must go! Good day to you.'

He turned and was about to shut the door when perhaps he caught sight of my expression. I do not think it was particularly friendly towards him. He pulled a face and offered me a cup of wine to help reinvigorate me, but I refused it and turned away, off down towards St Paul's. On the way, I passed his master, Loughgren, but turned my gaze away from him.

I had a feeling of sickness deep in my stomach. In my mind's eye I could see Alice's smile, the way she looked as I lay back and she squatted over me, the way she raised an eyebrow after making the most salacious proposals, her filthy laugh . . . The thought of wine was enough to make me want to hurl up all the ale I'd drunk in the tavern with Humfrie.

No, I didn't want wine. I wanted to avenge her. It was so wrong that someone could have taken her. And why? She was a mere servant girl. She had no money to make her worth attacking or killing. Why would someone have murdered her?

FIVE

Monday 15th August

I was up early the next day, and began my day with a visit to the church. The attitude of the priest the day before had persuaded me that I should make more of an effort to show willing. He had been unwelcoming, or so it had seemed to me. In the past year, he and I had not always agreed on matters. His predecessor had believed I was responsible for a murder, which tended to spoil any pastoral relationship between us, and his replacement was a younger, rather thuggish sort who looked like he had enjoyed happy pursuits, such as standing alone against a charging football team before destroying the entire side. In short, he was the sort of man who could have held Calais against the French army on his own.

Today he was on his top form. Which is not to say that his competency was ever of a high standard. He ran more to insults and issuing threats about his congregation's likely demise on the Day of Resurrection, when they would inevitably be cast into the inferno for eternity.

It was not a cheerful sermon.

He was the sort of priest whom a fellow would see in his nightmares. I have occasionally thought that he was a warning to all: *If you do not wish to see this face again, turn from your sinful pursuits, because this is the kind of demon the Devil employs to torment his victims.* It was a relief to leave the church and cross the road to walk to my home.

I was almost there when I saw a small group of men at the entrance to my street beside the church. I offered them a 'good afternoon', ducking my head politely, since none of them was familiar. There was no sign of my blackmailer or his remaining mobile rock, and I was about to walk past them to my house, when one, a particularly fretful-looking cove in his middle fifties, with a head all but shorn of hair, and an apprehensive expression on his long, donkey-like face, stepped in front of me.

'Are you Master Blackjack?'

'Yes. Why?'

'I am the parish constable, and you are suspected of murder in . . .'

'*Murder?*' The rest of his words washed over me. He was telling me that I was required to go with him to my old parish to answer to the murder and robbery of a Dutchman called Vanderstilt. My mouth fell wide at this unwelcome news. 'But . . . I thought there was no body. Everyone thought he had run away, to escape his debts to me!'

'So you admit it? Where did you put the body?' a man demanded.

I stared at him, then back at the constable. 'I have no idea. I haven't seen Vanderstilt for days, but he was fine when I saw him last!'

'Others say different. You were seen outside his house, you were heard to threaten him, and since his debts have increased, it's likely he was killed by someone owed money by him,' the constable said. He was a pedantic old donkey, I reckoned.

'I had nothing to do with it! I have been here all the time. And he repaid my debt. Ask my servant!'

'We did. He said you had no money from him.'

You recall I said I would regret telling Raphe not to mention the payment Vanderstilt had made? I did now. 'Let me speak with my servant; he will speak the truth now—'

'Oh, yes,' said number two. 'So you can tell him what to say to us, eh? I don't think so, master!' He was a nasty-looking fellow, all black hair and beard, with a vicious squint. I didn't like him.

'Look, it must sound curious, I admit . . .'

'You confess, good,' said the constable, and suddenly my wrists were gripped, and I found myself being led back towards my old haunts, the innocent victim of a vicious twist of fate that was entirely unamusing, and somewhat ironic, bearing in mind my assumed occupation.

And there, under lock and key, I was to remain.

PART TWO

John Blount's Chronicle

SIX

take up my pen in this difficult time in order to hold a record of the events in London, during the previous week, and the subsequent matters pertaining to Jack Blackjack and the queen.

First, Sir Thomas Parry had invited me to visit him at Longleat to discuss certain matters relevant to our Lady Elizabeth and her future. The kingdom was in a state of great confusion and dismay. The queen was considered to be unwell, and her physicians had recommended bleeding and cupping and to the best of their abilities had sought to improve her physical health and general wellbeing. However, it was known that she had made out a new will, and in that she exhorted her subjects to defer to her husband, Philip of Spain. This was not an injunction that could easily be obeyed.

Queen Mary was, of course, a staunch Catholic lady, and adhered to her creed with determination and conviction. She saw it as her maternal duty to her subjects to ensure that they were all obedient to the Pope, and sought to gently persuade them to follow the Holy Catholic church by use of pyres, whips and brandings.

It need scarcely be said that Lady Elizabeth despised such treatment of the people of her realm. She was convinced that the church of her father was the true church, and she was of a mind to allow all those who agreed with her to follow the church services as King Henry had provided. That itself was known to many in the land, and the fact led to a number of men declaring that they would not support Lady Elizabeth.

For that reason Sir Thomas Parry and I were engaged with other men who were also devoted to the safety and protection of Lady Elizabeth. We were dedicated to ensuring that, were Queen Mary to die – may the good Lord protect her soul – there would be enough men to serve Lady Elizabeth. Were the throne to fall vacant, many would vie for it. The throne of England was coveted by many – by the French, by the Spanish, no doubt by the Scots too. Sir Thomas had warned me that there were suspicious movements of weapons throughout the realm, but especially around York, Gloucester and even in the Scottish Marches.

Our bounden duty was to remain with our lady and see to it that no assassin's knife could find her. And to plan how to foil any attempt by militants to wrest the throne from Mary, for the succession could easily be broken, and a new pretender could try to take the realm for his own.

Thus there was a need to ensure that our own men were capable of fighting to protect her, in some cases possibly removing those who could become obstacles to Lady Elizabeth's safety.

This was the reason for many of my visits to Sir Thomas Parry and Lady Elizabeth: to ensure that the armouries were filled and prepared, but also to meet to discuss those who wished harm to our lady, and decide whether one or two could be removed in a non-temporary manner.

On the seventeenth of the month I was once more discussing affairs with Sir Thomas at Longleat, when a messenger arrived. I have a small contingent of loyal servants in London, and had left firm instructions that if any matters required my involvement, I wished to learn at once.

It was some four years before that I had first encountered Jack Blackjack – or Peter the Passer, or Hugh Somerville, or Jack Faithful, or Jack of Whitstable, or John of Smithfield – the damned rogue had an alias for every day of the week. At first I was wary of the man. He was plainly the worst form of vagabond, a sly type who would dip his hand into a purse as soon as smile a greeting. When I met him, during the time of the rebellion against Queen Mary, he was useful in discovering a message that could have had significant importance for many in the realm, and it became clear to me that this was, behind the duplicitous, woman-izing, drunken exterior, a most competent intelligencer and assassin. Rarely have I seen a man so efficient at the task of ending other men's lives.

I proceeded to employ him, thinking that he could be useful in a number of situations – such as removing foreign agents, or

English activists eager to destabilize the queen's realm. Now, with the queen's apparently increasing frailty, there was a need to see to it that those who would obstruct Lady Elizabeth's accession were removed. That meant that a man like Blackjack could be usefully employed. He was the paviour that filled the potholes in Lady Elizabeth's path to the throne, potentially. God forbid that Queen Mary might die, of course. But were she to slip from this mortal coil, Blackjack could be utilized to smooth the safe rise of Lady Elizabeth.

The news from London was not, therefore, to my taste.

'God's ballocks!'

Sir Thomas eyed me coldly. 'Master Blount, I trust you have reason for such an outburst?'

I passed the letter to him. He took it, eyeing me, and cast a glance over the paper. 'Damn his eyes! Could he not have rescued Jack from the damned constable? What do you pay him for?'

He referred to my man, Sam Cutpurse, a man named for his skills, who had been posted to watch over Blackjack and protect him from harm. And *this* was how he viewed his task: to allow Blackjack to walk into a waiting posse and get arrested.

'Where is he being held?' Sir Thomas demanded.

I could not assist him. There was no news as yet, but we both knew that it would be an insanitary and unhealthful gaol. Death by starvation or prison fever were still considered natural causes in the coroners' rolls, and Sir Thomas had no desire to lose a useful servant any more than I did.

'You have to have him released,' he blurted, hands in the air in quick anger. 'In God's name, with the kingdom teetering on the edge of a precipice, I do not wish to have to procure a fresh assassin!'

'No, Sir Thomas.'

'What will you do?'

'I will have to ride back and see what is to be done. Sometimes a constable can be bribed to release a felon; sometimes a felon can be set free on a magistrate's order. I will see what must be done to secure his discharge.'

'Very well – you had best succeed, Blount, or I'll be having *your* ballocks on a plate!'

'Yes, Sir Thomas.'

He glared at me, as he would when trying to assure himself that his message was received. 'Very well. Let us complete our discussion before you have to depart.'

After I sent the messenger to find food and drink to refresh himself, and ordered that my own horse be prepared, Sir Thomas and I discussed the weapons in Lady Elizabeth's armouries, the noblemen who could be relied upon to join her cause, those who might be persuaded with gifts or the promise of future honours, and then, finally, those who were not to be trusted, those who had set their faces against her utterly, and those who were so devoutly Catholic that they would see any possible rise on the part of Lady Elizabeth to be anathema.

'There are too many in London who claim to support the Catholic Church and have declared themselves opposed to our lady's stance,' Sir Thomas mused. He had written eight names on a parchment, and now stared at them as if mulling which would be the most dangerous, which the least. 'These all have access to men and arms. Sir Edmund de Vere is utterly against our lady. He has a number of friends who are possibly not so strong in their views, and who could be brought to our cause. But while de Vere is there, he is likely to pollute their minds. If he were out of the way, it would assist us.'

'I will see to it.'

Sir Thomas looked at me. 'Ensure that it is not a matter that can bring embarrassment to our lady. There must be no hint that this is a political act. I understand a man can easily fall into the river of late. The banks of the Thames are notoriously treacherous. I understand that de Vere is a keen supporter of the stews down by the bear garden.'

'I have heard that he is a keen patron of the Cardinal's Hat,' I said.

'So I believe. It would be a good place for him to meet with a terrible accident,' Sir Thomas mused. 'Perhaps he might fall into a bear's cage, or into the mastiffs' pit? Do make sure he enjoys his last evening, Master Blount.'

I smiled grimly. 'You want him to enjoy his last hours?'

'No. I want him too exhausted to defend himself.'

SEVEN

Thus it was that I found myself returning to London that afternoon. The way was miserable, with a sudden storm bringing filthy rain that made the roads treacherous and delaying us for half a day because of trees fallen over the road. They, and the mud, were a sore annoyance, but we rode faster on the second and third days, and on the following Friday we reached the city – too late to begin to investigate what had happened to Blackjack, but at least I could speak to Sam Cutpurse.

It was natural enough that the office I held often meant I must communicate with the lower classes of the city. As an intelligencer for Lady Elizabeth, it was often necessary to question the dregs of the population. Few, in my experience, were more loathsome than Sam Cutpurse.

He was a weedy, spiderly fellow, with a constant squint as if expecting at any moment to be struck heavily. Which, given his society and his companions, was all too likely. I admit, it was a sore temptation to strike him now, as he came into my room.

'Well?'

He had a whining voice, much like a child demanding a new toy, a wheedling tone that hurt my ears as much as chalk on a slate.

'I'm sorry, master, the fool went walkin' 'ome and met the constable, and was arrested in a trice, and marched 'way.'

'You said two were killed.'

'Yeh, 'is tenant, and they 'eard him threatenin' 'im. Jack had no means of denyin' it. There was witnesses. And then a maid 'e 'ad been seein', she were murdered 'n all.'

'Who is this maid?' I asked, frowning. Jack had always been over-keen on chasing after any woman – provided she had a pulse.

'Some 'ousemaid called Alice. 'Er worked for a man called George Loughgren, up near the wall.'

He had little more to impart, and I was glad to be able to send him on his way.

So, Sir George Loughgren's maid was dead. I knew of George Loughgren – few in London would not. He was a man with strong views, a large treasure chest, and many retainers. A man like him had enemies, and perhaps one of them had tried to pick the brain of a maid in his household? Someone seeking to hurt him. It was possible, but I really had little idea whether that was the case, or whether a comely maid had come to her end because she was attractive and crossed the path of a drunken scoundrel, just as I had no idea why Jack's tenant might have died – but I was sure of the fact that coincidences are rare. The fact that Jack was now being held in gaol because of these two deaths meant there must be some reason, some connection between all three incidents.

I resolved to begin my investigations with the girl's death first. If there were two murders, I could believe one: his tenant. If the maid was some wench he had been regularly battening against a wall, it would not surprise me. He was ever determined to climb up beneath the skirts of any maid he saw; he had the urges and lusts of a broken-down alley cat, and could be relied upon to try his fortune with any woman in his vicinity. *But* . . . the idea that he would murder one was both repellent and, so it struck me, unlikely. He was ever soft-hearted when he spoke of his lovers.

Perhaps I should go and speak with the household and see what I might learn about this dead woman. I must speak to George Loughgren.

Jack would have to wait until I had learned more and perhaps discovered why he had been suspected and arrested.

EIGHT

George Loughgren was a large man with a genial look about him, but as soon as I walked into his hall, it was plain to me that he was also a powerful figure, an impression he must have been keen to project. He was the sort of man who would wish to create an air of imposing authority on any visitor.

The house was modern, with fresh golden oak panels on the walls, and light oak beams at the ceiling. All the gleaming plaster was freshly limewashed, and the light from the diamond-paned windows glinted from silver plates and goblets at the sideboard. Yes, he was wealthy. But it was not only the proof of money and authority: he was built like a strongman. He had the arms of a wrestler, and a short, bull-like neck, so he appeared to lean forward aggressively, as if about to grab and grapple an opponent. Yet when he saw me enter, he rose politely, grasping my hand in his and welcoming me effusively.

'Master Blount, I believe? I am glad to welcome you here to my house. This is my wife, Judith.'

His wife was a tiny, fine-figured lady with the bright, alert eyes of a shrew. She was the opposite of her husband, with delicate bones and features. I was left with the feeling that Loughgren could crush her in the marital bed, were he to be careless.

'How may I serve you?' he asked when we were all seated, and his steward had passed around glasses of wine.

'I have heard that a maidservant of yours has died,' I said. 'Could you tell me more about the incident?'

'You mean little Alice? That was a terrible, sad matter,' Loughgren said. He threw a sharp look at his wife, and I had thought he might ask her to give me more information, but he continued without giving her an opportunity to speak. 'She was a sweet woman. Some eighteen years, I suppose, wasn't she, Judith? Yes, I thought so. A little inexperienced in the ways of the world, and perhaps too friendly to strangers.'

'What happened to her?'

'She had gone out that afternoon. I thought she was shopping, but we heard later that she had a romantic entanglement with some fellow called Blackjack. He is from St Helen's, a trader or some such. No doubt he is the sort of man who has a finger in several pies. He certainly doesn't appear to have a trade or a business of importance.'

'How did you hear of her meeting him?'

'The constable told us when he came to let us know that the miscreant had been captured and was being held. Poor Alice was captured not far from our door, it would seem. She was tortured, from her appearance. She was not raped, but she had been beaten, and her body thrown into a midden near the city gate.'

'Why should Blackjack do that, I wonder?'

'Who can tell? These felons are ruled by their passions. There is evil in their hearts: whether it's there from birth, or inspired by the Devil, who can tell? You would need to ask the priest what leads men to such horrible violence. Why murder your lover? Yet many men will slay their own wives. Perhaps he thought Alice was too demanding, that she wanted too much of his time – or maybe she was not compliant enough for his tastes? Perhaps he will confess the reasons before he hangs.'

'Did she have other swains? You mentioned that she was overly friendly.'

'She was no whore, if that's what you mean!' Loughgren snapped, a sudden anger darkening his face.

'Not at all,' I said. 'I was taking your words. If not, what did you mean?'

'My apologies. I have been under some strain of late,' Loughgren said as his wife put her hand on his arm to calm him. He took some deep breaths. 'My business keeps me heavily occupied, and now I am involved in the City's administration.'

'I see,' I said. 'What is your business?'

He fixed a gimlet eye on me. 'I buy and sell. I buy from Holland and elsewhere, and bring goods to England. Recently I have been much involved with some large trades. They have been

troublesome. It is difficult. You see, we are a happy household
here, and we treat our servants as our family. No, she was a
young woman, and enjoyed the usual, natural pleasures: singing,
dancing, drinking. And she was friendly, yes, but I mean no more
than that. She had no other lovers that I know of. Only this
black-hearted devil, Blackjack.'

I have often found, over my many years of working as intelligencer for Lady Elizabeth, that it is best not to listen to one
account only, but to ensure that as many opinions as possible are
gathered. Only then can a full picture be obtained.

The area was quiet when I left Loughgren's house. A short
way along the same street was a baker's shop, and I walked to
it, selecting a small cake that was still hot, fresh from the oven.
While chatting to the baker, I ate half, and could compliment
him on his skill. By degrees I managed to bring the subject away
from cakes and to his neighbours in the street.

'I am sure you must sell a lot of cakes here, with so many
wealthy families in the area. They will all have a taste for such
delicacies,' I said.

'Some do, yes. There's Master Gilbert along there, with five
children. He has his maid come every day – I reckon, if he di'n't
come fetch them, he'd start a riot to beat all the 'prentice nonsense,
the stink them brats could start. And his missus – God's pain,
but there's little peace for the poor soul when 'e's 'ome.'

'Ah, it's a terrible thing, to marry a termagant,' I said know-
ingly.

'You'd best trust to it, master.' He chuckled indulgently. He
was a man who clearly enjoyed his own produce as much as the
five horrors from Master Gilbert's house, from the way that his
belly rippled, and the enormous chin wobbled.

It was some little while before I could run my mind along the
street, speaking of each house in turn until I reached the
Loughgren's.

''E's an odd 'un, 'im,' the baker said, shaking his head, ''ardly
ever see 'im or 'is folks.'

He expanded, informing me, between customers, that the
family had no children, so there was little in the way of business
to be had from them. Most houses where business was conducted

would often drop by and pick up dainties for clients, but not Loughgren. No, he had many deliveries, and there were regularly men with heavy carts arriving throughout the day, delivering items, but only rarely did anyone buy cakes.

'I heard that a maid from the house was murdered,' I said tentatively, biting into the cooling cake.

'Aye. Poor chit! I knew 'er, moderate well. Pretty little thing, 'er was. And a wicked sense o' 'umour. Oh, 'er could tempt the birds from the trees, 'er could. And tempt a lot else,' he added darkly.

'What is Master Loughgren's business? Does he run a wine shop?' I asked innocently.

'Not 'im, no! 'E's more in the arms business, 'e is. Buys and sells all sorts of weaponry, so I heard. Certainly 'as a lot delivered, day and night. Enough to arm a small host, I'd reckon.'

He had given me much to mull over. In those troubling times, there was always a need for caution. After all, there was no law against buying and selling of weapons. Weapons don't hurt people, it's people that do that, and it doesn't matter what is to hand – if a man is filled with the Devil's hatred, he'll commit murder with whatever is to hand, whether it's a sword, spear, cudgel, dagger, or even his bare – well, hands.

However, just then, while the queen was unwell, there were many men angling for position. It was like watching masters of defence in the arena, swords glittering as they sought the best position. With the queen rumoured to be suffering from some illness, many lords, barons and knights were looking to take advantage. One method of winning advantage involved storing stocks of weapons and gathering servants and retainers to use them. Few would dare to try to begin a rebellion – the events of the Wyatt attempt to wrest the throne from Queen Mary were still in many people's minds, as were the bodies which had hanged from gibbets for months afterwards – but were the queen to grow much more weak, or even die, then all the gamblers would be considering who to bet on. Some wealthy men, like Loughgren, may well decide to arm their retainers and ensure that their houses and warehouses were secure. Others might think to arm rather more men and attempt to take over the city – or the kingdom.

Sir Edmund de Vere was one more of that ilk, which was why Sir Thomas Parry had instructed me to ensure his removal from the board, in the hope that his destruction might persuade others to halt their plotting.

Of course the alternative possibility was that removing one knight from the board might simply embolden three others.

I proceeded to Newgate to enquire of the prison guards as to whether they held a prisoner called Jack Blackjack, but there was no one there who could help me – not that I was surprised. I knew that London had at least fourteen prisons, with various buildings set aside for debtors, vice-related criminals, state prisoners, ecclesiastical offenders and others. So, with a sigh, I turned away from Newgate and chose to make my way to Jack's old haunts in the east of the city.

It would appear, from the letter I had received, that Jack was being held under suspicion of the murder of a man who had been his tenant as well as the maid Alice. This fellow was known to have several debts – but that was common with a certain type of merchant. They would invest all their possessions in a ship, intending to see the cargo sold for a rich profit. This man, Vanderstilt, was apparently one of that kind, who had put a large sum of money into one cargo going to Holland, and then all the rest of his money into a second, which he had anticipated paying off with the proceeds from the first. However, the first ship was held up for some reason, and now Vanderstilt was dead, and certain men had heard him threatened by Jack. That led to immediate suspicion, and he was apprehended outside his new home in St Helen's.

His old haunts were nearer Aldgate, I knew, so I went there next. Perhaps if he was captured and taken to that parish, he would still be held there. Of course, all the various parts of London had their own prisons, usually little more than single-cell gaols. They were not needed for long, since they were merely for holding suspects until they could be tried, and then released or hanged. Aldgate had a small chamber in which I discovered five men squatting on the damp packed earth of the floor, gloomily awaiting their fate. None was Blackjack.

'I seek a fellow who was arrested last week,' I told the turnkey.

'Oho? What's that to me?' He was a short, thickset man holding a blackthorn cudgel, with one eye and grey stubble for hair. His eye was not that of a man with compassion and kindness, but it would be hard to find any gaoler in the land who had the look of an amiable priest. He was fat with the look of a man who enjoyed his ale but without the amiability normally associated with such a build. His nose was large as a plum, and the same colour; his guts swelled over his belt like grain in a sack. I was speaking to him before the cell, where one man stood mutely, a hand outstretched through the bars in the window of the door, begging for money for something to eat. As I watched, behind him another prisoner tried to catch a large rat that scurried across the floor. The odour from the pail was enough to make a man gag. The gaoler smacked the begging hand almost without looking. It was plain to me how well he treated his inmates. His cudgel looked well-used.

I turned back to the gaoler. 'He goes by the name Jack Blackjack, although he has used others. He is a little taller than me, perhaps, with clothing of a good quality, and he has a pleasant face, with only one small scar,' I said, about to point, but before I could the turnkey scowled.

'Him? Oh, I dare say you'd like him. So would I, master. The lying, conniving, dishonest . . .'

He was plainly of a mood to continue for some little while, but I cut him off. 'Where is he?'

'The Devil's prickle 'scaped. He knocked down my companion and made for the river, so I heard.'

'Where then?'

He rubbed his stubbled chin with the sound of a rasp smoothing oak, but remained speechless until I brought a coin from my purse. 'Thank 'ee, master. I understand he made it south – maybe to the Clink, to claim sanctuary, the bastard! My companion was sorely injured when he was knocked on the pate. He won't never be the same man again. He deserves compensation for the trouble and his injury.'

The average turnkey makes very little money. He is a man who has no profession or livelihood other than what his prisoners pay him. Some gaol keepers can become wealthy. They charge prisoners what they want for food and drink. The gaoled with families could have money brought for them, while those who had no relatives must starve. From the look of this man's inmates, he was taking much of the money and not providing them with any sustenance. A gaoler is not there to give comfort and ease to his inmates, it is true. Yet I was struck by the drawn features of the man in the cell's doorway. His eyes had that hunger which is only held by the horribly malnourished. I have seen that look before.

'He might be able to tell you more,' the gaoler added hopefully.

'Bring him. I will have a coin here if he can help me,' I said.

The gaoler rolled away as fast as his short legs could bear him, and as soon as he was out of hearing, I dropped a penny into the beggar's hand. He snatched it away, wide-eyed, as though terrified I might take it back again. Instead I held a second coin for him. 'You know my friend Jack?'

He nodded, his eyes fixed on the coin.

'Did you see what happened to him?'

'He was here. In here with us. Turnkey came, and told him he'd be here till he died, and beat him. Your man was hurt and said he'd pay to be released. They took his money and let him go, then raised hue and cry about his escape and set the constable to catch him back.'

'Did they bring him back again?'

'No, I think he got south of the river.'

I passed him two more coins, and as I did so, the turnkey returned with a smaller man, slight of figure, with a shock of tallow-coloured hair. He had the look of a hound that had been beaten too often. When the older man glanced at him, he cringed.

'Here he is; you question him.'

'Where did he hit you?' I asked.

The fellow looked up at the turnkey with obvious fear.

'Tell him!'

The assistant pointed to his leg. His master snarled and smacked his cheek. 'Your head, you guffin! He hit you on the head, didn't he? Knocked you down and scrambled your brains, didn't he?'

'Aye, my haid. Hit my haid!'

'Really,' I said, and it was obvious that I did not believe him. I walked from the gaol.

'Oi, what about the money?'

That was when I turned and marched back to the turnkey. He was strong and capable of scaring his associate and prisoners, but I have endured enough bullies in my time. I continued approaching at a fast stride, and he was forced to retreat until his back was to the wall. I pressed forward until my nose was almost on his. His odour was only a little better than the cell's pail.

'I have *already* paid. Be thankful I do not increase my payment to the level your behaviour justifies. And you should be glad. You were holding one of the most dangerous men in all England. Be glad he didn't kill you both for your insults to him.'

I was angry to have heard of the gaoler's treatment of Jack. If I was to find Sir Edmund de Vere and ensure that he posed no risk to my Lady Elizabeth, I needed Jack back and working, and that meant fit and well, not beaten and injured.

The gaoler had said that Jack might be at the Clink, over the other side of the Thames. This ecclesiastical prison was a sanctuary for any felon evading the law, but only for forty days. If I was right, Jack had been there since Tuesday or Wednesday – I had not asked the prisoner when exactly Jack had escaped. Clearly sometime between Monday, when he was arrested, and presumably Wednesday or Thursday.

I proceeded quickly to the bridge and passed over into Surrey. The Clink was a liberty originally owned by the Bishop of Winchester, and free from the authorities of London north of the river. I had no need to ask directions. The sanctuary was famous. To be so close to London, and yet free of the officers of the law, it was known as a hotbed of licentiousness, and for the quality of the whores who patrolled the streets. These 'Winchester Geese' – named as such because the land was owned by the good Bishop – were much favoured by Jack, I know. He had friends all over this area.

And he must have gone to hide with some. When I reached the Clink, he was not in the church grasping the altar cloth as a sanctuary seeker should.

A cleric was sweeping the aisles, and I enquired of him what had happened to Jack.

'A penitent seeking sanctuary? I do not think we have had one for a few days.'

'This would have been in the last week.'

'No, there has been no one in that time, I am sure.'

'You are quite sure?'

'Certainly. When a man comes here to find freedom, we are most careful to make a note of his name and the date he arrives. He can only remain here for forty days, and then the coroner is entitled to demand that the fellow submits to imprisonment or must abjure the realm. We have to keep accurate records. But there has been no one here.'

It was enough to make me grind my teeth in frustration. Without Jack, I would have to seek another assassin, or undertake Sir Thomas's mission myself.

Where was Jack?

PART THREE

Jack's Tale Continues . . .

NINE

I t had been a hard time.

To be told that I was arrested for two murders was worse than appalling. Especially when I realized they were not talking about the death of the troll who fell through the bridge into the sewer, but in fact meant *Alice* as well as Vanderstilt.

Poor Alice. She had been such a keen rattle, and I would miss her. Who could have killed her? Who would want to? I mean, a foreign merchant was understandable. The more dull-witted of London's population were capable of taking against any foreign gentleman for the slightest of reasons, but a young, appealing maid like Alice? That made no sense.

In any case, back to my travails.

You will find this astonishing, but when I was captured and taken to the lockup, the gaoler actually *beat* me. I mean, I was dressed as well as *any* gentleman, I had the clothes of my new suit, and it was obvious to the *meanest* intellect that I must be a man of quality, but the fellow had the temerity to take a stick to me, and would have broken my head if I had not boldly stood in opposition to him and told him to show some respect. Obviously my words had the desired effect, and he agreed to accept a small indication of my gratitude in coin to release me.

However the scoundrel immediately blew his horn to call the hue and cry. I barely had time enough to escape from the immediate locality, and then it was a matter of simply running. I made my way to London Bridge, thinking to escape to the Clink or some similar church, but as I pelted over the bridge, I suddenly bethought myself that the Church of St Saviour's at the Bishop's Clink might not be the best place of safety. Kneeling on a stone floor for forty days was unappealing, and in preference, after crossing the river, I turned right, along the line of the Thames, until I came to the bear pits, and thence to the Cardinal's Hat.

Piers, the apple squire at the Hat, was a short fellow with a bald pate surrounded by a mass of grizzled hair. He had been a successful barber, but drink had seen off his wife and family, and now he guarded the Hat for the lady of the house. And the other ladies, of course.

'What you doin' 'ere?' was his immediate response.

While I explained the sad events which had brought me to his door, he whistled and stood aside. It was a relief. After all, any man with blood in his tarse would find it hard not to be affected by the harpies in the Hat. I knew many of them, from Nan to Rose: Rose in particular, a busty, long-legged redhead with the come-hither look of a professional of twenty years' standing – or lying – yet she was only some nineteen summers old. I could easily and happily have lost a few days in her company, but just now my business was more pressing.

'Piers, I need a place to hide 'til I work out a means of clearing my name.'

He blew out his cheeks and poured himself a large pot of ale from a flagon. Noticing my expression, he grudgingly filled a small cup for me too, and leaned against a wall, his bloodshot eyes narrowing with the effort of thought. 'Aye, well, reckon you can bide 'ere a while, then. But if constables come, you'd best make yourself scarce. Away over the roof and off, I reckon.'

'Of course.' His room was up in the eaves, in a room that the Hat's clientele would be reluctant to go to swive the hostesses, being cold in the winter and boiling hot in summer. However, there was space on the floor for me.

'What'll ye do?' he asked, having sunk half the contents of his pot.

'I . . .' It was a good question. I had no idea. Without protection, I was in danger wherever I may go. I should have been able to call on Lady Elizabeth's household to take me in, but she was nowhere about, and with the threat of the strangers who had accosted me, I had no idea what I could do.

Mark had suggested that I should speak with Lewan de Beaulieu, the competitor to Vanderstilt. And now I realized there was another man I should see: the steward, Peter, had said that his master was on his way to meet Sir Edmund de Vere. I would have to find him and learn what I could about Vanderstilt. He might know *something*.

I would have to find him.

I had been shut up in the Hat for five days when I finally made my way out, desperate to learn what I could. Who could have wanted Alice dead? Was her death a coincidence – an unfortunate event, but not an uncommon one. She was small, young and attractive. Women like her were often assaulted, sometimes killed. Trying to learn about her death would be difficult. Vanderstilt was perhaps a little easier. Where could he have run to – or had someone killed him? I needed to find out, that much was certain.

If he ran, he must have fled in a hurry to escape his creditors, and that must mean he had gone into hiding, which would be no mean feat for a stranger and foreigner in a city like London; or perhaps he had decided to go to the countryside? But that was hard to believe. No man would want to escape from a city like London to go and immerse himself in the misery and grim life of a peasant's village. Not a man of style and elegance such as myself – nor Vanderstilt. He was not the sort of man to endure peasant conversation for long.

Besides, they may take him for a dangerous alien and kill him. I assure you, some of these rough country folk are ridiculously superstitious and hidebound in their approach to matters such as a foreign accent. When I was in Devon, the peasants were wary of a man with an accent from seven miles away. Not that I could understand any of them, no matter where they came from. They were so ill-educated!

'You goin'?' Piers demanded when he saw me in the doorway.

I nodded, setting my hat on my head once more. At least in my suit of clothes I felt a gentleman again. Once I was walking the streets once more, I would feel more myself. The truth is, being shut away in the brothel was not ideal for me. I enjoy the sight of doxies as much as any man, but the idea that I was locked in the building with no sight of the sun, only the heat of her rays beating on the slats of the roof, left me feeling little better than I had while I was incarcerated in that cell.

'Where?'

I explained about my need to learn all I could about my tenant's disappearance. 'He was visiting this man de Vere,' I said. 'He's a knight.'

'Yes – I know.'

'You know of him?'

Piers looked at me pityingly. He was soon able to tell me that he knew that name very well. Sir Edmund was a patron of the Hat; he was an important man in the city, a politician, and possible intelligencer.

Having imparted these words of wisdom, he gave me a lingering look.

'You goin' out like that?'

His words rankled. After all, I was a gentleman and dressed in the manner of a man of property and value. I was about to say this, when he spoke again.

'They'll have reports of your clothes. Every constable will be seeking you.'

'Ah.'

I took my leave of the Hat a half-hour later. It was embarrassing. I could barely move without curling my lip, and had to avoid the view of any reflections.

Now clad in noisome hosen, with a surprisingly clean shirt of some dubious provenance and a jack of rough leather. On my head I wore a hood, like a peasant. It was a humbling experience.

Making my way to the river, I discovered a wherry with an ancient, wheezing wherryman who looked as though he could barely make it halfway across the river. He scowled at me, plainly considering me too poor to afford his time, muttered some imprecation under his breath, but when I offered it, he accepted a coin for the crossing, and soon we were into the main stream.

My initial concern appeared to be confirmed, when the vessel was suddenly snatched up by the eddies of the river about a mudbank, and we were almost spun about to fly down the river in reverse. The boatman sneered at me as he struggled with his oars, and then laughed aloud, I assume because he saw something in my face that gave him amusement, and then he chuckled again, hawked and spat over the side, and manoeuvred his little vessel back into the main flow, and soon we were coursing over the water to the farther bank. I hopped out at the pier and gave the rower a sour glare rather than a tip.

These wherrymen get worse every year. If you find one who is moderately polite, you will soon find both ears bleeding from the nonsense that he spews; if you find one who is less polite, you will find yourself abused for the entire journey. I have experienced many of them in my time, and I confess that I am less than enamoured of them generally.

I knew these alleys and streets well from my life here four years ago. Slipping from one to another, I made my way moderately quickly to Ludgate Hill, and stood gazing at the throng in the roads about the St Paul's Cross. There were two priests holding forth at the passersby, but as usual in London, not many paid them any interest or attention. I sidled in amongst the crowds, feeling exposed the whole way. It took me a little while to realize why: when I had been arrested, the first thing the constable had done was take my sword and dagger, and I was now walking the streets of London with no defence. It was a more than slightly alarming prospect. The idea that I might bump into the blackmailer at any moment was not remotely appealing, especially while unarmed.

First, I resolved to go to my home and fetch whatever weapon I could. The obvious one was the old dag, my wheel-lock pistol, but it contained only one shot, and I was reluctant to carry that on its own. I had a knife that should serve, so perhaps the two together would suit me. With that in mind, I set off for Bishopsgate and St Helen's.

I went to the garden gate, slipping into my garden quickly and going to the back door, which was bolted.

Gritting my teeth, I knocked, feeling thoroughly exposed and in danger. Only a couple of seconds before I had been struck with a conviction that this could be a mistake. After all, the constable had come here and captured me with his posse only a few days ago. He may well have received a report to say that I had broken free of gaol – which had merely involved the payment of four shillings to the corrupt gaol keeper, and I would ensure that his complicity in releasing prisoners would be brought to the attention of the authorities once I was sure that my own safety was secured again.

However, I could not walk the streets without a weapon for my own defence. I knocked again, louder.

I heard steps, and then a suspicious voice. 'Who's there? Why are you at this door?'

'It's me, Cecily! Let me inside!'

'Who?'

I rolled my eyes. Pointlessly, I know, but her attitude was infuriating just now. 'Me, your master!' I hissed. 'Let me in!'

There was the sound of a bolt being slid reluctantly, and then a second, and at last I could sidle in with a sigh of relief. 'What made you take so long?'

'You didn't sound like yourself. You don't look it neither,' she replied smartly. 'What are you wearing?'

I wasn't going to explain that these were the clothes of a patron of the Hat who had not enough money to pay for his bedding, and instead demanded to know where Raphe was.

'He's gone out with Hector' – that was Raphe's adopted mongrel – 'but he should be back soon. It was just to buy some eggs and meat for our supper.'

She wore a grumpy look as she said this, and I was suddenly aware that for her and Raphe my disappearance must have been rather a blessing. After all, with me out of the way, they had the house to themselves and could treat the place as their own. They already lived as man and wife – which still confused me since Cecily was one of the most religious, pestilential women I have ever met, and the fact that she was living with Raphe not only betrayed a dreadful lack of taste on her part, I also felt it would be behaviour deprecated by the parish priest. Still, that was not my concern just now. My main concern was the whereabouts of my gun.

Pushing past her, I hurried up to my chamber, where I found the bed made up in perfect order, the sheets and blankets turned and the counterpane spread neatly. Looking at it, the temptation to throw myself onto it and close my eyes was all but over-whelming. It was over a week since I had slept in a real bed – any bed, let alone my own.

No. There was no time to be lost. I found the dag under some clothing in my chest and thrust it into my belt, then pulled the straps for the powder and shot over my head so the two dangled on my left hip. Then it was back downstairs to the kitchen, where I sat at the table and cleaned and loaded the gun, checking the flint in the dog's jaws, and seeing that the wheel span easily. With the gun ready once more, primed and loaded, I went to my room and hunted about for my knife. Once that was installed on my belt as well, I felt better prepared to confront the world at large.

Having left instructions that Raphe should not allow anyone into the house under any circumstances, I went out by the same route I had entered. That way, I could see the street clearly while concealed by the garden gate. I saw no one to cause any concern – nobody loitering and watching the house; no suspicious fellows walking back and forth; no young urchins who could have been paid off to keep an eye on things. Most of all, no blackmailer and his accomplice.

I opened the gate and slid out into the street, making my cautious way to Aldgate, where I soon found myself in my old road.

Pulling my cowl's hood higher over my head, I strolled along the road towards my old house, and knocked sharply.

The sound of shuffling feet approaching recalled to my mind that last visit, when the fool of a servant had chosen to fight me. Glancing about me at the quiet street, I took hold of my dag. As soon as the door opened a crack, I thrust it into the gap. 'Open the door!' I said. I might even have snarled a bit. I was not in a good mood.

Vanderstilt's steward, Peter, expressed no emotion on seeing the gun's barrel, but stepped back from the door as I pushed it open and closed it quietly behind me, still pointing the weapon at him. 'Through to the kitchen,' I said, and he turned and shuffled out to it. His act did not fool me. I had seen how swiftly he could move when he had the desire to, from how he had bested me last time I had been here.

I had him sit on a stool with his back to the fire, and took my own seat on a bench at the table, pointing my gun at him. There was cheese and a ham on the table, and I used my knife – somewhat clumsily with my left hand – to cut chunks from both. I was starved.

'You know why I am here.'

'No.'

'Men have accused me of killing your master. I have to find him so that I can prove my innocence.'

Something glinted in his eyes, and I hefted the pistol again. 'Don't try anything. This is cocked and ready.'

'So I see.'

'You know about handguns?'

'I was a soldier.'

'Oh. Well, in that case you'll know that this will kill easily at this distance.'

'Yes.'

'Where is your master?'

'I don't know.'

'You said he left here on the Thursday after you brought my money to me. Is that right?'

'Yes.'

'But he didn't return?'

'No.'

'And you told me he was going to visit a customer.'

'Yes. Sir Edmund de Vere.'

The sound of his name renewed that block-of-ice sensation in my bowels. Piers had said he was a politician and intelligencer as well as enthusiastic patron of the Hat. I didn't like the sound of him. 'How did your master know Sir Edmund?'

'My master was a proficient merchant. He was renowned for some of the items he brought to England. I imagine Sir Edmund was interested in some of the goods he was bringing with the latest shipment.'

'You think he went to fulfil an order for something Sir Edmund had demanded?'

'No.'

I frowned. 'Why not?'

'He took nothing with him. I don't think he carried anything of any value or interest. I believe Sir Edmund invited him as a guest because of past items delivered, or perhaps to discuss a future order.'

'Ah!'

That meant it was possible that Vanderstilt had been paid for something, and had been on his way home with money in his purse. Which also meant that a wayside robber could have seen an opportunity and knocked him on the head to take his purse. Suddenly a logical flow was occurring to me. If the man had walked down certain dark alleys, it was likely that a thief could have taken advantage of his being alone and struck. What then? Once he realized the value of the purse, the felon would have bundled the body into a ditch, or concealed it in an alleyway before making off with his profit.

But if a body was left in the open, it would surely have been noticed by now.

'What was he wearing when he left home?'

'Wearing? A pair of hosen in blue, with a jack that was also blue, and a black cloak with hood. He did not want to look important or a suitable gull for the thieves and vagabonds who live about here.'

I was tempted to point out that this was a good neighbourhood, but instead I ventured another question: 'If he was going out and returning with money, would he have arranged for a guard to go with him?'

'Yes, I am sure he would.'

'So you don't think he returned with money?'

'I don't know.'

'What does that mean?' I blurted. 'Either you think he did or he didn't!'

His rheumy eyes studied me for a moment or two, then he said, 'I don't think he intended to collect money, but if it was offered to him, I have no doubt he would have taken it. But he had no bodyguards with him because he had not anticipated being given money. If he came back alone, and was set upon, he would have defended himself. Perhaps an assailant took his chance, knocked him down, and robbed him.'

'Is that more likely than he ran away?'

'I do not think my master would choose to go to a house to eat and drink, and then go to hide. The city gates would be shut and barred. How could he leave the city? If still in the city, why not return to his home? No, I believe he has been killed.'

'Where does Sir Edmund live?'

'I believe his residence is down towards the river, near St Botolph's.'

I recalled the second man. 'What can you tell me about Lewan de Beaulieu?'

'Him?' The gaunt features wrinkled as if in surprise. He gave me a glance as if wondering whether I had a prejudice against all foreigners. 'He is a merchant from Amsterdam.'

'Is he a friend of your master's?'

'They often talk, I suppose about business.'

'Where does he live?'

'In St Margaret's Lane.'

Armed with this information, I instructed the man to keep his mouth closed about my visit, but if any news came to him, that he should immediately send a message with it to my new house.

I knew St Margaret's Lane. It was just beyond St Mary's Fenchurch and, London being the small city it was, it was almost directly on the way to Sir Edmund's house. I could visit the merchant and then go on to the knight's, I thought.

Lewan de Beaulieu was one of those merchants you meet occasionally who had the appearance of genteel elegance, amiable comradeship, and a patina of generosity that almost, but did not quite, cover the avaricious, mendacious, scheming and devious soul beneath. As soon as I met him, I disliked him intensely.

Perhaps it was the way that he welcomed me into his hall with a courteous wave of his hand, the way he commanded his quiet, rather fretful-looking servant to fetch me wine, but all the while kept his eyes on my hosen as though fascinated by the array of stains and threadbare patches.

'How may I serve you?' he enquired. 'Does your master wish for me to help supply something for him?'

'No, no. I am a friend of a fellow countryman of yours, Master Geoffrey Vanderstilt. Did you know he has gone missing?'

'Geoffrey? Ah, how sad.'

The eyes glittered, but registered no compassion or especial interest.

'Yes, he went to a meal at a client's, Sir Edmund de Vere, but never arrived back at his home.'

'Really. Ah, the wine. Yes, very good, Charles.' This to his servant, who withdrew to the wall, head downcast. 'And what of it?'

The little eyes were suddenly intent upon me.

'I wondered whether you knew anything about his disappearance?' I said lamely.

'You suggest I knocked him on the head as he passed? Nay, I would not this do. He was a compatriot, as you say. We competed in business, it is true, but beyond that, *pfft*! We rarely socially met.'

'You had his ships held up by officials, he told me.'

'He lied.'

Again, the hardening of those eyes. They were like chips of flint now.

'So you didn't see him on his way home that evening?'

'Of course not.'

He didn't even ask which was the relevant day.

The walk to St Botolph's was not lengthy, but it did give me a little time to review what I had learned. I confess, I was bemused. Perhaps the fool Dutchman had not run away as I had first assumed, but instead was now languishing and rotting in an alleyway on my way – or had been thrown into a ditch en route. I might be passing him even now, I thought, and my eyes began to search about for any flash of blue by the side of the road.

There was nothing.

The de Vere house was imposing. My own two properties were both of a good size, and yet this made me feel overawed. Not me alone, either. It was the sort of house that made men stop and gape. Two men even now were gazing up at it from the opposite side of the street, one in the mouth of an alley, the other in a doorway.

It stood three storeys tall, a great mansion with fresh limewash over all the timbers and daub, and jettied upper levels that gave increased floor space. Flags with the de Vere coat of arms fluttered gently in the mild breeze, and when I knocked on the door, the lintel above, carved of stone, held its own representation of his arms. This was a property designed to make any visitor comprehend his insignificance, and I felt sure that even Sir Thomas Parry would feel that. Then again, knowing the Welsh windbag as I did, perhaps not. As I thought of him, it struck me that he had similarly cold, uncaring eyes to those of the Amsterdammer. The reflection made me shiver.

A tall, austere man opened the door to me. His gaze flicked over me and behind me, as though searching for any indication that house breakers might follow closely behind me, before his attention returned to me, an expression of distaste on his face.

'What do you want, fellow?'

'I wish to speak to Sir Edmund, your master.'

'*Re-ally?*' He managed to make the word sound as long as a paragraph, the way he drew it out. He glanced down at my feet, then up the worn hosen, over my shirt and jack and up to the cowl. Suddenly I realized that my present appearance was not the sort to inspire confidence. I was not clad in my new suit of clothing, but in the cast-offs of a number of sex-starved customers of a brothel. It was a good brothel, a place of quality wenches and good wine, but that did not mean that my attire was necessarily suitable for a man living in a place like this.

I pulled an ingratiating smile to my face. 'It is to do with the merchant who came here, Geoffrey Vanderstilt.'

'What of him?'

'I just wanted to speak to Sir Edmund about a matter of some delicacy to do with his visit.'

'What matter?'

'It is delicate,' I said stubbornly.

'Wait here.'

The door slammed shut and I heard a bolt shoved home. After that there was little for me to do other than cool my heels on the doorstep. I had to wait some little while, and then came the sound of the bolt sliding back and the door opened. The man stood aside and I entered. Almost immediately both my arms were grabbed, and I was pushed against a wall, cheek flattened against it, hands behind my back, while a man methodically went over my flanks, back, breast and hosen with light fingers that found everything of value on me. My dag, powder and shot were removed, my knife and belt too, and I was gripped by both upper arms and wrists, my hands behind my back, and then the two holding my arms followed the doorman, the light-fingered searcher behind me bearing my possessions.

They took me over a large hallway with a black and white tiled chequerboard floor, up to a new oak door that glowed golden.

After knocking, the doorman stood aside, opening the door, and I was frog-marched inside.

I have been in wealthy chambers many times. This, however, was the most curious room I have ever entered. In part it was rather like Mark Thomasson's, with masses of papers on all surfaces, and racks of halberds, swords and other weapons prominently displayed. I imagine that the Tower of London's armouries have more weapons, but only just. This was the largest selection I had ever seen in a private home. It was enough to take my breath away. Not because I had any intimation that I was in the presence of greatness or anything like that, but purely because I was suddenly very aware that I was unarmed, with both arms securely gripped, and in the presence of more means of ending my life than I had seen gathered together in one room before.

'Well? What do you want to speak to me about in confidence?'

This was from a tall, angular man. He had the square shoulders and narrow waist of a professional fighter, and aquiline features above a pointed little beard that made him look like a man from the church – one of the educated ones, not a mere shabby rector. His eyes were like gimlets, and he stood on my side of a table with one hand clutching a sheaf of papers, which he returned to the table as one of his minions passed him my handgun.

He took it and cast an eye over it with a professional's attention to detail. I saw him move the dog up and down, test the feel of the grip, glance along the barrel, and then he turned to me. 'Well? You said you wanted to speak with me. Here you are. And here I am. But I am concerned that you came here carrying a weapon designed for assassination.' His voice hardened. 'Who are you, and what do you want?'

'I . . .' My voice lacked a certain firmness, I felt. In fact, I suppose you could say I squeaked somewhat. I swallowed and tried again. 'My tenant, Geoffrey Vanderstilt, came here to dine last Thursday, I believe, but he never returned home. I am trying to learn, did he run away after your meal, or was he waylaid while returning home?'

'That is not information that interests me,' he said. He took up the pistol and aimed it at me. I could feel his two servants withdrawing slightly from me as he did so, but both kept a tight grip of my arms.

'All I want to know is, did he come here? And if he did, did he mention anything that was concerning him?' I said. 'Did he feel endangered?'

'There is no need to sound so pathetic, man!' he said, and set the gun down on his desk. It served well as a paperweight, apparently. 'Yes, he came. We had a good meal, and discussed matters of interest to us both. Mostly ships and trade, not that it matters. But concerns? No, none at all.'

'Do you know of his ship which is being held in Holland?'

'No. One ship was delayed, but it was released soon after, and he had a second commissioned. I received some of my goods on Wednesday, and was to receive the next shipment this coming week.'

'Oh. When he left, did he have a bodyguard with him?'

'Not that I know of.'

'Did you send anyone with him to protect him?'

'He was happy to go home alone.'

'Oh.'

'Master Blackjack, he ate, we chatted, he left. No concerns were raised, other than the trials of finding good servants in this city of layabouts. And now, I wonder what I should do with you?'

I swallowed. It sounded much more that he was debating with himself what he should do *to* me, rather than *with* me.

'You can go,' he said.

'What about my things?'

No doubt others would not have shown the same bravery as me, but you have to recall that I was a bold fellow. I have always had the courage of Hector, and besides, I wanted my weapons back.

He raised an eyebrow at my temerity.

'My dag? And knife.'

Sir Edmund took up my handgun again, nodding to himself. 'Give him back his knife. However, this pistol is, I think, above your station, knave. You should not be walking the streets of London with a toy such as this. No, I will keep this for my own use.'

'You can't do that!'

That was not the right thing to say. He looked at me then with a very straight and cold expression. It was as if all human feeling and emotion had been sucked from him in that moment. 'There was a lawyer who worked in Exeter until recently. He had a dispute with a wealthy man in the city on behalf of his client, and pursued this man for some months until he grew to be a nuisance. Do you know what happened? This man went to the lawyer and knocked on his door. While the lawyer prevaricated, the rich man had his servants set afire to the lawyer's stables. All his horses died. And still the rich man knocked. Eventually the lawyer let him in, once he had won an oath that the fellow would do him no further harm. But the rich man was infuriated with the lawyer, and told him so. The lawyer gave him and his men food and drink, and all the while the rich man abused him, telling him he was no better than a toad. What did the lawyer say? What did he think? We do not know. The fellow was stabbed and beaten to death there in his hall. And the rich man had his body carried to the city by the lawyer's own servants, singing a bawdy song about their master – on pain of death, were they to refuse.'

He peered at my gun contemplatively.

'Now: that lawyer died horribly because he had made himself a nuisance to a rich man. It was foolish behaviour. You would not wish to do the same, I am sure.'

I was none the wiser about my tenant's last hours. However, I was more certain than ever that this man must have been involved in Vanderstilt's death. Everything about him spoke of his sense of entitlement and conviction that others would do his bidding and submit to him. He was a political fellow, that was certain.

But he also had an armoury as if he was planning to begin a small war. That was a horrible thought. As I have said before, I had experience of the rebellion four years before, and I had no desire to see the realm fall into such a terrible catastrophe again. And on whose side would he join battle, were he to try that? Was he the sort of man who would take power for himself, perhaps? Could he be planning to overthrow the queen? Or was it possible that he knew more about the queen than most, and that he sought to take over the government were she to fall ill once more?

He aimed my gun at me again, smiling. 'You can leave,' he said after a few moments during which my cods shrank to the size of peas. 'Please, don't let me detain you.'

'Um . . .' The threat in his words was enough. I left. Partly of my own volition – and partly because of the two servants who still held an arm in each hand and pulled me from the room.

I think they realized they were dealing with a dangerous man, though. They dared not try to beat me, but only took me to the front door and threw me into the street.

It could have been worse, I reflected, as I stood rubbing the dirt and ordure from my knees and jack.

I stood outside his front door in the street, wondering what this all meant, and came to only one firm conclusion: I needed a whet.

Outside, on the road that led to London Bridge, I saw there was a tavern, and made my way to it. I ordered an ale, and stood with it in my fist bemoaning my fate. Here I was, an innocent, accused of murder, forced to wear these foul clothes (I was starting to itch, and I was sure that it was some creature left inside the hosen that was responsible), robbed of my sword and dagger, robbed now of my gun, powder and shot, and all the while without a tenant on whom I relied for my own livelihood.

It was indeed a very grim and dissatisfied Jack who ordered a second ale and scowled at the window, wondering how best to clear my name, bring revenge to Sir Edmund, return my weapons, and go back to my old life of ease. John Blount was ignoring me, so I could not turn to him. No, the only people who would consider helping me were Mark Thomasson and Humfrie.

A hand clapped me on the shoulder, and I almost emptied my entire second pot of ale in shock. The hand of the law is a heavy hand, so I have heard.

'So, Jack. I think we need to talk.'

I was all but unmanned as I turned to meet the serious gaze of Humfrie. 'You nearly killed me!' I gasped, once I had regained the power of speech.

'How?'

It was pointless to try to explain. I paid for an ale for him, which seemed to disappear without any effort on his part, and had to refresh it before we could make our way to a free table away from the other patrons.

'Humfrie, I think my tenant was murdered up here,' I said. 'He came to meet a man for . . .'

'Aye. He went to Sir Edmund de Vere's house.'

'How did you know that?'

'I've been asking about Vanderstilt. He was bringing arms to the country for de Vere.'

'Eh?' I gaped. 'Who told you that?'

'A seaman at the docks. I went to talk to the men who worked for your tenant, then heard about their cargo and who had ordered it.'

'I think this de Vere's involved in some unpleasant business,' I said decisively. 'His house is full of weapons, enough to arm an army.'

'How many men does he have in his house?'

'I don't know. There was space for a lot,' I said.

'Enough for all the weapons you saw?'

'Well, no, but . . .'

'So you think he's gathering a force, but there's nothing to show it other than the weapons. What if he merely bought in the weapons so that he could sell them on?'

'He didn't seem like a man to just want to make a profit. He is a gentleman. A *knight*.'

'Men are rarely what they seem.'

I morosely sipped ale. 'Then, what should I do?'

'Tell your master, perhaps, but for now I would go somewhere else and leave it to me. I can go where you cannot. You have the accusation of murder hanging over you.'

'They cannot hold me in prison without a body. The coroner cannot report without a body,' I pointed out.

'True. What makes you think a body won't soon be discovered?'

That, I have to admit, was a new thought. It should have occurred to me sooner, of course, but so much had happened, what with the disappearance of Vanderstilt, then my capture and the theft of my rapier, before the discussion with Sir Edmund and his men taking my dag. All in all, I was confused by the rapid series of disasters.

I agreed that Humfrie was possibly better placed to investigate Sir Edmund de Vere, but that left me at a loose end. My mind turned to young Alice once more. I could really have done with another assignation with her. Her fair hair, tumbling over her shoulders, those minxish eyes tormenting and tempting all at once, her splendid little perfectly formed body . . .

Something was niggling at me as I left the tavern. There was a comment someone had made – or was it a conversation? Somebody had made a reference to Alice, and it had seemed out of place. Not that much seemed to be correctly in place just now. All I knew was that the world was a darker place.

Without thinking, I retraced my steps up St Mary's to Fenchurch, past de Beaulieu's house. As I went, I saw a scruffy, nondescript, rather gaunt figure leave the house and hobble up the lane before me. It was Peter, the servant to Vanderstilt. It struck me immediately that the poor fellow must be seeking fresh employment, and where better than in the company of another Dutchman?

Yes, the world was a darker place without Alice. Of course footpads were a constant threat to all. Any solitary man or woman was fair game. The queen often stated that she wanted the streets to be made safe for travellers and local folk, but that had little impact. It is one thing to state what is wanted, and something else to actually try to acquire it.

Then it struck me – it was *the blackmailers* who had mentioned her! They had not known her name, but they did speak of my – how had Perkin Bagnall put it? My *dalliance*, I think. The nerve of the scruffy beggar! But if they knew I had a meeting planned, even if they didn't know her name, that meant that they must have decided to learn as much about me as they had. Could they have been responsible for her murder? And if so, for what? To make me angry? To avenge the hurt my boot had inflicted on their weedy leader? But they had discovered my movements before the confrontation near the inn. What possible reason could they have had for removing a young woman like her?

I could not tell you how I got there, but almost before I knew it, I was at Rose Street once more, outside Mark Thomasson's house. Perhaps it was mere good fortune, but I think it was more likely that as my mind circled around the problem, my feet knew where to go to discover answers. After all, my mind was fully occupied with Alice as I walked, and I did not pay attention to the road or other people on it.

Before long I was in his house, standing before his fire, keeping a wary eye on Peterkin. The brute had come to my side and sat now on my foot, his eyes fixed on my face with a kind of sullen suspicion.

Mark was as usual in his seat behind a castellated wall of papers and rubbish that would have looked more in keeping with the King's Bench than a private house. But he was always scribbling and reading his curious little notes. I think it was a form of illness. He could not believe anything until it was written down.

'Master Blackjack, how can I aid you this time?' he had asked as I entered, and I told him all – the missing tenant, the merchant Beaulieu, the suspicious knight de Vere, and now Alice's death. I mentioned my own capture and imprisonment, and my subsequent flight to the brothel – it was one of his own favourite haunts, I knew. I had first met him at the Cardinal's Hat, when he came to visit the doxies. But I did not mention the troll who had drowned in the Thames while trying to follow me.

'What can I do?' I said as I reached the end of my tale. I looked at him helplessly. At my side, Peterkin appeared to sympathize. He rested his great head on my thigh, leaving a smear of drool.

'You have been having adventures again, haven't you?' Mark said. He idly picked up a quill as if to start writing, but then caught sight of my face, and set it aside. With a look of earnest determination, he sat upright and leaned both elbows on his desk.

'Your tenant's servant stated that his master never returned; no one else saw him return. He visited Sir Edmund de Vere, since Sir Edmund admitted as much to you. However, he has not been seen since he left Sir Edmund's house. If he left that house after dark, any sensible host would have sent men with him to protect him on the way homewards. It was a fair distance to walk from the river up to Aldgate and your house. If he had left

Vanderstilt without a guard, that would be suspicious. If he *did* send men with him, he could vouch for Vanderstilt's return to your house. But you say he stated that no one walked with Vanderstilt. That shows us that no witnesses saw him go to your house.'

'I could have told you that,' I said.

'But what, then, is the obvious inference?' he asked mildly.

'That he didn't care about Vanderstilt's safety,' I said, shrugging helplessly.

He peered at me rather like a priest staring at a confessor who admitted and begged forgiveness for . . . something horrible. 'Possibly. Or, more likely, I venture, we can assume that the man never left de Vere's house. You say that his house is right on the river? How difficult would it be to murder a man, carry his body to the water, and let the Thames take it out to sea? If de Vere had no desire to honour his dealings with Vanderstilt, that would be his most elegant solution. All he need do was tell anyone who asked that he had waved Vanderstilt off that evening. Any constable would believe him. He is, after all, a knight, is he not? A member of the watch or others would assume he must be telling the truth. So, there it is! He slew Vanderstilt and threw the body into the river.'

'What of Alice?'

'Ah, that was likely the sad misfortune of a young woman. A man desired her, attempted to persuade her to join him, and when he failed, he decided to rape her.'

'But he didn't rape her. The steward at her house was quite insistent on that.'

He shrugged. 'Her assailant wanted to rape her, and struck her down. Then he realized that she might be able to speak about him, give a description, perhaps, and so he stabbed her to silence her forever. Or perhaps he was so steeped in wine and brandy that his Roger wouldn't rise, and he found himself incapable of assaulting her. You are better informed on such behaviour. If I am right, that was that.'

'I don't know.'

'There is much you don't know,' Mark agreed somewhat rudely.

'But all this – Vanderstilt's death, Alice's death, the three men attempting to blackmail me, it is all too much of a coincidence.'

'Is it?' Mark shrugged and surreptitiously stole a sheet of paper to glance at with a frown. 'Perhaps. But coincidence is the logical answer. Obviously his body is somewhere along the river, on the northern shore, I would guess. Many bodies end there after they have been washed away from London. I suppose they enter the water on the north bank, and are likely to be snagged on that bank as they move downriver.'

He selected another sheet and frowned at it. It was my dismissal. I stood, offered my salutation, and walked out into the gathering gloom of a late-August afternoon with a firm conviction that there was more to this matter.

I turned to the river, cowl over my head, shoulders hunched, deep in thought. I knew I was no nearer a solution to the two deaths, and although Mark was convinced that the blackmailers had nothing to do with Alice's death, I was growing more and more convinced that they had. They had threatened me with blackmail, and had mentioned her. Would it be a surprise if they had realized I was to meet her at the inn, and they followed her afterwards, murdering her as a means of getting to me?

No. These were clearly dangerous felons.

PART FOUR

John Blount's Chronicle

TEN

On the Sunday, I had already sent a report to Sir Thomas Parry, advising him of the difficulty with which we were presented owing to the disappearance of our assassin. Accepting which, I proposed that we should seek another man to achieve our ends of removing Sir Edmund de Vere.

In my experience of lower London circles, I had often been in contact with the outcasts, Egyptians, rogues and vagabonds who populated that cesspit of criminality. Many were the men I have met who would gladly accept a penny to thrust a knife into a man's back or cut his throat. Usually, in my experience, they could be discovered in the meaner alehouses, especially near the river, where sailors would congregate. There were men there who depended for their life and sustenance on a constant diet of strong beer or brandy. Most were barely capable of speaking without lengthy pauses while their addled brains tried to keep up with their mouths, and usually failed.

I repaired to a notably foul tavern, the Hawser, near Puddle Dock, and sat on a stool, eyeing the others in the room. None of the characters was inspiring.

It could be said that Jack Blackjack was my best acquisition for Princess Elizabeth's household, a man capable of mingling with the richest in the land as well as the poorest. He had a certain elegance, which translated to many as a proof of trustworthiness. To my certain knowledge, a large number of his victims had been persuaded by his easy-going appearance and open smile, to their cost. His was a face which men and women felt they could have faith in. They would believe in his honesty up until the moment when their lives ended. Only then would they recognize their error.

Key aspects of his brilliance as an assassin were his apparent stupidity, evident cowardice and clear incompetence. Better still, for my purposes, was the fact that it was contrived. He was a profoundly clever and devious agent. Many were the times when I had sent him on a task, and later, when the deed was done, discovered through multiple witnesses that he was a mile or more away from the scene of the assault. Perhaps he was a most competent briber of witnesses, but I doubted that. Which meant that he presumably was able to ensure that the victim was dead earlier or later than others assumed. It certainly made him, so far, one of my most prolific intelligencers, and probably the most fortunate.

Certainly there was no one in the tavern who could compete with him. Jack would never stand out. He was one of those men who was suited to the shadows, but when seen in broad daylight, he was all but unnoticeable. His was the type of face and demeanour that was simply easy to overlook – rather like a trusted retainer, or bottler or maidservant. They may be there in the room, but they were as worthy of attention as a candlestick; no more than dumb, insensate artifacts. Here, however, all the drunks were as unobtrusive as flaming torches at dead of night. All were loud, crude, uncaring and foolish with drink.

Reluctantly, I stepped out of the Hawser and into the alleyway. De Vere was a problem that must be resolved. I had other men I could call upon, but this was a matter of some delicacy. I did not wish de Vere's murderer to be a fool who could be caught and identify me or any others from Princess Elizabeth's household. That lady was too dear to me to see her put at risk. She had suffered so much in her short life, born as a princess, raised in a happy marriage until the King her father decided to find a new wife to grant him the son and heir he so craved. After that, Elizabeth had fallen out of favour. When her half-sister took the throne, her position worsened still more.

Mary had been Henry's first princess, but after his wedding to Mary's mother was declared null and void, and his subsequent marriage to Anne Boleyn, Mary and her mother had become non-people. Once a royal princess, now Mary was declared illegitimate. If Henry's marriage to her mother was illegal, Mary had no status. Her jewels were taken and given to Elizabeth, she was dismissed from the royal court – even her title of 'princess' was removed – and all were given to Elizabeth in her place.

But when Mary was crowned queen, she showed the same cruelty to her half-sister. Where Princess Mary had become Lady, so now did Princess Elizabeth discover what it was like to lose title, jewels, lands and freedom.

It was clear that, were she to be discovered to have plotted to remove a confidante and ally of the queen, her own life would be forfeit. The weak blood ties of the half-sisters would not be enough to protect her. And de Vere was definitely an ally to the queen.

I must seek another man like Jack. A reliable, competent fellow who could be trusted with this bloody deed.

It was just as I reached this decision that I heard the steps behind me.

I am a competent traveller. In my days I have wandered far and wide through the kingdom, and rarely had to worry about my personal safety. However, there were more than a single person's steps behind me, and this was a haunt of rogues and jacks. I was not going to take chances. I turned into a slender alley. It would be hard here for two men to come upon me at the same time. I ran up this to a still narrower section between walls, before turning to face the danger.

It gave me a good distance to gauge the threat. I was correct: there were two of them, one bareheaded, one wearing a wide-brimmed hat. The latter had a staff in his hands, while the other carried a sword. The quick dash to this point had given me time to prepare, and now I drew my sword, a short but serviceable weapon with a heavy blade. I held it before me and waited. If I had the opportunity, I would welcome closing with the man with the staff first, because although the sword was a more fearsome weapon, the staff had a longer reach.

To my relief the man with the stave pushed forward, snarling, the weapon held forward in the quarter staff attack, one quarter held between his hands, half facing me. He looked competent, but I waited as he approached, watching his movements. As he was almost with me, he jerked the staff at me as though it was a spear. I grabbed at it with one hand, deflecting it to the left of my face, and lunged. My sword entered his shoulder, and I wrenched it sharply, hearing his scream of pain with satisfaction. He shouted some sailor-like language about my parents as I withdrew my blade.

His companion took his place with considerably less confidence. He watched me with great attention as I slowly changed my position, and then reached behind me to unsheathe my dagger. It had extended quillons bent back to lie parallel with the blade, which could trap an opponent's blade. Twice, when I had used this, I had actually snapped a cheaper sword. I didn't know whether I could do so today, but it was a fearsome weapon, and with that in my left hand, my sword in my right, I began to proceed slowly towards my foe.

'Who sent you?' I demanded as he gave way before me.

'Don't tell him anything! Just kill him,' the man with the staff spat. He had relinquished his weapon now, and was trying to staunch the flow of blood from his wound, leaning against the wall near his friend.

'Who?' I repeated.

As I did so, his blade flashed at me. I blocked it with my sword, trying to cut at his flank, but he withdrew quickly, panting. He was slow, too slow for his own good, I felt. Probably the drink had done for him. It would be easy to finish him off. Thinking that, I stepped forward briskly.

It was a mistake. His apparent slowness was nothing more than a ruse to tempt me closer, and I was almost eviscerated as his sword's point flashed to my belt.

However, my reactions were not dulled, and as the blade rose past me, I pressed onwards fast, trapping his blade in my dagger, twisting it sharply, and thrust firmly with my sword. Its point caught him in the breast, and I felt the resistance as the point pushed between his ribs. He gave a sigh, then a gasp and a cough, and fell back. 'You've killed me!'

'Yes,' I said, kicking at his sword, sending it out of his reach. The blood was smearing his shirt and jack, and he sank to the ground as I strode past him to his companion, my sword all bloody as I pointed it at him. 'Who sent you?'

'We just saw you in the tavern.'

'You weren't in there. I would have seen you,' I said. It was a guess, but the way the two had launched their attack, especially the way that the swordsman had feinted like that, persuaded me that these were more than common footpads.

He sneered at me. 'How many enemies do you have?'

That would have taken some time to consider. All of Queen Mary's men, certainly, and probably a number of others too. I sheathed my dagger and set the edge of my sword on his throat.

His eyes widened as I slowly dragged the edge across his flesh. 'Stop!'

'Who was it?'

'I don't know. He paid us in cash to kill you.'

'How?'

'We was in a tavern up Aldgate and he pointed you out and told us to follow you and kill you.'

'How did he know you would agree?'

'He knew Bold Bob. They'd done it before.'

'Who is Bold Bob?'

'Him,' the man said and pointed to the other, now-expired assailant.

It was a source of irritation, I confess, to learn I had killed the wrong man. If this one had died and the swordsman survived, I might have learned more.

'What did this man look like?'

'I don't know. It was Bob saw him, not me. He was a merchant. Man called Luffrin or some such.'

I allowed him to live, and left him there, gripping his punctured shoulder. He was no more risk to me, and his companion Bold Bob was even less of a threat. Meanwhile I still had the problem of finding a suitable assassin for Sir Edmund de Vere.

And I must wonder about a merchant called 'Luffrin' or some such – and then I wondered – Luffrin: could that be Loughgren?

The attack was enough to persuade me that remaining down towards the docks was not a sensible plan. In preference I made my way homewards where I could sit and think through the men I knew who might be able to assist me in finding a man who could replace Jack Blackjack and remove de Vere.

At my house I have several men who are well-versed in all the martial arts. Two were members of the Masters of Defence under the good King Henry, and it was partly these two who taught me my skills at fighting.

I entered my house, pushing past the man standing at my door, and strode into my parlour. Sitting at my desk, I called sharply for Joel.

Joel is one of those men who looks like a small mountain come to life. I have heard foreign tales of giants built of stone, and Joel is one such fellow. He came to me after a lifetime of fighting for small purses. His ears have long since been pummelled into miserable rags of flesh, his nose broken so often that it lies squashed over his features, and his brows have been so regularly punched and cut that they project almost as far as his nose, so scarred are they.

However, Joel's brain is as clear and sharp as ever it was. He entered now, gave the room a quick glance, and then walked to my desk. Joel always stood close. For such a large man, he was surprisingly quietly spoken, and he appreciated the benefits of caution when discussing matters of importance. He also knew that when I called him to my parlour, it was usually for reasons that were better not bruited about.

'Joel,' I began, 'we have a need of a man who can remove our enemies, but someone who can do so subtly. A man we can hire, someone who is not immediately obvious as a man of Elizabeth's.'

'I will do it.'

I looked at the cragged – or cracked – features. It was tempting to think of using him, but were anything to go wrong, it would immediately make people think of me. All knew that Joel was my servant, that he worked for me. If I sent him to kill de Vere, it would immediately be clear to the meanest intellect that it was my fault. No, I must seek another.

'I am grateful, but no,' I said, explaining my reservations.

He nodded, his brows drawn into a fierce glower of concentration. 'There is one man I know of,' he said.

I took his advice and, with him leading the way, was soon in a tavern not far from St Paul's cross, where a vicar was giving an interminable sermon, and after asking the man at the bar, I was directed to a back room where, as soon as I entered, I was confronted by a shadowy figure leaning back against the wall opposite.

'I seek Master Humfrie?' I said.

The man nodded. He had a worn face, like a man who has seen too many summers, but his expression was affable enough as he looked from Joel to me and back. I walked to him and sat opposite him at his table. 'I understand that you can be hired for certain functions,' I said.

'Oh? Well, that would depend.'

'The sum I would offer would be substantial.'

'That would help,' he said. His eyes went back to Joel. 'Perhaps you would like to discuss this in private?'

'I trust my companion.'

'Who you trust ain't any interest to me,' Humfrie said.

It was enough to make me give a fleeting scowl. 'I would prefer to have him with me.'

'That's fine,' he said. 'In that case, master, many thanks and God speed.'

'*What?*'

He was rising. He set his empty pot on the table and picked up a hat. 'You have a need of help. I have a need of privacy while discussing such matters.'

It was tempting to command him to sit again, but there was a certain set to his shoulders that told me it would be a fruitless effort. I looked at Joel and said, 'Wait in the main bar.'

Joel, understandably, was irritated to be dismissed since our presence in that tavern, talking to Humfrie, was his idea, but there was nothing to be done. I jerked my head towards the door, and he lumbered out.

'That man has seen too many fights,' Humfrie said.

'He has seen his share.'

'And lost many, from his face. What can I do for you?'

'There is a man who . . . how can I put it? Who would be of greater service to me and my master if he were no more.'

'You would like him removed?'

'Yes.'

'There will be a goodly fee.'

'I understand that.'

'And it will take me a little while to arrange.'

'Be as quick as you can.'

'Tell me who and where I can find him.'

I left him some minutes later, lighter in my purse, but happily confident that my problems would soon be cured. Humfrie struck me as a most competent fellow. And cheaper than Jack.

PART FIVE

Jack's Tale Continues . . .

ELEVEN

On Tuesday, I had to try to work out what was happening. Who had killed Alice? What had happened to Vanderstilt? The idea that someone could have killed both just to get at me was so shocking that I was half tempted to put it from my mind. But you see, I have a great clarity of vision and can often see through other men's machinations and stratagems.

Oh, I know that some consider me dull-witted, but that is merely my ploy, to allow them to think of me as a dolt who is of no real threat, whereas in actual fact I have a sharp, keen brain that is like a razor at cutting through nonsense. As soon as I put my mind to it, I realized that I must be the real target of these deaths. Poor Alice had died as a means of upsetting me, perhaps – or could it be jealousy? A man who saw that I was so popular with women, and Alice in particular, and who decided to punish me by removing her? Vanderstilt, obviously, was targeted because he had money or something. But wait – the killer may have known he owed me money. I would be the assumed guilty party because of the overheard threat. That meant the murderer could escape and leave me to dance the Tyburn jig in his place. So someone had a desire to see Vanderstilt dead and out of the way, and I was a mere clot thrown to the constable to distract justice!

Thinking through all the possibilities gave me a sore head.

After Sunday's excitement, and my interview with Mark, I made my way down to the river, crossing in a wherry that looked and smelled as though it had spent the last ten years at the bottom of the river or some similar sewer.

Yes, I was going to the south side of the Thames again. It was not a view that gave me any pleasure or inspiration, but I was in need of some protection. My pistol was in Sir Edmund's hands, and I needed it back. I could, of course, have tried to acquire another gun, but that would have been expensive, and not terribly easy. There are not that many gunmakers of renown in London. The mechanical device of a wheel-lock pistol is complex and prone to failure. I needed a weapon that would be reliable.

Besides, I knew my own gun. And I was annoyed that this man dared to steal it from me.

I was going to go and fetch it back. Not on the day he stole it, and not on the Monday, but today. I felt sure that he would have been lulled into a conviction that his theft had succeeded, and he need not fear retaliation. I intended to show him he was wrong.

At the same time, I wanted to find the man responsible for murdering Alice. She was much in my mind. And I wanted to learn who could have killed Vanderstilt and left me to carry the weight of justice's incompetence.

But first I needed to rest and plan.

I know what you are thinking. Yes, you are rolling your eyes and gazing heavenwards because you think I was nothing more than a fool, that I had been duped by Sir Edmund de Vere, and that I was walking back into his trap.

Ah, but you have not thought this through. Of course, in the first place, he had shown himself to be a dangerous man who would be prepared to remove an innocent fellow's firearm without compunction or offer of compensation. But there, you see, that is the point! I realized that while sitting in the parlour of the Hat with one of the tarts and Piers, enjoying the warmth of the fire all that long Monday.

This is why I was in the post I enjoyed. I could reason through things, and from all this, it was clear to me: de Vere was a thief.

If he had been a murderer – if he had killed, for example, Vanderstilt – he would have wanted to silence me for harbouring suspicions against him. He would have had his men tie a weight about my waist, bind my hands, and throw me into the Thames. That is the sort of thing a madman with power would do. Instead, he had purloined my gun and released me. That might have been because he saw before him a tatterdemalion in foul clothing, a wastrel who could not realistically be a threat to him. He did not consider that I could bring any harm to him – even if I had a posse and pointed to him. No, not even if I had seen blood on his shirt, or Vanderstilt's feet poking out from beneath a cupboard. I was nothing, a nobody. Certainly not someone who could inspire fear and concern in the heart of a knight. Especially a knight who was at the height of his power and authority, as this fellow appeared to be.

No, I was convinced the fact that I was alive now meant that he was no murderer. And if he was no murderer, he could not have killed Vanderstilt.

But he did still hold my handgun, and I wanted it back.

The house was bright with lamplight when I stood there in the darkness and considered the best way to enter.

It was a perplexing question, of course. Where was my gun? Was it in the room where I had seen him, the room converted to an armoury? Or was he carrying it on his person? Not many would bother, admittedly. The handgun was a massive piece of metalwork, and must have weighed over four pounds. It would spoil the look of most suits of clothes, and from all I had seen of Sir Edmund, he was a man who cared about his appearance. On the whole, I felt it most likely that my gun was in that same room still, with all the other weapons.

The question was, how best should I enter, and how should I escape once more, considering the number of men in the building? I had seen four at least when I was borne in, as well as Sir Edmund himself, and I was sure that there would be many more about the place. It would be a hazardous place to enter unwanted.

I stood there a long while, staring at the building, wondering what would be the best way to gain access, while farther up the lane three scruffy urchins played with hoops, knocking them along the roadway with sticks, watched by a loafer squatting idly on a box and drinking from a flask. The cobbles proved seriously disinclined to allow the hoops to go far, and the jeering and laughter gradually began to annoy me, until I suddenly had a brilliant idea.

I accosted the largest of the three. He and his confederates eyed me suspiciously as I approached, allowing their hoop to roll to a rock, where it bounced and fell to the ground, whirling around and around until it settled with a rattle.

'Would you like to earn a penny?' I asked.

The middle-height lad to the left stepped forward in front of the other two. This one had a face sharp as a weasel's, and he peered at me, head tilted, like a sergeant eyeing a new recruit and not liking what he saw. 'Why?'

'I have a need of help.'

'What you want 's t' do?'

I explained my needs, and on the payment of tuppence – an exorbitant sum, but better than the cost of replacing my pistol – I contracted the three to my task.

Soon, I was hidden in the dark outside the house, waiting. Suddenly there was a flash of light, and I saw a small column of smoke begin to rise from an empty building over the road.

Fire is one of those dangers that no man can ignore. In a city like London, in which all the properties tend to be built of oak and wattles, a small fire can easily lead to a conflagration, and all residents know that their primary duty is to go and assist those attempting to put out the flames. Thus it was tonight.

Suddenly the front door burst open, and three men darted out bearing buckets. There was a horse trough just along the lane, and the three filled their vessels with that, running to throw the water on the flames.

I did not wait to see more, but made my way swiftly to the open front door. Inside, I recognized the screens passage, and crossed to the chamber where I had seen Sir Edmund. I could hear nothing. There was not a breath of air, and the whole house was still and silent. When I put my hand to the door's latch, it opened without difficulty, and I slipped inside.

There was no light in there, and I stood still until my eyes started to make out the shadowy outlines of weapon racks, tables and chairs. As soon as I could, I began to make my way forward to the desk where I had last seen my powder and shot and pistol. Here I patted the table, hoping that my search would soon be rewarded, but came across nothing but pieces of paper. I continued on, tapping at the desktop in my increasingly urgent search, but could find no sign of them. Frustrated, I fell into the seat behind the desk and struck something with my shoulder. Feeling for it, I found the strap of my shot wallet and powder flask. I pulled them on.

If they were here still, then surely so was my gun. I renewed my efforts, hunting all about me, until suddenly my fingers found a shelf behind me and, running my hand along it, praise the Lord, suddenly I found it.

And just as my fingers settled on it, the door opened and light from a horn lamp filled the room.

What? You expect me to say that I dropped to the floor and concealed myself? Or that I should have darted beneath the desk and hidden myself there? Or maybe I should have brazenly pointed my gun and threatened him?

I confess, each of these thoughts did occur to me later, when I was at my ease and could reflect on my situation with time on my hands. As it was, I did all that I could: I froze.

Sir Edmund appeared unsurprised to see me. His moustache was twisted up at one side as if in wry amusement, and he set his lamp on the nearest cupboard. 'So, you are a thief as well as an accuser?'

'I am concerned to retrieve what is mine,' I said hotly.

'Don't squeak, little sewer rat. You have no one to help you here.'

Shaking rather, I grasped my pistol firmly. I think he saw, because his eyes opened a little. 'So, you found it?'

I saw little point in responding to that, but shivered slightly as I set the dog on the wheel. If I pulled the trigger, the wheel would spin, striking sparks from the chip of stone in the dog's teeth, and as soon as a spark hit the pan where the powder lay, it would erupt in smoke and flame, and likely give de Vere an injury he would regret. His face told me that he was aware of the danger of such devices.

He grimaced, and walked to a chair, where he continued, sitting, 'What shall we do now, then? Your three friends in the lane told us you set fire to the building over the road and came in here as soon as the alarm was raised, so I came straight back, as you can see. Perhaps you should seek more reliable accomplices? In any case, you are here, in my house, so I am within my rights to defend myself. I think I should have you executed here. I dislike the thought that you might return here another evening. Put the gun down.'

'Not if you're going to kill me,' I said, I think quite reasonably.

'What is your name, little rat?' he asked, I think more than a little rudely.

'You can call me Jack Blackjack,' I said proudly.

He shook his head, tutting a fair bit, and then called out to someone called Will. In no time at all, a scrawny, greyhound-like, miserable character appeared in the doorway. His watery grey eyes took in the scene at a glance, and then he stood staring at his master with a troubled expression on his face.

'This fellow is Jack Blackjack, so he says. Go and get my gun from him,' Sir Edmund said.

Will looked at me, which seemed to involve staring for quite a long period at the gun's muzzle, before saying, 'But he's pointing it at us.'

'So, take it from him,' de Vere said with heavy patience.

Will looked at the gun again. I began to develop a liking for Will. He had his heart in the right place, and he plainly wanted to keep it there, unpunctured by a large ball fired from a weapon like mine.

'Go, *fetch*!' Sir Edmund said more sharply.

He may have looked like a hound, but Will disliked being commanded like one. 'He'll shoot me!'

'Then move quickly!'

He took a step forward, his face twisted like an old man's clenched fist. 'Would you give it to me?' he asked plaintively.

'No.'

'He won't give it me,' Will said to his master.

'In God's name!' Sir Edmund burst out, and started towards me. I lifted the gun to aim along the barrel, and Sir Edmund subsided, scowling. 'What will you do, you dunghill rat? I have twenty men at my beck and call, and I can have you trussed and thrown into the river in a trice!'

'Then I might as well shoot you now,' I said with, I think, elegant logic.

This appeared to strike Sir Edmund for the first time, with all the force of a lead hammer. 'Me? You can't shoot *me*! I'm a knight, you knave! I have the ear of the queen herself! Do you realize who you're dealing with?'

'No,' I said, and I think my honesty was transparent, because suddenly Sir Edmund looked still more anxious.

I stepped forward, towards Will, who remained in my path, until I motioned with the gun for him to step aside, and then I was past him and making my way to the front door at some speed, which was fine until Sir Edmund bellowed from the doorway behind me, calling for his men. I put on a fresh burst of speed, and went through the door.

At least, I entered the doorway, and would have continued through it, had not a large figure appeared in the way. I hit him in the lower breast with my head as I hurtled through, and he retreated with a loud '*Oof!*' of pain, to fall on his rump. I had rebounded a little, but now he was out of my way, I carried on past him, over the yard and out into the lane.

The three boys were all there, jeering and making sarcastic comments about the value of my money compared to the three pennies Sir Edmund's men had given them, and then they were behind me.

I did not stop running until I had passed near London Bridge, and there I turned up and back towards Aldgate without thinking.

I stood outside my old house and stared at it. The hour was late, and I knew that the bridge over the river would be closed. I would be apprehended as soon as I tried to cross that way, and the wherrymen would have stopped working by now too. I could not make my way over to the Cardinal's Hat, and instead must find somewhere else to rest my head – because I did need to sleep. The excitement of the day, the thrill of stealing back my pistol, the run all the way from the river to my old home, all had made me weary. If there was a good tavern nearby, I would have gone there to drink wine and fall into a stupor, but the ones nearer my house here in Aldgate suffered from the fact that I was moderately well known. If I were to enter any of the local hostelries, I should be recognized immediately and, from past experience, slung into the Aldgate gaol once more.

I needed to go somewhere else, and my eyes wandered over the street to Susan Appleby's house. It stood only a matter of paces away, the building rising opposite my own. Many were the times I had woken in my bed, looked across the street at her bedchamber, and seen her carefully undress just to torment me.

She really was a delightful bed mate, a lusty wench with a wayward eye and imagination to match.

It was tempting to go to her now, but if Saul, her husband, was there, I would have some explaining to do. Not about me and his wife, but about my arrest, and how I had escaped. After all, as far as anybody here knew, I was a fugitive from the law.

In the end, it was a neighing horse that brought me to my senses. I had two houses which I could not enter: neither the one here, nor my new property at St Helen's. However, I also had outbuildings, and the rear of my house here had a small barn and hayloft. I had always maintained a good hayloft, even though my horse had been held in a stable south of the river, where stabling was cheaper. In case I brought my own beast, or a visitor appeared with a horse needing refreshment, I made sure that there was plenty of fodder available. And just now, that hay seemed enormously appealing.

I made my way to the rear yard quietly, and thence into my barn. The hayloft was reached by a ladder, and I propped it against the boards of the loft space and climbed, dragging the ladder up after me.

How long was it since I had last slept in hay? Thinking back, it must have been not since I had taken a certain miller's daughter to have a frolic. It was she who, next morning when her father found me in her bed, denied knowing me, which was enough for her father to decide to see whether he could untwist my head from my shoulders. I only escaped with my life by the skin of my teeth – or, rather, the skin of my left cheek. In the act of fleeing, I stumbled and tripped, giving me the scar I wear to this day. But I do not regret it. How could I? I have often told new conquests that the scar was honourably won when I defended a maid from being ravished by a madman with a dagger . . . or a sword, sometimes, depending on my audience. Alice had been convinced easily enough that it was earned in defending two maids from a gang of roughs who sought to injure me for defending their virtue. I had, as I told her, been forced to kill two and injure three more before the remaining fellows realized their danger and ran from my justified fury. She had been most accommodatingly impressed and demonstratively grateful for my act of courage and honour, and rewarded me by losing her own virtue. That memory was enough to bring a little smirk to my lips.

I settled back in the hay. It was warm, and there was that odour of summer pastures when the scythes have gone through, which always makes a man feel randy. I would have given much for Alice to be beside me now. She had been such a willing mattress-walloper.

And that was enough to make my eyes open and frown.

She had been a good companion, yes, but more than that, she had been a very generous-hearted, kind young woman. What was the need for anyone to hurt her, let alone kill her? She did not deserve it. I was angry – yes, angry – to think that a man had taken her away. Why, for jealousy? It could not have been for her wealth. And why just now? There was a curious circularity to the facts of Vanderstilt's disappearance and then Alice's death. I know it has been said that bad things come in threes . . .

A shiver ran down my spine. It felt like icy aspic, slowly trickling, until it met the base of my spine, where it rested, leaching into my flesh.

Did death also come in threes? Would the next one be my own? Or was Vanderstilt already dead, taking the staircase to Heaven with Alice, while no doubt the moving lump of rock that had followed me to the Thames and drowned was already finding the afterlife much warmer.

That was a satisfying thought to conjure with.

TWELVE

I woke to pain.

There are a few rules to which I will adhere through my life, and one of the key ones is: do not go to sleep with a handgun shoved into your belt. It felt as if I had been stabbed with a halberd, and at the same time slammed in the backside with a heavy maul. I rolled to my right, trying to escape the agony, but it only seemed to exacerbate things. Giving an involuntary yelp, I was forced to rest on all fours, head dangling, while I caught my breath.

It was some while before I could struggle slowly to my feet, feeling like a man three times my age and ready for the coffin. It took a lot longer for me to manage to deploy and descend the ladder, and even then I was forced to stand clutching at a convenient pillar for some time before I could walk. I pulled the gun from my belt and moved it to the front of my body, considering that I really ought to draw the ball and replace the powder and priming, but just now I had other things on my mind. First among these was the matter of Vanderstilt's body.

He must surely have been discovered by now, had he been murdered. It was not as if a body could go unnoticed by the roadside, and there had been plenty of time for anyone to notice if a body had been thrown into their yard. Yards in London were not enormous, after all. The gardens of the palaces and massive houses further along The Strand were big enough for a body to get lost, perhaps, but not the usual little hovels and gardens here, towards the east.

Of course, a body thrown in the Thames would be lost forever, but a footpad coming across Vanderstilt would have the problem of carrying his victim's body to the water. Vanderstilt had left Sir Edmund's house, according to the knight, and headed homewards. He might have taken the route eastwards, but he would have to turn up along the wall at the latest, and there were not that many alleys leading to the water.

It struck me that many of those that did exist between houses did not have regular passersby. Perhaps a murderer could have stabbed him and slung him into the nearest alleyway? It would save him the effort of dragging or carrying the body to the water's edge. And if it were a quiet, unobtrusive alleyway, maybe no one had seen him. If they had, of course, they might have decided to 'unsee' him. The first finder of a body was invariably fined to ensure he would appear before the coroner and justices for future investigations, and many chose to walk by hurriedly rather than be exposed to the inevitable cost.

Thus it was that I made my way back towards the river, carefully noting how far I was from Sir Edmund's house, and determined to avoid any risk of seeing him. From Tower Hill, I started methodically searching all the little byways that led away from the main road, those heading towards the river, and those heading away. I found trash and garbage of all types: broken barrels, animal bones, old and worn leather buckets, several broken tools of different types, a number of dead rats – and on one notable occasion a body, which reeked of putrefaction. But it was that of a dog, not Vanderstilt.

I was almost at Sir Edmund's house, and about to return the way I had come, when I heard shouting and turned to see Sir Edmund in the street, while a man stood shaking his fist at the knight. Sir Edmund appeared unimpressed by the display, and shortly afterwards raised a hand. One of his men stepped forward immediately and slammed his fist into the stranger's stomach. I could hear his gasp of anguish as he folded up like a poorly constructed chair. Sir Edmund stepped over him and continued on his way to where a groom held a horse for him. He mounted and trotted past his agonized victim, ignoring him in much the same way that he ignored the three urchins who were playing farther along the street again, this time throwing stones to hit a target – I could not see what. I slid myself back into the alley, out of his sight.

When the knight and his small retinue of four men had passed by, I peered out after them, and was relieved to see that they were already disappearing around the next curve in the street. I quickly hurried out and along the way to the man, who was now on his knees, dazed.

'Master, are you well? Can I help you up?' I said.

He declined my offer of a physician, but was grateful for my hand to support him. 'What was that about, master?' I asked as he tottered with me to the nearest wall. I was keen to lead him away from Sir Edmund's house, and away from the Tower, since that was the direction Sir Edmund had taken, but the fellow was not in a condition to rush. His breath came in painful little gasps and whistles. Besides, my own back was hardly up to a mad scramble from the place.

'He owes me money. Usual thing: rich bastards think they can get away with thieving from the small fellows like us. Can't trust these *nobles*.' He made it sound like a very rude comment on the knight's birth. 'Not one. They all think to steal just because they have men behind them who'll enforce their thefts!'

'What is your profession, master?'

'I am a master armourer. He had weapons needing work, and I dealt with them, but now he refuses to pay my bill. Well, I'll never work for him again, and I'll tell the others in my guild to avoid him too.'

'What did he want done?' I asked, trying to manoeuvre him away from the wall. 'Look, there is a tavern over there. I could do with a refreshment – what of you?'

He graciously assented. I had already had an opportunity to weigh his purse – it was my old profession, after all – and before long we had entered the Wherryman's Retreat, a lively little drinking house at the top end of London Bridge. I knew this place from many years before, and I knew it to be frequented by cheerful workers from the docks, boats and wherries. It was the sort of alehouse where a fight could break out at any moment, and many faces would be bloodied and noses broken, but owing to the size of the landlord, a short but broad Scotsman with a temper so vile none would gainsay him, all fights tended to end swiftly, with those desperately keen to fight soon knocked on the pate by the owner and slung from the door.

My companion, William ('call me Bill') Paynter, was a shortish, sallow-complexioned man of some four- or five-and-thirty years, with shrewd, dark-brown eyes that measured and assessed a fellow while he spoke. He accepted a pot of ale from me with a show of reluctance, since, as he said, he owed me the drink, but we agreed that he could provide the second drinks, and with that arrangement we settled to discuss Sir Edmund.

'He's a vile, paltry bastard with the makings of a second-level peasant,' was his considered opinion of the good knight. 'He spends his time in that house, riding off to see the nobs, and trampling ordinary folk on his way.'

'What nobs?'

'Oh, he is very keen on all the big families. Stuck-up, arrogant arse-wipe!'

'I suppose you meet many men like him.'

He grunted, sank a quarter pint. 'Not like him, no. Plenty of men want good weaponry now, but most pay cash on the nail. Him? Never.'

I murmured sympathetically.

'There's a man up near Bishopsgate, Master Loughgren, I was working on some items for him until last week, and he paid without muttering. Hard cash. Thought de Vere'd be the same, but oh, no! No, he said I was late, and he'd wanted his things earlier. I told him, I was held up by this other contract, and he went all sniffy with me, the God-poxed . . .'

He hesitated and gave me a sideways glance. No doubt he had been about to curse the man for being a Catholic. Since the queen's crackdown on protestants, and her father's new church, which he'd only created to ensure he could throw her mother from his palaces and take the younger Boleyn woman to his bed, I suppose Mary's dislike of the church was unsurprising – still, it seemed over the top to keep burning the religious to death to avenge herself on her father. He'd been dead some while.

I gave a quiet comment, indicating that I was also not enamoured of the latest experiment in religious zeal, and Bill nodded. 'A man's faith should be his own, and not punishable by any,' he said, glancing about him truculently. 'Master Loughgren thought the same, so he said. This de Vere was from a different mould. Always changes with the wind, that sort. Carried his rosary like it was tied to his wrist, but go to good King Henry's religion, and he'd be all for breaking the altar stones and melting the chalices!'

He went on: 'Used to be only the queen whom de Vere cared about, but now he's keen on seeing all the high-ups. The Earl of Pembroke, John Boxall . . . all those important to the queen. He ingratiates himself with them, visits them. Even now, he is on his way to the Tower for a meeting with someone. Probably Boxall, the queen's secretary or whatever it is he does.'

I knew of Boxall, the Secretary of State. Not a man I had ever met, but he was well enough known up and down the country as a keen ally of the queen, and busy imposer of the harshest laws. In the same way, the Earl of Pembroke was counsellor to the queen, and implacable foe to Lady Elizabeth. These were men who would be problematic for Elizabeth at any time. It made me wonder what de Vere was planning. Clearly he wanted to advance himself in the queen's estimation, I guess, since he was trying to get close to her supporters.

'You know the queen's health is despaired of?' Bill said. Our second drinks arrived and he paid before laying a podgy finger aside his nose and narrowing his eyes. 'I've heard she won't see out the week.'

I was sceptical of that. 'You know how many times I've heard her life is despaired of in the last year? If the woman sneezes, she has the plague; if she stubs her toe, she has leprosy – if you listen to the rumours.'

'Aye, you can scoff, but this time 'tis different. She has a babe, so they say, but we know what happened last time. She lost it, didn't she? And now rumour is, she's made a new will. Must mean she thinks she's going to peg out. Maybe childbirth will do it. A childbed is often a deathbed, isn't it?'

'I suppose so,' I agreed. After all, who didn't have a friend or relative whose mother, sister or daughter hadn't died in labour? It was the curse of women, and not something I begrudged them. The thought of nurturing a babe in the womb was curiously repellent, and the pain involved in birth . . . well, I was happy to be a man.

'How will you get the money you're owed?'

'I doubt I'll ever get it back. All that work – sharpening, strengthening the staves, oiling and ensuring they were all ready for use . . . It was a lot of work.'

'I can imagine,' I said. I had bought a third round of ale, and we were getting on famously. I liked this fellow Bill. He was a good man, friendly and open, I thought. The sort of man with whom it would be pleasant to while away some hours. We chatted; we drank. He ordered a fourth round.

'Why did he want so many weapons?' I mused when I had bought the fifth. 'He doesn't have that many men about him. Is he going to sell them to the Tower armoury?'

'Nah, I heard one of his men talking, saying they needed the arms for when the queen dies,' Bill said. He yawned, blinking rather owlishly, and looked offended when I chuckled, but then he began to laugh as well. He bought the sixth round; he really was a splendid character.

'When she dies? Why?'

'Oh, in case of rebellion or war, I suppose,' Bill said with a light shrug. 'It would be hard to avoid, I suppose. I mean, all the nobs now, they won't want to give up everything, will they? What'll they do? Invite the queen's husband back here? A bleedin' *Spaniard*? You reckon London would let him in? The nobs, they'd want Philip back, just so they can keep fleecing us all, like Sir bloody Edmund.'

I think it was about now that I bought the seventh round, but I confess our conversation was too involved for me to be absolutely certain. 'What if he doesn't come?'

'Oh, well, there's only Lady Elizabeth now, ain't there? Who else could take the throne? She's Henry's blood, God rest him. No one else, now his son's dead already. No, I reckon it'd be down to a fight 'tween Lady 'Liz'beth on one side and the nobs on t'other. And all of us in the middle.'

'I don't want another war,' I said plaintively.

'Nor me neither.'

'I was in the fight over Wyatt's revolt. I didn't like it.'

'Me too.'

We clasped hands then, and even had a brief, manly hug, as befitted comrades-in-arms.

Bill looked at his pot. 'Think we'd better have one for the road, eh?'

* * *

When the pail of water hit me, I was startled to full wakefulness in an instant. Standing over me was the ape-like features of the Scottish landlord. There was a kind of vicious grin on his face at the sight of me with water dripping from my upper body. 'Are ye awake, ye drunken sot? Be off wi' ye! Ye've been snoring like a sow in shit since noon.'

I would have liked to have passed comment on him, his ancestry and many of his vile attributes, but just at that moment, I discovered I required something to moisten my mouth. My tongue was apparently cloven to my palate, and I found speech difficult. At least my purse was still on my belt. I clambered to my feet, making free use of the assistance offered by a stool and table, and at last stood, swaying gently in the breeze from the open door. My hearing appeared to have dulled, as had my brain, and I lumbered over to the bar with the gait of an eighty-year-old stevedore bearing a heavy bale of wool. Have you ever tried to lift a bale of wool? Trust me, the buyer gets value for his pennies.

'What?' the landlord demanded.

I managed to indicate, by degrees, and with the croaking harshness of the thirsty, that I would appreciate a pint of his finest beer, and soon I had a mug of strong, dark ale before me. I sank the first quarter swiftly, but the remaining liquid took rather longer. For some inexplicable reason, I felt desperately thirsty, but at the same time my desire for ale was heavily diminished. Finishing the drink was mostly an exercise in determination.

Outside a thin drizzle had begun to fall. It was, I suppose, mid-to-late-afternoon, and all I knew was I had a desperate need of a comfortable bed. I made my way, rather haltingly, to London Bridge, over the new drawbridge, built to replace the one demolished during Wyatt's rebellion – although I personally reckon they retrieved all the timbers they could, and supplemented those which had fallen into the Thames with any old rotten spars they could find, while charging the city for the best oak.

Aldermen and officials are quick to see any opportunity to pocket a profit.

Still, I managed to avoid the carts and horses coming over the bridge, and kept on going to the south bank, where I wandered along the river to the bear pits and thence to the Cardinal's Hat, where I gratefully made my way to Piers' chamber in the roof, and collapsed on his bed roll.

In my time I have often heard it said that the best drinking sessions tend to be those which have not been planned, but which evolve after a chance meeting. I can certainly confirm that my lunchtime drinking with Bill had been immensely pleasant, but it had depleted the energy with which I am usually so filled. As soon as I closed my eyes, I was out like a pole-axed bullock, and it was not until Piers appeared, some little while after dark, that I woke again, this time with a pounding in my head as if someone was cudgelling me unmercifully.

'What've you been doing?' he demanded. 'You've got eyes like piss 'oles in snow, and you're almost see-through, like a ghost.'

I expressed my gratitude for his loud welcome, and slowly swung my legs to the ground, showing the caution of a prudent man. I did not want my head to fall from my shoulders.

'I had a meeting with a man,' I said. 'I helped him when he was attacked, and he insisted on treating me to a drink.'

'A drink, or a barrel?' he asked rather snidely. It was jealousy, of course. 'Who was this fool?'

'A man called Bill.' I swallowed. 'He's an armourer,' I added.

'And he was attacked by footpads?'

'No, by a *respectable* knight – Sir Edmund de Vere.'

'You be careful with 'im,' Piers said suddenly. I was surprised to see that his face was serious.

'Why?'

'De Vere's the sort who'd pull your fingernails out, not to torture, but just to see 'ow you'd react.'

'He'd best not try it with me,' I said. I had left my pistol this time on the floor by the bed, and now I picked it up and patted it.

'You think that'd scare him?'

'It did,' I said smugly, and told him about the meeting in Sir Edmund's house.

'I think the ale 'as addled what brains you had,' Piers said uncompromisingly. 'Are you moon-struck? He's rich, he's got the ear of lords and all, and—'

'I know, and he's got a huge armoury of weapons he's collecting in his house,' I said.

'What?'

'That's what I found when I went to talk to him. He has a large armoury he's collecting. Bill reconditioned some of them for him. Vanderstilt brought them over from Holland, so I suppose they were old weapons. Bill is obviously good at his work. He has other clients, like a man called Loughgren, he told me, and—'

'So what?'

His words made me feel a little flat. 'I just thought de Vere might be planning to sell to the Tower's armoury, but maybe he has another buyer?'

'Or perhaps 'e hasn't,' Piers said. He was frowning now, concerned.

'What?'

'You 'ave the brain of a mayfly, don't you?' he said. He picked up a small cask, shook it mournfully, and let it fall. 'No more brandy,' he said.

'At least you won't get charged like the gulls who come here to nail the wenches,' I said. The last time I had been here, I had been appalled to be presented with a normal client's charges.

'All I was thinking was, if he didn't have someone else to sell to, what would he need all those weapons for?' Piers continued. 'Change his name to Wyatt, and what would you think?'

'Wyatt? Why would I change his name to Wyatt?' I said, somewhat confused. 'Wyatt the rebel, you mean?'

He looked at me sadly, as though mourning the man I had become.

My mouth fell open. '*Oh!*'

Because, although this may not have occurred to you, there is little doubt that Piers might have had a point. It was quite possible that Sir Edmund de Vere was collecting weapons so that he might himself start an insurrection. And perhaps he had learned from the past. When Wyatt tried to raise the kingdom against the queen, he managed to have the men of Kent join him, and anticipated that London would also rise with them – but he was wrong. His rebellion, and life, ended when he reached the gates to London. His little army had achieved much, but that availed them nothing because, with no siege machines, there was no means of breaking into the city, and with the citizens' determined defence, Wyatt could not enter. Instead, his force broke on the walls like waves on the shore.

It was not a thought that gave me any pleasure. But it did have the merit of making sense.

'He wouldn't dare. The queen would have him beheaded in the blink of an eye,' I pointed out.

'Do ye walk the streets with eyes and ears closed? What if the queen were not on the throne? 'Ave you not heard the rumours of 'er illness?'

And of course, that made perfect sense. As Bill had said in the tavern, if it were true that the queen was dying, or that she was expecting to die in childbirth, there would very likely be fighting again to resolve the succession. Spaniards invading, English Catholics fighting the Church of England congregations, perhaps even the French coming to take part – they always enjoyed a chance to tweak the English tail – or the Scottish?

I sat back with my head in my hands. 'Oh!'

Bill had mentioned some men – Boxall, the Earl of Pembroke and Cardinal Pole, I think. They were all enthusiastic supporters of the queen – and of the Catholic faith. If Mary were to die, the three could perhaps use arms from someone like de Vere to wrest control of London and Parliament, preventing Elizabeth from taking her rightful place as heir to the throne. Suddenly my belly roiled with acid.

'You need to tell your master. John Blount will know what to do,' Piers said.

'Yes. Yes, I should.'

But what I was really thinking was that I needed to escape London. Much though the thought was anathema, I wondered whether I should depart and make my way back to Devon. At least that was a long way away from any possible fighting, even if it was equally far from a decent tailor, barber, cook or brewer.

There are times in every life when the simplest of plans goes slightly awry.

In my life I have often experienced that kind of problem, from the time when I managed to pick a purse and discovered that its bulging contents involved solely wooden counters; or the time when I sought to protect a fellow proposed as my victim, and the fool stepped backwards from a jetty and drowned when I tried to save him; or the time when I was looking after a Spaniard, and the fool had himself murdered before me; or . . .

But you take my meaning. There are times in everyone's life (very commonly in mine) when events conspire to throw a man's life into extreme danger, with no reason that is obvious to the poor fellow involved. He is merely the unwitting victim of events that are outside his control.

That was the situation today.

Leaving Piers, I went down to the bar. I had need of refreshment, and something that would help me plan my escape from London – for it was clear to me that I must escape, and make my way elsewhere. Not only for the dangers of a revolt in the city, but also because I was wary of the risk of becoming imprisoned once more. Justice can move slowly, but on occasion it can prove effective.

The Hat had a large hall below, where the doxies all displayed themselves for the clients. Some were fussing over a man in a seat, while others, in various stages of undress, were chatting quietly in a corner, no doubt discussing the more foolish gulls they had entrapped and fleeced. All I saw immediately, though, was the man at the bar, a thickset fellow who was set to pouring drinks and opening flasks for clients. The girls were expected to stay as sober as any of them were capable. It didn't always work, but they were not supposed to drink too much of the wine unless the gulls were paying. The profit on such drinks was one reason why I had often thought of opening my own brothel. It would prove a useful investment for some of the money I had acquired in the last few years with my alternative career.

I spoke with the barman, gaped at the price of one cup of wine, and paid. Turning, I sipped the drink just as the two harpies about the man in the seat moved aside, and I almost dropped my drink.

Their client was Sir Edmund de Vere.

Choking as the wine was sent along the wrong channel, I turned back to the bar quickly. I would finish this drink speedily, I decided, and leave. I could make my way out towards the river, and disappear among the alleyways there. Sir Edmund need never know I had been here.

What misfortune was this, that he should arrive here on this evening? It was so unfair, so unreasonable, that it was tempting to run to a church and complain to Him. I mean to say, we are told always that we have free will, and thus those who behave sinfully are fully responsible for their own actions, but take my situation here: it was hardly *my* choice that Sir Edmund should follow me to my favourite brothel. How could anything happening here be my fault? No matter: I would leave, and quickly at that.

I gulped the wine, pulled my cowl over my head, and made my way from the room, head down and trying to move as swiftly as possible without attracting any attention.

In this I was successful. I stopped in the doorway to make sure, and when I glanced back, I saw that the knight was fully engaged in a spirited communication with a red-haired whore whom I recognized: Rose. I confess, I was a little put out. She was one of my favourite tarts in the establishment, and I would have liked to spend an hour or two with her myself, but it was plain enough that Sir Edmund intended to monopolize her that evening.

With a little sigh of regret, I turned and sped on my way.

Or would have. Unfortunately, my swift movement meant I was unaware of the young apprentice goose who was at that moment entering bearing a metal tray full of drinks. I turned, felt a soft body with one hand, heard a gentle scream, stumbled over a long leg, and tumbled to the ground, my fall heralded by the brazen clatter of a metal sheet striking the floor just before five expensive glasses and goblets and a silver jug all joined it.

The pleasant aspect of this was that the young wench had rather delightfully fallen over me. The more immediate, and unpleasant, aspect was that she prevented my swift escape. She was a delicious little strumpet, but even delicious little strumpets can be moderately heavy when lying across a fellow lying on the ground.

And even a delicious little strumpet can be forgotten when a face like Sir Edmund's appears above a fellow.

'Oh, er . . .' I spluttered, and gave a smile of welcome as the wench climbed off me, naturally with a show of reluctance. Perhaps her apprenticeship had begun? Or, perhaps she was not keen to leave me because that must involve a discussion with the madam who owned the Cardinal's Hat, about who was going to pay for the spilled drinks and broken glasses. I have met the madam of the Hat, and I would not wish to upset her – but then, I am a fellow who is reluctant to offend the fairer sex. Perhaps she would be better and kinder towards a young trainee.

The chit scurried out, and shortly afterwards I heard a slap and a yelp. Perhaps the madam was not so gentle and kindly, after all.

'Master Blackjack. How pleasant to see you once more,' Sir Edmund said, and took a step nearer.

I would have scrambled to move away, usually, but just now I was painfully aware of broken shards of glass lying on the floor, and I was reluctant to put my hands on the ground in case I slashed myself. I can stand almost any pain, it should be said, and my courage knows few bounds – but there is no reason to inflict additional pain when it's unnecessary. I climbed to my feet cautiously, wary of a blow from the knight, but it seemed that he was on his best behaviour, and did not wish to assault me in the brothel.

'Come with me, Master Blackjack,' he said. 'I should like to refresh you. There is no need,' he added as he led the way to his table, 'for us to be enemies. I understand your desire to find Vanderstilt. I had not appreciated your position, when you came to visit me. You should have said that you had been accused of his murder. I thought it was purely your concern, as his landlord, for the wellbeing of your tenant. If I had realized that you had another reason for finding his body, I would have offered to aid you, rather than protecting myself by removing your weapon. When you retrieved it, and did not kill me, I realized that you were not just an assassin sent to kill me.'

'Why would you think me an assassin?'

He chuckled. 'Master Blackjack, I think we can set aside pretence? We are two gentlemen discussing matters of importance to the state. You have a certain reputation amongst the lower classes of the city. They talk about you behind their hands, quietly, and with great respect. Obviously, when a man like you appears in my house, I am going to suspect your reasons for coming.'

Well, put like that, there was a degree of common sense.

He continued: 'And, of course, when I discovered you

possessed an assassin's weapon, I felt sure that my suspicions were confirmed. As a wealthy man, I have, alas, built up a considerable array of enemies. As you saw, I have been forced to accumulate weapons for my own defence. If it were to come to pass that a small force decided to attack my house, I am confident enough that I could defend myself and my people. Not that I anticipate any large assault, of course. The queen's peace must not be infringed. Hah! Especially when she is close to her lying in!'

'If she is to have her child, she and the boy may well need protection,' I said.

'Boy? You feel sure that it will be a boy?'

'It is the rumour,' I said. 'I have no more knowledge than my butcher, but we can hope that the succession will be secure. The country needs a strong hand to guide it, and a man would obviously be preferable. Women,' I added slightly owlishly, for my host had provided me with a goblet of strong wine, and on top of my previous imbibing the fumes were enough to make my head whirl, 'are altogether too flighty and flippant. They seek fripperies, not fighting. Hah! Look at how quickly Queen Mary lost us Calais!'

'Yes. Quite,' Sir Edmund said, rather coldly, I thought. 'I was there.'

Hastily, I added, 'And I have little doubt but that you were courageous and fought like a lion – like all the other defenders of the queen's lands – but to fight when you know that your mistress . . . Well, if you were fighting for our old King Henry, that would be different. That would put fire in the belly of any soldier in his army.'

'You think we lacked fire in our guts?'

'Yes . . . *no*! I'm sure you were all keen to best the Frenchies. I mean, they are hardly fearsome, are they? The French are the sort to turn and flee at the first sight of English steel. It was . . .'

I became aware that I was painting the English army at Calais in a less than favourable light and quickly clammed up, staring at my goblet miserably.

'The men were brave enough, but we were unfortunate,' Sir Edmund said quietly. 'I was in one of the outlying forts, and the French moved past us, to take the town itself. It was terrible!

Like watching the sea enveloping a castle built of sand. But we stood strong and determined. And I will never again see the queen's wishes thwarted. I know how grievously she felt the loss of her French territories, and if possible, I will ensure that she never suffers like that again. While I breathe, I will support her and her legacy. And if she were to have a boy child, I would see it as my duty to protect and serve him, too. Were she to be attacked, I would be in the first line of defence – and damn all God-foresworn traitors!'

I nodded emphatically, indicating my total agreement.

'What of you, though, Master Blackjack? Whom would you support?'

'Me?'

'Yourself, I suppose. In your profession, the most important person has to be yourself.'

'I am a loyal subject,' I protested. And it was true, to an extent. My loyalties were occasionally divided, since I suffered from my attachment to Lady Elizabeth, but I saw no need or reason to upset my queen.

'Well, I am sure that you will want to continue to support her, then.'

I am no fool. While Queen Mary was maintaining her teams of experimenters dedicated to seeing how much effort was needed to break a man's body as well as his will in her famed chambers at the Tower, I was never going to argue with a comment of that kind. 'Of course.'

'Good. You may soon have an opportunity to prove your support of her. One never knows when such opportunities may arise.'

I left him relieved that he so obviously saw in me a useful ally. It was, after all, vastly preferable to be a friend to a man who could see to my destruction in a moment. He had not tried to hurt me, nor even steal my gun, but instead had behaved perfectly reasonably, as one gentleman to another.

Admittedly, looking down at my clothing, it was hard to believe that he had recognized in me another man of equal status, but I suppose my innate courtesy and obviously cultured manner persuaded him immediately that I was the perfect example of a gentleman. It takes a gentleman to recognize an equal, of course.

It's not something a tradesman would understand, but fellows like Sir Edmund and I can instantly spot someone of similar position.

Then again, he might just have been disinclined to start a fight in his favourite brothel. The madam might have banned him from returning, should he start a brawl.

I left the room and went outside to get some fresh air. For some reason, after the day's exertions, I felt more than a little light-headed. Perhaps it was the impact of the young wench hitting my belly, but I was aware of a definite queasiness. I was glad to have made peace with Sir Edmund, but could not leave this odd feeling of discomfort. Perhaps it was just the amount of wine and ale I had drunk, I reasoned. Certainly, I had not drunk quite so much in some little while, what with lunchtime drinks with Bill, then more with Piers, and now wine with Sir Edmund. Perhaps it was tiredness. Maybe I needed more sleep.

Piers was once more back on the door, guarding the way to the wenches. I decided to go for a walk along the river to clear my head a little again, and then go to bed with a fresh perspective on things.

I walked up, past the bear pits and the slobbering brutes held in the mastiff cages, before reaching the shore and turning west, following a little track that took me along the edge of the river. It must have been an unpopular path, for there was no mud or unpleasant pools along it. Mostly I had to negotiate my way past the detritus of broken ships: spars, barrels and other garbage that had collected at the river's edge.

If I could, I would have left the path and taken a more inland route, but just here there was a thick hedge at the side of the path, and I had no option but to continue.

The smell was foul, it has to be said, but there were many people living in London, and the excrement was enough to create its own river. Which is to say that the majority of the Thames was just that. The waters were grey and dismal in the dark, and the occasional candle or rushlight in the houses on the opposite bank only served to emphasize the grim scene. It was enough to make me shiver, and I turned to return to the Hat, when I saw something I had not expected – nor hoped – to see.

Emerging from the gloom was a monstrous figure, a terror from the dreams of Satan himself. I gave an involuntary start, and was about to run, when a voice behind me said, 'Wait, Jack.'

I span to find myself facing the blackmailer. When I looked back, I realized that this monstrous figure was in fact the second brute from the day when these two had threatened me with blackmail.

'Master Blackjack, wait. We ain't goin' to hurt you – I think we can help each other.'

You may be assured that I was not of a mind to trust him. His words were honeyed, but honey can be used to trap animals, and I had no desire to be a victim of this pair. Besides, if they knew that I had been responsible, sort of, for the death of their comrade, they might well change their tones.

However, we were all on the same path. The hedge was a barrier on one side, the river on the other. The thought of diving into those befouled waters was, believe me, thoroughly unappealing. Yet it was plain enough that I would not succeed in passing the blackmailer or his tor. Both were aware of my speed, agility and courage after our last little battle in the alleyway.

He bowed and offered his hand. I took it reluctantly. He still had his troll behind me, and I was not going to try to pick a fight with a monster that size. Not unless I had an escape route available.

'What did you do to Alice?' I managed at last.

'Who?' Perkin Bagnall said, and he looked frankly baffled as he spoke. When I explained, he shook his head. 'I heard she'd died – that was when the coroner was called – but I swear on me mother's grave we had nothing to do with her. When we saw you last, we wanted to talk to you, that was all. We'd been watching you for some little while, and it seemed the best way to gain your attention, to mention her, but I assure you we had nothing to do with assaulting her.'

'You want to blackmail me.'

'No!' he said, but gave me a sly glance that seemed to disprove his denial.

'What do you want with me, then?'

'Look, you're a sensible fellow, ain't you? We want your help.'

'How?' My head was beginning to hurt. The nausea that had afflicted me before had returned with full force, and I felt sweaty and uncomfortable. And chilly. I wrapped my arms about my upper chest.

First, he gave me a straight look. 'I've heard you was loyal to the queen in the rebellion.'

'Of course,' I said. That was an easy one. I didn't see the need to mention that now my loyalty had been bought by her half-sister.

'You'd do whatever necessary to protect her?'

This was much like my conversation with Sir Edmund. Everyone seemed to want to confirm my allegiance. 'Of course,' I lied. *Whatever* was a very large and deeply unsatisfactory word for me. I did not intend to risk my life, after all. But saying such things can be hazardous.

'So you'd be happy to assist her, protect her?'

'What do you want of me?' I snapped at last. The nausea was griping at my stomach now.

'Her heir is soon to be born. Many of us want to see he can inherit his realm, but others don't. They want to see him lose it. People like that Sir Edmund de Vere, who plots to overthrow the queen's wishes. We need to show her officers he's a threat to her, that he wishes to take over the throne.'

'No, he wants to protect her and her baby. He is collecting weapons so he can guard her and the boy.'

'He's collecting weapons, yes, along with others, to take over the throne.'

'He has told me that he wanted to defend her.'

'He lied.'

'How can you tell?' I demanded. 'He seemed convincing to me.'

'I know he lied because we've been watching him for many months, ever since we first suspected he was plotting against the queen. Sir Edmund de Vere and his men think that because the queen is unwell, they can usurp her throne for their own purposes.'

'He told me he was entirely loyal to the queen,' I said heatedly.

'What else would a traitor say, eh? He protests his undying loyalty? Of course he does! Else he risks the rack, and any one of the other interesting pastimes the torturers can dream up. Yes, we've been watching him and his house for an age. That is how we knew you were here. We have followed you from the moment we saw you today, when he left to visit the Tower.'

'If he had reason to fear the torturers, why would he go there?'

Bagnall gave me a very straight look. 'He is not known to be under suspicion, yet. He is thought of as a loyal subject still. His plotting has not been bruited abroad – yet.'

'But I have heard that he regularly meets with the queen's own counsellors – Boxall, the Earl of Pembroke and . . .'

'All them, yes.'

'You mean they too are involved?'

'De Vere and others will sell the throne for a great purse and titles. He has persuaded the queen that he's supporting her and her child, but when she's gone, the child will disappear and de Vere'll sell the crown to the highest bidder. If he waits for her to die.'

'You mean . . .' There was no need for him to spell it out. I was fully aware of the implications: *regicide*. 'What do you want of me?' I said wearily.

'We know you, master.' A sly sneer returned to his face. 'You 'ave been into his house. We can show he's planning her overthrow, that he and other plotters ain't to be trusted, and he ought to be arrested at once.'

There have been times – many times – when I have found myself in danger through no fault of my own. On such occasions I have always found that a certain icy clarity springs into my mind. I can see things, understand things, more readily than most. It is a particular asset of mine, and a great advantage when dealing with thieves and vagabonds who are, obviously, not so fortunate in their mental capacity.

'*Me?*'

'Yes. You've seen the weapons he's collected, ain't you? Your words'll carry weight.'

'I don't want to get involved! *You* know the man well enough – *you* report him!'

'How can we? She don't know me, nor *my* loyalty. You, though, *you* could explain to her. You is known to 'er.'

Yes, I thought. Of course I was. I met her once, briefly. She might listen to me – at least for as long as my head remained on my shoulders.

Trying to denounce her chief advisers was a short path to pain and the Tyburn tree. I had met Mary the queen, and she was ever devoted to her religion and her legacy, and denying the religious choice and legacy of her own half-sister. Some hundreds had died in the flames for disputing her view on religion, and many others died while in prisons. Then again there were almost a thousand who had fled the realm and her reign. From the little I knew of her, I felt sure that she would be as determined as ever her father was to punish those who sought her harm. And if they threatened her child too, that would only exacerbate matters as far as she was concerned.

However, a man informing her that her chief advisers were all corrupt and determined to overthrow her child's inheritance as soon as she was dead – that was suicide. Her advisers would be consulted, and I doubted that their evidence would support my own.

I had a vision of red-hot brands, of a rack, of pincers and other means of destroying bodies, and swallowed hard. Once more the acid in my belly started to roil like water in a copper, and I had to fight to control a shudder that threatened to overwhelm me.

'Of course,' Bagnall mused, 'it'd also mean you'd have all charges against you quashed. You could plead clemency, and she would be certain to give you a fair hearing, was you to convince her of the truth of your accusations. And you'd once more be a free man. No suggestion of murder hangin' over you.'

'No.'

'You'd be doin' the queen a service. And the country.'

'No.'

He looked at me quizzically. 'There's somethin' else. That maid what was killed, Loughgren's maid. Looks like de Vere had somethin' to do with her death.'

'What? Why?'

'Because he thought she could tell him what her master was up to, mayhap. Loughgren was workin' with another Dutchman, Lewan de Beaulieu, bringing weapons. De Vere didn't want competition against his own plottings.'

I recalled Vanderstilt talking of this man. He had said that his
ships were late because another Amsterdammer had held them
up, and that was why he couldn't pay me. And de Vere's weapons
were in those ships. Could he have captured Alice and tortured
her to find out what her master was doing? Piers had said he
would pull out my fingernails to see how I responded . . .

I felt seriously queasy again.

It was a most tempting vision: the chance to escape the threat
of arrest, to be able to return to my past life – this time, quite
possibly, with a large sum in my purse as a reward for my loyalty
and reliability – but also to avenge poor Alice.

Still, the reality was, I was going to throw myself into a mael-
strom of danger. Better by far to leave London and escape the
nets of these plotters and other political fools. And perhaps I
would have fled, were it not for Piers.

I returned slowly to the Hat, thoughtful and perplexed. The
only information I had about Sir Edmund was the view of the
weapons in his armoury, and the allegations made by Bagnall
and his walking mountain. Bagnall himself had declared his utter
devotion to the queen, as had Sir Edmund. For that matter, so
had I, although I was sworn to support John Blount, and through
him, Sir Thomas Parry and Lady Elizabeth. For all that I knew,
my Lady Elizabeth was herself planning to overthrow her half-
sister, and it would be no surprise to me whatever, were she to
have hired Sir Edmund de Vere to find the weapons, the men,
and the opportunity to take the throne for her.

But there was that niggling sense at the back of my mind that
something was wrong. My stomach had the same impression, and
it was only a short period after Bagnall left me that I had to
succumb to the insistence of my belly and vomit up everything
in it, adding to the foul contents of the river. Wiping my face
afterwards, I was left with the absolute conviction that either man
could be telling the truth, but in all likelihood both were lying.

There were some aspects of Bagnall's story that did ring true.
Sir Edmund de Vere did not seem like a man to fully submit to
a woman – even a queen. It was easier to believe that he had a
plan to steal the kingdom from both half-sisters. The weapons
meant he had gathered, presumably, a small force of men who

would also support him. Who were they? Mercenaries from abroad? More Amsterdammers? His own men from his estates? He must have lands to have earned his title, surely. Or perhaps the men were to be provided by his accomplices – Pembroke and Boxall and others. The armourer, Bill, had spoken of the man Loughgren, and how he had also accumulated weapons – perhaps Loughgren was a second man involved in this plot? Or were they competitors? Did De Vere guess that Loughgren's supplier was holding up his own weapons, and suspected Loughgren was deliberately putting de Vere into a difficult position by accumulating weapons while de Vere's were still in Holland?

But Bagnall himself probably had ulterior motives. Perhaps he had a grudge against the knight? Was there something that drove him to want to see de Vere destroyed? Or did he have his own plan to destroy the queen and put himself in her place? It was hardly likely, for the man was only a lowly fellow. But he might represent someone else of a higher station. Or was he himself an agent of Elizabeth, perhaps? Her agents rarely knew of each other – that was a simple means of protection for all, ensuring that we should all have our identities concealed so that even were one of us uncovered, the others would all remain safe.

I did not know. And that was enough to make me throw up again. I was a poor reed on turbulent waters, thrown this way and that, and unable to force my own route to safety.

Well, the one thing that Bagnall had said was that, at least with the queen, my courage in informing her of his suspicions might lead to a pardon for my accusation of murder. Not that I was guilty, but with accusations of that sort, there was always the likelihood that a poor lawyer might perform such a bad job that I would be hanged in any case. That was unappealing.

It was a reluctant Jack who came to the conclusion, but it seemed obvious to me that it was the only one I could come to.

I would have to accept exile to escape the accusations of murder, and ensure my safety from men like Bagnall.

With that thought, I was sick again.

At the door to the Hat, I saw Piers. He looked relieved to see me, and bustled me indoors. Ignoring my protests, he shepherded me up to his room, and once inside, pushed me in so that I fell with a thump onto my backside.

'Did you see him?'

I stared at him goggle-eyed. 'Who? Bagnall?'

'Is that his name? De Vere sent him after you as soon as you were out of here. Said he had a message for you.'

'Yes, we had a long talk.'

'A "talk"?'

'Yes.'

He stared at me. 'This Bagnall, is he about my height, broader in the chest and shoulders, wearing a long ballock knife and green jack with a stain at the heart?'

'No, he's a—'

'De Vere's man was looking for you, and if he found you, you'd not be here now,' Piers said with conviction.

That was when I realized that trying to merely run from the city would not be enough. De Vere intended to remove me before I could share news of his plotting with others.

The only safe route for me was to gain an audience with the queen and persuade her that de Vere was not her loyal subject, but a man determined to wrest the throne from her and her son.

I felt sick again.

PART SIX

John Blount's Chronicle

THIRTEEN

Wednesday 24th August

After arranging for the murderer Humfrie to deal with Sir Edmund de Vere, I allowed myself to return to the conundrum of my assassin and what could have happened to him.

Jack must have realized the danger he was in, and bolted after escaping from the gaol. I knew from experience that Jack was inventive and more than capable of hiding when he wanted to. Before I knew him, he had lived amongst the worst denizens of the city, the pickpockets, the whores, the robbers and rogues. He was competent at shaving dice, at using cards to gamble, and many other means of winning money. More, he knew those sorts of people.

There are some who can pass through the strata of the city with ease. They can converse with the poorest beggar, and then straighten their backs and chat amicably with a lord. Jack was one such fellow. He had the gift of charm and elegance that could pass in a royal palace, and on leaving change his clothes and mingle happily with thieves. It was a distinct skill, and ideal for a man like him, who was dedicated to fading into the background and never materializing. As an assassin, he needed to be able to disappear, just as he had now.

It was quite likely that I would not be able to find him. If Jack was determined to remain hidden, I could do little about it.

Fortunately he was only a servant, when all was said and done, and not even a particularly loyal or devoted one. Jack was a creature of his own devices. He followed his urges. Whereas many of my servants have been quite canine and obedient in their behaviour, Jack inclined more to a feline independence. When I thought of him, it was of a man who would seek his own interests first. Others, like myself, would concentrate on furthering the interests of our masters. Certainly there was a degree of self-interest in doing so, for as our masters – or my mistress – advanced, so would we in their service. Jack had none of that desire.

For him, it was more important that he should remain secure, independent, a free spirit. As an example, he would not divulge to me how he had committed his murders, no matter how often I enquired, occasionally threatening him. No, he was not prey to any concerns as to what I might do. In fact, often I would see a cool, remote look come into his eyes when I threatened him, and although I was sure that he did not mean to do so, it left me chilled. When such discussions occurred between us, even when I had tried to instil some fear in him, that look would return, and I would know that I had not only failed, but that were I not cautious, the threat might redound to my disbenefit. At such times, I was aware of a rising anxiety, and usually ensured that I had a number of my men with me for my own defence.

Still, I sought him as best I could for three days until, on Wednesday, I chafed at hearing nothing from my many informers throughout the city. Mark Thomasson told me that Jack had visited him, speaking of a blackmailer threatening to expose Jack as an assassin, but I could learn nothing more. A servant was left at the door of the Cardinal's Hat, and a second at the entrance to the Clink, but beyond that I saw little that I could usefully do.

But inactivity was anathema to me. On the Wednesday I visited Jack's house with a view to seeing if there was more for me to learn there.

I set off for St Helen's.

The way was busy. Bishopsgate was full of carts and sumpters, with young apprentices and trades boys idling about as they will. The church soon rose before me and I turned to the side of it to walk down the street to Jack's house, and knocked loudly on the door.

It should take only a few moments for a good servant to come and respond to a knock, but Jack's servant could have baked a loaf of bread in the time it took him to come to the door. He opened it, and when I saw the familiar, surly face, I cuffed him about the ear. 'Why did you leave me standing here so long, Raphe?'

'Ow!'

I do have certain rights when it comes to Raphe. He is my sister's son, and his position here was as a result of my machinations. I wanted a man in the household I could rely on to tell me what Jack was up to. It was not my aim to have my own nephew there ignoring his responsibilities to me, his uncle.

His blasted dog, Hector, immediately began to bark at me until I stared at him. He slunk off behind Raphe, tail down, growling still, but not threatening.

'Fetch me wine, and be quick!' I said, and followed Raphe through to the kitchen.

In there, Cecily, Jack's cook, stood cutting up meat for a pie. She held the knife threateningly, but I ignored that, staring at Raphe while he drew off a jug of wine from the barrel, picked up a cup and brought them to me. I sat at the kitchen table, aware of the dark looks I was getting from the pair of them.

'What do you know of your master's disappearance?' I demanded of Raphe.

'He went to look at the old house, but I haven't seen him since,' Raphe said sulkily.

'You didn't report him missing?'

'He told me – express, like – not to speak to anyone.'

'You did not think to let me know?'

'How could I? I didn't know where you was.'

'You could have told my men and they could have forwarded the message to me,' I snapped. 'As things are, why did he think to go to his old house?'

'He didn't say to me.'

'What else can you tell me?'

'I don't know . . .'

'Any instructions which he has given you?'

'Only to keep the place locked up, nothin' else.'

'Just tell him, Raphe,' the cook said with asperity. 'Don't you want your master to be released and come back here?'

'Yes!'

'Then tell him all you know! Oh! He came back here,' she said, throwing down the knife and setting hands on hips. 'He said that he was going to the Cardinal's Hat. He looked awful, dressed like a butcher's boy, all mucky and besmottered with filth, not at all like his usual clothing. While here, he took his gun, powder and shot, and then left by the garden, and told us not to let anyone else into the house. I suppose he didn't mean you, though,' she added doubtfully.

'He said nothing more?'

'Only that he was going to his old house, and he meant to find who had slain the tenant so he could preserve his own good name,' she said. She set her head to one side as if listening to a voice in her head, and then nodded to herself and picked up the knife again. 'That was all. Just a suggestion that he was going to find the actual murderer.'

I left them a little later, once I had consumed the rest of the jug of wine, pensively turning over all she had said while I did so. It made little sense for Jack to return to the place where the crime was supposed to have been committed, and the parish must have been on tenterhooks looking for him, or indeed for any man who could be thought to have been involved in the disappearance of the Dutchman. He must have been a respected man. Those who came to England to trade generally came from good families and brought with them money which smoothed their business dealings.

Perhaps it was that which had led to the man's death. Rich men from outside the city were prey to all kinds of wild animals – most on two legs, although some few might be on four.

By then it was already late, and I was torn, but in the end I decided to return to my house to receive the reports of my spies. Jack's tenant would have to wait until morning.

FOURTEEN

That night I learned that my spies were all but useless. Only Sam Cutpurse had any information, and that was hardly helpful. He had tracked down an armourer who had accepted the weapons supplied by Vanderstilt to Sir Edmund, and after speaking to him at some length over several pots of ale – which he expected to receive compensation for – heard that another merchant called Lewan de Beaulieu was engaged in a similar business, supplying arms from his own ships to men around London.

Early the next morning, I was at Beaulieu's house. It was one of the newer brick buildings just off Cheapside, and I stood on the opposite side of the street staring at it for some time. It was one of those places which had been designed with a view to trade. The windows were shuttered, a sensible precaution against the London mob, and I could see that an archway led around to a yard area behind – not that I could see anything. The gates were solid, fitted the gateway perfectly, and were barred. There was no view of the space behind, although there must have been space for a London cart without difficulty.

I was soon admitted to the merchant's counting house, where I found him, an elegant man with a black cap and heavy coat, shivering in a room that had no fire. Two clerks were adding up his profits, and they cast anxious eyes at me as I entered.

De Beaulieu welcomed me with the sort of look that spoke of his suspicion that I was not likely to add to his profits that day. 'Yes?'

I explained that I would like to speak with him in private, and he very reluctantly told his two assistants to make themselves scarce.

He was not an unpleasant man to look at. His paunch spoke of his wealth, and his genial smile told of his good nature, but there was a glint in his eye that also said he would not tolerate having his time wasted, and also that he was a man who would not appreciate protracted politeness. It would be best to come to the point. I explained that I was investigating the disappearance of a countryman of his, and asked if he could help me.

'I am also from Holland come, yes. So too are many others. Holland is no small nation,' he said. 'What do you want to know?'

I explained I wanted to find Vanderstilt. 'I have heard that you are in competition with him. You trade in the same goods.'

'He has disappeared, you say? That is terrible. We are both merchants, it is true. As to competition . . . occasionally we may find we have similar goods to sell.'

'Such as weapons?'

'It is possible. We sell what we can, and if we have requests for certain items, we attempt to supply them, naturally. It is our function.' His eyes, I noticed, had hardened, giving the lie to his amiable expression. A servant brought us wine in pewter goblets, simple and unadorned, but very delightful, and I sipped as I considered him and the room.

It was plain. Tables stood against three walls, one swamped with papers, one holding ledgers, the third covered in bags and towers of coins. There was little ostentation, and I looked about for signs of his religion. A crucifix hung on one wall opposite a window, and I saw that a rosary of bright beads dangled from Beaulieu's belt. Yet in the present religious climate, many would adopt the trappings of Catholicism without necessarily the beliefs. It was safer.

'What can you tell me about him?'

'Vanderstilt? He is a young man making his way. His father helped him set up in business, and loaned him money to help him start, and when his father died some years ago, Vanderstilt took over the family business, and advanced his own trade. I helped him when he was new to the trade. I assisted him in memory of his father, advised him and even lent him men from my own business. He has two ships now, and plies their trade between Amsterdam and London.'

'What sort of a man is he? Friendly, amiable?'

'Outside business, yes. But in business, he's as grasping as a miser. Few can beat him. In a tavern, he will buy the best wine for all, and think nothing of paying for all his friends, but in business, count your buttons before leaving him. He might take them all,' Beaulieu said, a grin breaking over his face.

'His competitors may not like him, then?' I said.

'Yes. I myself managed to hold off one of his ships. It is a grim side of business, but sometimes a man must do what he can.' Seeing my confusion, he grimaced and continued, 'You see, if a man can bring his cargo over sooner, he will benefit from the higher prices. If there is a glut on the market, the price will fall. If it is still a rare item, because no other merchant has managed to dock yet, the first in the markets will command higher prices for their rarity. So for some little while, I have been bribing an official at the Dutch port to raise questions about Vanderstilt's cargoes. It has held him back but increased my profits.'

It sounded like a sharp practice to me, but what could I know? Besides, it was something done in a foreign land, and not under the jurisdiction of English justice.

'Did you hold him in contempt, then?'

'No. For my part I think him a likeable rogue. He is a pleasant fellow, good company, and although he sails close to the wind on occasion, he is yet an honourable businessman, I think. I liked his father, too.'

'But others might have troubles with him?'

'Ah, who can say, but that someone in business might resent his profits at their expense?'

'Did you lose business to him?'

'Many times,' Beaulieu said. 'But if I were to attack all those who have taken business from me, I would have no time to conduct work of any sort. It is a part of life. Not every deal can be won. We win some, we lose many. He was the same. We merchants tend to be practical; phlegmatic. There is enough trade for all.'

'So you can't think of other merchants who might have wanted to harm him?'

'No! I think you will find he returns soon. I expect he has been travelling to make a trade somewhere.'

'You don't think he could have been murdered?'

'Not Geoffrey, no. It seems unlikely to me.' He paused and

looked at me very directly, and while the genial smile remained on his lips, his eyes were as cold as diamond. 'What exactly is your official interest in this matter?'

I sipped wine and considered him. He appeared to be the sort of man who would be honest. I had seen no indication of his trying to mislead me. As I set the goblet back on the table, I had made up my mind to be frank.

'A friend of mine has been accused of Vanderstilt's murder. He was arrested and held, and I seek to show him innocent.'

'What is this friend's name?'

'Blackjack. He owns the house which Vanderstilt was renting.'

'Oh? Why should he be suspected of murder?'

'He was heard, foolishly, threatening Vanderstilt because he was a little late with his rent.'

'I see.' He took in my attire. As usual, I was clad in plain clothing, with little ostentation. After considering, he set his head to one side and studied me again. 'I am aware that Geoffrey had some people who were displeased by his efforts. A knight had been arranging for weapons to be brought into the city.'

'Who?' I asked, but I knew the answer.

He quickly confirmed it. 'Sir Edmund de Vere.' Seeing me nod and make as though to leave, he leaned back in his seat. 'You know, I like this city. It is a place where men can live side by side and not fight. Foreign men like me are welcomed, if we accept the city's laws and obey them, and if we pay our taxes and customs. It is friendly, safe, and a haven for the persecuted.'

I nodded, thinking the fool clearly had not spent much time in the places I knew.

Continuing, his eyes went to his goblet as if he was speaking to it. 'I would be displeased to think that a man might desire to overthrow the command of the city or the country. This kingdom is precious to me.'

'Is that why Sir Edmund did not go to you for his weapons? Or did you refuse him?'

'Oh, I only learned of his plans afterwards. You see, I had another client who wanted a similar cargo, and I was not aware of Sir Edmund's.' He looked at me closely again and appeared to make a decision. 'The man I was working for was another who wished for a large consignment of swords, halberds, lances and guns. When I heard Sir Edmund was seeking the same, I was immediately struck with the one thought: the two men must be arranging for shipments to arm soldiers. But they did not work for the queen. So they were planning their own army – and that could only be for one reason.'

'To overthrow the queen,' I breathed.

'No. Perhaps that was so with Sir Edmund de Vere, but my own client is beyond reproach. I know him well, and he is not a man to foment rebellion. His arms were to protect the throne.'

'I see.'

'However, he is not a knight, and therefore more . . . affected by the laws of the land. Perhaps he might fear that his own venture could become his downfall? If one conspiracy was discovered, his own life might be at risk? They say a man can be tarred with the same brush, I think?'

'Perhaps,' I said. 'Who was this?'

After some minutes of reassuring him that I would not allow his own name to become known in relation to any criminals' acts, he finally grunted and admitted.

'George Loughgren.'

After that interview I proceeded to Aldgate. I confess that I was chewing over the interview with Beaulieu all the way.

So, according to Beaulieu, Loughgren was also accumulating weapons. He and de Vere were – what? Planning insurrection together? A rebellion against the queen? I do not believe in coincidences: if two men in London were collecting weapons for armed uprisings, surely no matter what Beaulieu thought, the two must be acting in accord.

Her 'own forces'! The army was a nondescript aggregation of every churl, thief and vagabond who was prepared to take a niggardly salary for the benefit of a limited amount of power. In truth, they were ill-equipped and disorganized: in essence, a rabble. She had some good bodyguards, the city of London had its own militia, but against a coordinated attack by well-armed and drilled soldiers, they would be helpless. Those who had fought in the queen's wars in France and elsewhere were disbanded as soon as they returned. They could be of no use.

The others, the men of fighting age, were untrained, and of those, how many would seek to uphold the queen's position? It was likely to be all too few. De Vere could likely raise a small army from the disaffected in Kent; Loughgren must be moderately wealthy, or was backed by others who were, from the sound of the orders he had put through Beaulieu. How many others were there about the country? Sir Thomas Parry had spoken of men up and down the country who could be tempted to help remove the queen: from the Scottish Marches, from Gloucester, from York – if de Vere and Loughgren were aware of them, they could make common suit with them.

And if so, where would that leave Lady Elizabeth? Very likely held either as a prisoner, or perhaps executed, unless she had some contacts with the rebellion.

I would have to write a lengthy note to Sir Thomas, outlining these new threats.

I continued on my way and was soon rapping sharply on Jack's old door.

Vanderstilt's servant was an elderly man who looked as if he had already died, but whose mind had not yet caught up with the fact.

'My master?' he said, glowering steadily like a man who suspected I might be a thief, damn his cods! He gradually opened up a little and told me that he was sure his master must have been waylaid on his way back from Sir Edmund de Vere's house.

'Are you sure that was where he was going?'

It seemed a most significant coincidence that the fellow was going to the same house where Sir Thomas Parry had told me to arrange a death. Everything seemed to return to de Vere.

'Yes, yes. But he never returned. My poor master disappeared that night, and I have not seen him since,' the man said. He looked like a fellow in mourning, clad in his dark clothes, and with his face gaunt and strained, but a glitter in his eyes. 'He has never been away so long before. Some, they say he has fled because of his money troubles, but that is a lie. He would not run from the town for such a reason. He would ensure those he owed money to would be paid.'

His voice carried conviction. I said, 'What of the money he owed Jack Blackjack?'

'The landlord? He paid it.'

'You have told the sergeant that?'

'No one has asked me. Somebody did say that Master Blackjack threatened my master, that if he was not paid, he would take revenge or some such, but I did not hear that. In any case, the money was certainly paid. I took it to him. He came here soon after.'

'When?'

'The Saturday after my master disappeared.'

'He came here?'

'Yes. He demanded to know where my master was. He insisted on looking in my master's money chest.'

'And?'

The old man gave a sour grimace, which I took to be a smile.

'It was empty. When my master was not home, after two days I took his money to a safe merchant to see it guarded.'

'Who?'

It took him a while to answer that one, but after some moments he admitted, 'Master Lewan de Beaulieu. I would not trust my master's money to an Italian or other banker.'

'I see.'

'The girl, I do not know of.'

'What girl?'

He looked surprised. 'There was a maid up near the Bishopsgate, murdered, so they say. They say Master Blackjack killed her.'

It struck me suddenly that Loughgren's house, where the maid Alice had worked, might well be a reason for her death. If she had overheard a discussion between Sir Edmund and her master, and realized that the weapons were all being collected for a battle for the throne, she might have decided to tell the authorities, and her decision may have become known to her master. He might have killed her for listening. Or maybe she saw a chance for profit, threatening to blackmail her master – and he took the precaution of removing her.

Or he desired her and she was unwilling to participate in his natural desires, so he killed her. The opportunities and motives for murder were far too broad and commonplace. But neither explained why Loughgren, or "Luffrin" might have sent two men to kill me.

The steward's voice was harsh and guttural, but there was no doubting his earnest conviction. He could not tell what had happened to his master, only that he had left to visit the knight.

I left the house with little further information, and stood for a short while outside, casting an eye up and down the roadway, wondering what I should do next. I was determined to find my assassin. If Jack was in serious trouble, I must help him. After all, it was quite possible that I could bind him to my service for some time at a reduced cost, were I able to save him from whatever fate he found himself suffering.

Jack had always been most cautious about sharing information about himself. He was a naturally reticent man. But I had spent a considerable amount of time watching him to learn all I could, and I knew there was one person who knew him probably better than any.

I crossed the street and knocked on the door opposite. Before long I was in the parlour of Mistress Susan Appleby, a cheerful, pleasant woman. She at once made me at home as we spoke, and I can safely assert that she was impressed with my authority and general demeanour.

PART SEVEN

Jack's Tale Continues . . .

FIFTEEN

Thursday 25th August

Thus it was that the next day, freshly clothed in my suit, now cleaned and of good appearance, thanks to the careful and solicitous efforts of the brothel staff – for an exorbitant fee, I must add – I made my way by wherry over to the north bank of the river, and by degrees, carefully keeping an eye open for any threatening-looking fellows who might have shown too much interest in me, up to the great gateway of St James's Palace.

I've never liked this palace. It's said that Queen Mary was in two minds about using it because her father had ordered it built, and over the arched gate were the initials H and A – Henry, and the A for Anne Boleyn, Elizabeth's mother, whom he married after having his marriage to Mary's mother annulled – thus declaring her illegitimate. But for all the unpleasant connotations of those symbols for the queen, it was yet a pleasant palace, built around a number of courtyards, the buildings modern and comfortable. It was no surprise that the queen would like to spend her time here, rather than the gloomy and cold Whitehall.

However, for a man like me, arriving before the red-brick gatehouse already filled with trepidation at the thought of the meeting to come, this fortress, elegant though it was, was daunting. If I could, I would have turned about and left to find a decent alehouse somewhere near. I felt the need of a stiff drink to settle my liver. I had woken with a nervous twitching, and my hands shook slightly, which was not helped by the dreadful headache that assailed me from the moment I first saw the sun that morning. I attempted a meat pie to break my fast, but most of that was deposited into the Thames during the wherry trip to the north bank of the river. It must have been the anxiety of needing to beg an audience with the queen.

Not that it was likely to be granted. I knew that, of course.

The queen would not make herself available to every – or, indeed, any – gentleman who appeared at her palace doors, as was made quite clear when I stood at the gate and tried to explain why I was there.

'Really,' the sergeant said. 'A plot, eh?'

'I have to speak with the queen, yes,' I said.

'Bugger off!'

I looked him up and down with all the hauteur of a duke meeting a peasant. 'Bring a grown-up for me to talk to.'

'You what?'

'I wish to speak to your superior about this.'

'Look,' the sergeant said. He was a tallish fellow of about three-and-thirty or so, with a scar that ran along the side of his face and pulled his mouth into a permanent sneer. For all that, he appeared a fairly kindly man, in the way that he took hold of my jack in both hands. Then he leaned forward, pulling me towards him at the same time.

He had eaten a lot of garlic recently.

'Sarn't!'

The shout came from behind him, and I could not see who it was, but the sergeant dropped me like a hot coal and stood at an approximation of attention. '*Sir.*'

When he reached us, I studied the newcomer with interest. He was clad in an old leather jack with heavy fustian hosen. His boots were of a good size, and the leather looked of good quality, and when I looked at his face, I thought him little more than a child, but when I glimpsed his eyes, my first impression was not a good one. He was one of those men who has a cold, uninterested look about him. Not that it matters hugely in general, but when you find a soldier looking at you with that kind of hollow-eyed expression, believe me, it's time to start running.

'Don't blame me, pretty boy,' the sergeant muttered from the corner of his mouth. It was enough to make me want to spin around and bolt for the open fields, but it was too late already. I felt a heavy hand on my shoulder, and the officer was connected to the fingers that pinched my flesh.

He had an amiable grin on his face. 'Now, sir, what can we do for you?'

'I am here to speak with the queen.'

'I see. Did you hear that, Sergeant? He has an appointment with Her Royal Highness. And you were going to hold him here, or worse, send him away. I hope you feel thoroughly ashamed! And you, sir. You are expected?'

'No, but this is a matter of—'

'Ah,' he interrupted. 'That sounds less hopeful. The queen is not expecting you. If that is the case, there are certain matters a guard should check.'

'I have met her before, you know,' I said forcefully. 'You can tell her it is Jack Blackjack here. I met her during the Wyatt battles. I was a defender of London.'

'Ah, the mouse squeaks,' he said, and I was irritated. This was the second time I had heard my protestations described thus, and it struck me as insulting.

'Look here, good fellow,' I said. 'Take me to the queen. I have intelligence for her which will protect her and her heir.'

'Oho! I'm a "fellow" now, eh? I should be wary, Sergeant. This pipsqueak wants to warn me of my danger if I don't listen to him, eh? Now, little squeaker, little mouse – or are you a rat? Rats are not scared of showing their teeth when they're cornered, after all. Do you have teeth, master?'

'What?'

Look, it had been a long day yesterday, and now, here I was, with an officer who was determined to speak in riddles. I had lost much of my patience already, and now, listening to this fool, I was rapidly losing the rest of it.

'This,' I said, 'is ridiculous!' I lifted both arms at the same time, breaking his grip of my shoulder, and began to stride to the entrance.

I say 'began', because suddenly I was aware that I was arrested in my progress. There was a sort of braking effect on me, and although my feet moved, they did not help to propel me forward. It was most peculiar, rather as though all the wine, brandy and ale of the previous day had suddenly returned to me with full force. I wanted to move, and tried to move, but I went nowhere.

Turning, I was just in time to see the officer, who was smiling with the sort of look I had seen on a crocodile's face at the menagerie some years ago, holding on to my jack. I would have remonstrated with him, but for the fact that he was currently engaged on swinging a cudgel at my head.

It struck. I felt a dullness at my brow, and then I blinked, and the world turned into flashes and sparkles, as if all the stars of night had come to earth and now circled my head. I vaguely remember thinking, 'They are pretty!' before they were all snuffed out simultaneously, and I fell into darkness.

When I came to my senses again, I was not sure at first that I had. First, I was aware of the pain in my head. That was, yes, the most obvious injury that I had suffered. Next, I became aware that my jack had been wrenched from my body, and now I was in hosen and shirt, with both arms above my head. Oh, and that was when I became aware of the pain in both shoulders, and at my wrists, since all my weight was being held by them.

Looking up, I saw that my wrists were bound by strong leather straps, both far enough apart to make it impossible for either hand to reach over to the other. I would not be able to unfasten the buckles on either. The anguish which had woken me was caused by my body's weight dangling from my wrists. My shoulders were being torn from my body by the simple matter of my own weight. I quickly lifted myself and, if I had hoped that the pain would subside, I was to be sorely disappointed. The pain continued: with the sudden easing of the strain on the shoulders, it appeared to exacerbate, as if now the tendons and muscles felt they could complain and let me know how much they had been suffering while I was happily unconscious.

I am a strong man, of course, but I could not help but permit a small expression of my distress to whimper from my lips.

'Ah, awake, eh?'

It was my friend from the gateway. He had been resting with his buttocks on a low ledge below a window, and now he walked to me with the lazy motion of a feline seeing a trapped mouse. There was no hurry; he was fully intending to enjoy himself as best he might.

'Master Blackjack, I believe.'

'Yes. And I have urgent news for the queen.'

'I am sure you did. Perhaps they involved this little toy?' he asked, and brought out my handgun from behind him. 'A devilish little device. Very cleverly made. A spring, a chain linked to a spinning wheel of steel, a dog gripping some pyrites or flint, and

soon you have a gun ready to fire. Sadly, you allowed the priming
powder to leak from the frizzen, but I have replenished it.'

'Yes, but I need to speak to the queen!'

'You had a sword, a dagger, and a gun when you came here
demanding to speak with her. Tell me, what were you going to
tell her? That lead or iron might end her life? There are other
fools who came here seeking to injure or murder the queen. We
will know who sent you.'

'No one sent me! I came to warn her!'

'Yet you are an accused murderer. All because a man did not
pay you enough rent.'

'Yes, he did! I had no argument with Vanderstilt!'

'Eh? A Hollander? You mean he was not a Catholic, but one
of the continental heretics? Are you also a heretic?'

'No! I am a loyal subject! I simply want to help Her Royal
Highness!'

'I think,' he said, and now he stood right before me, 'I think
you are an assassin, Jack Blackjack, and I don't like assassins.'

And with that, his gloved fist hit the side of my jaw, and I fell
unconscious again.

This was not a good day.

I don't know how long I was unconscious that time, but when I
came to, it felt as though both shoulders had been racked. I had
to stand up, groggy and unsteady. Both legs had turned to canvas,
and could barely support my weight, added to which the pain in
my arms increased as soon as I reduced the pressure on them,
as if they had waited patiently for me to return to consciousness
so that they could express their feelings at being left to strain on
their own. Then again, at least my hangover seemed to have
faded into the background. Sadly it was only because of the pain
in my head and swollen jaw.

There was no sign of the officer, to my relief. I could moan
without running the risk of a fresh punch. However, I heard steps
in a nearby corridor, and soon a shambling figure entered. He
was clad in a leather apron, rather like a blacksmith, and had a
kindly face. I tried to engage him in conversation, but he smiled
and shook his head, a finger to his lips, before making his way
to a brazier. He used flint and steel to strike sparks into some

tinder and blew on it carefully before setting it into the brazier, and adding a few sticks of kindling. All the while, he was silent, and barely even glanced in my direction.

It was an entirely domestic scene, and at first it was comforting. I felt the pain in my shoulders begin to diminish, and allowed my head to sink back to rest against the stones of the wall to which I was chained.

And then my eyes snapped wide and I could not prevent a wail slip from me as I realized that this was no servant preparing a meal – this was a torturer getting his tools ready.

Ready for me.

PART EIGHT

Susan Appleby's Testimony

SIXTEEN

Thursday 25th August

I had heard of Master Blount from Jack, of course.

Jack could be quite a chatty fellow, when he wanted. When he came to visit me, he was never one to hide his feelings particularly well, and had shared his opinion of his superior. Which was never particularly complimentary, to be honest.

Of course, it is often the way that a man will assess another as a matter of comparison. *Is he better looking, stronger, more virile than me?* Jack, God bless him, was no different from any other man. I know men can be astute, of course. However, sometimes it takes a woman to understand a man without competition. Looking at John Blount, I could understand Jack's stories of Blount's cruelty. Poor Jack was only a menial servant, something like a clerk, he always told me, and he perceived Blount as being a bleak, black-hearted devil. He did have black eyes, but I don't think they were those of a snake, as Jack often said. No, they were glittering with intelligence and some humour. He had deep tracks carved into his cheeks at either side of his mouth, and into his brow too, which showed that he was a thoughtful man, who had serious responsibilities. Yet, he had manners, too. It was good to see that he made a show of removing his hat and bowing respectfully.

'My husband is not here, I am afraid,' I said. 'Perhaps you would like to return when he is home?'

'No, mistress, it was you whom I wished to speak to. In private,' he added, looking over at my bottler.

I motioned to him to leave. I knew that he would stand outside the room, listening. My husband has, on occasion, formed an entirely unjustified suspicion that I might have been disloyal to him, and the servant was often keen to listen to my conversations in order to report to Saul. I allowed myself to take on a courteous but reserved demeanour and waved my guest to a seat while I took my own perch near the fire. 'How can I help you?'

His eyes had drifted to my blouse, and when I spoke his eyes snapped back to my face quickly. 'I believe you know Jack Blackjack, who used to live opposite you.'

'Yes, of course.'

'He was arrested not long ago, for the murder of his tenant.'

'So I have heard. He was taken outside my house here, but it is ridiculous! Who could think him guilty of murder!' I said somewhat hotly. If I were not married, I would have gone to the gaol to visit him and bring him a little comfort – but for a married woman that would not have been seemly. Still, any who knew Jack must be aware that he was as innocent as a child when it came to violence. He would avoid it at all costs.

There was a certain strange look in this man's eyes as I spoke, but he was a strange-looking man all over. I found myself wondering what his chest would look like. I have always rather liked strong, powerful chests on my men.

'Perhaps so. Yet the tenant has disappeared, and some suggest it was just as he owed Jack the rent for the property, and that Jack may have threatened the tenant because the payment was late.'

'Jack? Threaten a man for a late payment? I doubt that. Jack could speak from an excess of annoyance, but he would never allow his feelings to overwhelm him. He would only resort to violence if he was attacked. He is not the sort of man to assault another, and he would not murder. I am sure of that.'

'I am glad to hear it.'

There was a brief easing of his features as though he was relieved. I caught a glimpse of a little smile, and wondered how he would be in bed. Serious, certainly. Possibly quite a remote companion, determined solely on his own pleasures, rather than his partner's, but potentially exciting too.

'Where is he, then?' I asked. I slowly crossed my ankles, and saw his gaze move to my legs. He averted his face quickly, but not before I noticed. He crossed his legs.

'He – um – he was being held at the Aldgate, but he escaped, and now I do not know where he might have gone.'

'You mean he has disappeared?' He did have a good leg. I

liked his calves – strong, muscled. I always liked the sight of a man's legs.

'So it would seem, mistress.'

I felt the need of refreshment, and called at once for wine and two cups. While my bottler was hurrying to fetch them, I considered Blount – and all he had told me. I certainly did not believe that Jack could have killed the man in cold blood. It was ridiculous. When my bottler returned, I spoke generally with Blount while we both drank a little wine together. Of course, I knew that the tenant opposite had disappeared, and no body was found. Most, naturally, assumed the foreigner had performed a midnight flit to escape those to whom he owed money. Meanwhile, all suspicion had fallen on to poor Jack. Gossip can be so unfair.

Now I learned from Master Blount that it was also common gossip that Jack was accused of killing a woman as well. Well! I was shocked to hear this. After all, it was arrant nonsense! No one who knew Jack could believe him capable of any such behaviour. He was a lover, not a murderer.

Although I am no more than an innocent woman, with little knowledge of the world, I did have certain information of my own. For example, I had been a little . . . shall we say, keen to learn more about Jack's other assignations for some little while. I knew that I was not his only inamorata, any more than Jack was my only male friend. Some weeks before I had hired a man who was competent and trustworthy to follow Jack for a few days, and see where he went. Thus it was that I learned of a maiden who had apparently taken his eye. From all I had heard, she was a pleasant enough child, buxom, as Jack liked, and with a flirtatious, amusing manner. I had gone with the man to see her, and he showed me the house where she worked, and as luck would have it, she appeared and made her way to the baker's shop near Bishopsgate itself.

Yes, she was an appealing little trollop, and I could understand how she would have attracted Jack's eye.

Why does this matter? Why, if Jack were to disappear, it was more than likely that he would go somewhere he felt safe, but knowing him, he would also wish to be comfortable. A house like that where the maiden lived would be ideal for him. He may not be able to sleep inside, because he would be likely to be discovered, but if he could rest in a building nearby, she would be able to bring him sustenance, no doubt. And 'entertain' him too.

But now Blount mentioned this Alice, and that she was also dead. I had no idea. The little doxy had been such an appealing little piece. The idea that someone could end her life was shocking – almost as shocking as the suggestion that others thought Jack could have killed her. *Ridiculous!*

It was enough to make me resolve to go and visit her old home, to see whether I might learn what had happened to Jack. It was out of my parish, but not too far.

As soon as Blount left I told my bottler to bring one of my grooms to me, and armed with his company, and his stout cudgel, I put into action my intention to help him, if I may.

Some may ask what I was going to do. Jack was not my husband or family, it is true, but he was a friend. I had been . . . *close* to him for some years. I was quite sure that any allegations against him were unjustified and not fair. He was no murderer. If he was in danger, then I was resolved to aid him. I would not desert him at his time of greatest need.

We made our way up the street to the house where his maiden lived, and there I allowed my groom to knock loudly on the door with his stave. It was opened by a somewhat flustered and suspicious-looking steward, who gazed at my servant with an expression of intense dislike. 'Did you mean to try to break down the door, fellow?'

My man was about to square up to him, but I put out my hand and told him to step back while I spoke with the steward.

'I am looking for a friend of mine, a fellow called Jack. I believe he may have known a housemaid here, and wondered whether she could help us?'

'I am sure that no maid of this house would dare to be involved in some form of promiscuous relationship with a fellow from the streets,' the man said with a sneering contempt. 'Our maids are better behaved than that, if they wish to remain in this house. Any who forms unacceptable relationships would be cast from the door.'

He was about to slam the door in my face, so I put on a piteous display of concern, breathing heavily and shamelessly. I was correct. He was unable to divert his eyes from my heaving bosom.

'Oh, please, sir! Are you sure? She was a young girl, and perfectly well-behaved, I assure you,' I lied. Any wench who could keep Jack's interest for more than ten minutes would have to be as randy as a rabbit. 'But he has disappeared, and I greatly fear . . . that something must have happened to him.'

'I am sure that none of the . . .' He paused, and an uncertainty flashed across his face like a small cloud over an empty sky. 'I . . . perhaps it could have been . . . what did this maid look like? Do you know?'

I described her in fine detail. 'Very pretty, large eyes, and lips that smiled readily, with a slim waist but well formed in her upper body, if you take my meaning. I think she was fair-haired, for she had a very fair complexion.'

'Oh, I am sorry,' he said, and now he was flustered. 'I think . . . that is to say, it sounds much like Alice.'

'Has she been cast from your door, then?' I asked, and I opened my eyes wide to indicate shock.

'No, she has been murdered,' he said. 'She was found outside the house, her body all broken. A very sad sight. Someone must have waylaid her and killed her.'

'My God! Who could do such a thing?'

He went all mournful. 'Who can tell? The world is going to pot, I fear. The behaviour of youngsters is appalling. No respect for their elders and betters, whether it's an apprentice or servant, and the common folk have no understanding. They all seem to think the world owes them a living. Why, only recently I had a man threaten to punch me, just because I told him to stop pissing against the house's wall! Murders abound, and the watch and constables can do nothing to prevent them, and now we have soldiers returning from France with weapons and no job. What does the government expect them to do? They are warriors. If I had my way, they would all be sent back to France to retake Calais or die in the attempt. At least they wouldn't be clotting our streets, then.'

'She is dead – that is so sad.' And truth be told, I was sorry. She had seemed such a vital little thing, with her ready smile and flirtatious manner. She did not deserve to lie mouldering in a grave.

'Yes. Very sad.' The man sighed. 'I don't know where I'll find another maid.'

I almost kicked him in a sensitive place.

I did not, nor did I order my groom to knock the man on the pate for that comment, tempting though it was. Instead, against my better judgement, I turned and marched away.

Jack probably had a fresh hide-away. Where that could be was beyond me, of course. However, I was intrigued by the notion that there might be some connection between the maid Alice's death and Jack's own disappearance. It was ridiculously far-fetched to think he was responsible for any murders, let alone that child's. What was less far-fetched was the idea that there was something linking the disappearance of his tenant and the death of the girl. That seemed to me to be too much of a coincidence, that they had both disappeared or died on the same day, from what I had heard.

I knew nothing more about the disappearance of the Dutchman than Blount. That day, the Thursday, had been perfectly normal. There were no strangers in the lane, that I was aware of, and the man had gone to dine at a friend's house, but not returned, so Blount had said. Others had obviously searched for a body – the constables had been to enquire of my husband and servants whether they had seen or heard anything on the evening he had disappeared, but none of us knew anything that could aid the search.

There would be no purpose seeking the body myself. Instead, I was set to wondering how I could assist Jack. Perhaps I could devise a different approach that the men would not have considered. That was easy enough.

If men hold secret discussions or meetings, it is often noticeable that they ensure that they cannot be overheard by anyone. They will go to a chamber which is empty, and there have their deliberations. But just because they think the place is empty, does not always mean that they are alone. Many are the times that I have seen my husband sit in his chair before the fire and discuss matters of great importance, whether those of business or politics, confident that he was not overheard. Because, you see, he never thought of his wife or maids as being of any importance.

All too often people would ignore their servants or wives, because they were less than human, in their eyes. Yet a woman like me, or a maid like Alice, has perfectly functioning ears and eyes, and a working brain.

And others do too. Which was why I always sent my bottler from the room when I had matters of any delicacy to discuss.

Yes, I realized, I should speak to maidservants and wives, if I was to learn more about the disappearance of the Dutchman – and of Jack's own disappearance. And, further, that I should also learn all I could about Alice. For no matter what the steward in that house thought, I knew that murder was not so common-place for young, appealing women. So many men were convinced that any woman would appreciate their attentions, even if she continued to try to reject his advances, that they did not conceive of a need to murder their victims. They would knock the maid down, perhaps, and commit the act, and then leave her weeping, while they went to seek a fresh drink to celebrate – it was enough to make a woman want to carry a gun like Jack's wheel-lock for protection – but only rarely would they think to commit murder.

Was it possible, I wondered, that the girl could have been more open and friendly with many other men? Perfectly possible, I supposed. Some maids had a constant itch between their legs, and could behave disgracefully, flaunting themselves. No doubt that was how she had attracted Jack. Could she have come to know Jack's tenant? Perhaps the tenant had come to know of her, became infatuated, and tried to take her; she refused, and he murdered her, frustrated at her rejection, and then he ran away. It was possible, certainly. Or he ran away, concerned about some threat or perceived danger, and his assailant, knowing of Alice, decided to torture her to learn where the Dutchman had gone, but she knew nothing, and so the murderer cut her throat?

Or was it someone trying to find Jack, who thought she must know where he was?

That was enough to make me start to think very carefully. I had never truly learned how Jack occupied himself. I knew that he worked in some capacity as clerk for John Blount, but beyond that, I had little idea exactly what Jack did for Blount. It was interesting, and I really should have asked Blount while he was in my house, I realized. Knowing his business might help direct me towards the men who could have a motive to hurt him. After all, sometimes business competitors can turn difficult. Possibly this was a matter like that? I know that my husband, Saul, has on occasion found that other men in his line of work have turned nasty, and more than once he has hired men to protect himself and me.

It was then that another thought struck me. Or, rather, the realization that I was missing one vital aspect of the whole affair: if men had gone to Alice and killed her, thinking she might be able to tell them where Jack was, that indicated that they knew where she lived, but also that they had seen her with Jack.

If they had followed him and learned about her, they might well have followed him and discovered that Jack was friendly with me as well.

They may well come to question me in a similar manner.

I instructed the groom to walk a short distance behind me, as though we were not associated, and made sure he understood that there could be men watching me to capture me. He nodded, but I wasn't sure that he was any more intelligent than our carthorse. Still, he swore he would watch out for me and ensure that I was not attacked. He clutched his cudgel with enthusiasm, and I fear he was hopeful that we might be waylaid so he could get into a brawl. The way these young men behave nowadays!

But it wouldn't do. I may have to tell Saul to send the boy packing. It is one thing to have a defensive servant, and quite another to have a walking mêlée as a groom.

That was a matter for another day, however. First, I had to test my theory as to whether Jack's tenant had discussed matters of importance before his servants. It did not take us long to return to my house, and I was very glad to see no strangers loitering, no vagabonds suspiciously watching for me.

I walked straight to Jack's front door and had my groom knock on the door – this time with his knuckles, not his stick.

The door was opened by the servant. I had seen him often enough in the street, but never so close to, and I studied him with interest.

It was plainly obvious that he was concerned, as well he might be. If his master did not return, the fellow would have lost his home, income and protection in one fell swoop.

'Yes?'

'I live in that house. You have seen me before?'

'Yes.'

'Good. In that case, I would like to enter and speak with you for a short period. My man will wait out here for me to return.' I nodded to my groom and swept inside the house.

It was many months since I had last been in here, but it was as familiar as the fingers on my hand. I walked past the servant and into the parlour. Here I indicated that I would appreciate a little refreshment, and soon I held a large goblet of wine. I sat on a comfortable, straight-backed chair with marvellous carvings of ships on its back and arms, and sipped.

'Your master has disappeared. Often a man will give an indication that he might need to take a trip, and will tell others of his requirement. You heard nothing of that sort?'

'No, mistress. He never gave any . . . indication he was going to leave the house. He went to see his business associate, but never returned.'

'I have heard that he did visit Sir Edmund de Vere.' That was the little that Blount had vouchsafed. 'But that he left there to return home, but never reached this house.'

'That is correct.'

'I am aware that often a man, such as your master, will hold meetings in the presence of their staff. If they have a steward in whom they know they can place all their trust, they will often keep him in the room with them while they talk about business and other matters. Did your master trust you?'

'Yes. He always kept me in the room with him when he held discussions in case he needed wine or snacks. I was always trusted.'

'Who came to meet him in the days before his disappearance?' I asked, holding out my now-empty glass to be refilled.

'There was Sir Edmund de Vere, of course. My master's priest. A friend of my master's . . .'

'Is Sir Edmund de Vere a friend of your master's? It was on his way back from Sir Edmund's house that he disappeared, yet he had been here too only a little while before your master's disappearance.'

His language was occasionally difficult to understand, but I was given to understand that Vanderstilt had a professional interest in Sir Edmund. The knight had been procuring weapons from Vanderstilt for a while, and the latest shipment was due in from Holland, but had been delayed. Sir Edmund had come to demand that the delivery be made, and it was not a happy discussion, with the knight threatening Vanderstilt and pressuring him to find more weapons.

'Why?' I wondered. 'What was the urgency of Sir Edmund's demand?'

He had no idea. It left me concerned that the knight might have had some motive in the near future, naturally. Why should a man be demanding weapons at a time when the country was more or less at peace? There was no reason why a London-based knight should need to arm a small army, after all.

'What happened after that?'

'Sir Edmund invited my master to go and visit him once the ship had docked, and he was keen to ensure that the weapons were delivered urgently. My master went to meet him and arrange the delivery. Both men were happy, I think. Their last meeting here had been hard. The knight was . . . His language was *harsh*, you say? He was very angry and demanding. But when the ship docked with his cargo, he was happier.'

'So he was happy when the weapons were landed?'

'He was happy to hear that they were here, yes.'

'Did he want them delivered to his own home?'

'No, these were to go to a house in Kent.'

I left the house and returned to my own in a state of considerable confusion.

What was the knight's need for these weapons – and why did he have them stored so far from London and his own house? It made some sort of sense to have weapons in his own house for defence, of course; but to store them elsewhere was curious. Not only that, he had ordered many more weapons than any householder should need, according to the steward: two hundred each of pikes and spears, for example. Vanderstilt's servant had provided me with a list of the items ordered and delivered, and there was enough to arm a small army. Why would they be needed by Sir Edmund?

When my husband returned, I was eager to share with him all I had learned, and to chew over some of the tastier morsels of the servant's evidence.

He was back home quite early that afternoon, and you may be assured that it took little time for me to explain about the arrival of Jack's master, and my own investigations. It was necessary, for my dear husband, Saul, can be jealous. He would not tolerate having the cuckold's horns planted on his head. I know that not long ago Jack had been assaulted by men hired by Saul. Only Jack's cleverness had avoided a severe beating that time. And since then I had made it quite plain to my husband that he must not make such ridiculous accusations. It would, after all, cause comment and might damage my reputation as well as his own. Fortunately, he was easily browbeaten. Still, if he were to hear of someone appearing in the house without an explanation, such as John Blount, his suspicious mind could leap to the wrong conclusion. I knew full well that our steward was always happy to paint me in a particularly poor light. I really must remove that man, somehow.

'This servant of Vanderstilt – what is his name?' my husband asked.

I had to confess that I had no knowledge of the man's name, but our steward, who took a keen interest in the comings and goings of all in the street, not just our house, was soon able to provide his name: he was known as Peter de Clarke. Not that his name truly mattered. He was only a servant, after all. I didn't know why Saul would be interested in the fellow's name. He rarely worried about his own steward being present at private discussions – for him it was like asking for the name of a candle-stick.

In any case, I was able to tell him all about Peter's words. 'Why would a knight need to have so many weapons? And why have them delivered to Kent?'

Saul was bemused, I saw. He is a keen follower of business, but just recently he had grown interested in politics because there were opportunities for advancement for a man like him, not only within the guilds, but also in the city administration, and he had started looking at the potential posts as well as the men who were most likely to help him rise to them.

'I cannot imagine why someone would want to buy weapons now. The country is at peace,' he said.

'There are stories that the queen is not well,' I suggested.

'Oh, I am sure that they are nothing more than rumours. The people like to have something to gossip about,' he said with masterly disdain. 'But I have heard that the new alderman, Mark Coates, has been having an affair with a neighbour's maid. Scandalous behaviour, since the maid works for another member of his own guild. Hard to imagine such foolishness. Does he not have maids in his own household?'

I ignored that, as a wife must, although it did make me grit my teeth. As usual, he did not notice. So different he is from Jack, who would always know to be more careful in his speech, and show respect to me. He had his own failings, of course, but he also thought of others when he was with them. I had little doubt that the child Alice would have been grateful for his attentions, too.

'So you do not believe the tales about our queen's health?' I said.

'Oh, who can tell? She is a woman of a certain age, and she has a child in her womb, she says. She has believed this before, of course. I imagine most women must know when they are with child?'

He looked at me then, in a more than slightly accusing manner. I could say nothing. The fact that we had no children was a source of great dissatisfaction to my husband, who had assumed that I would fall pregnant as soon as we were married. I had thought I was pregnant more than once, in fact – but no. I was barren.

I nodded sadly. 'I wish that I could bring you a son, Saul.'

'It is of no matter,' he said, his heavy voice belying his words. 'But it does not detract from the fact that the queen believes herself to be bearing a child, and that must mean there is a good likelihood that she is. And ladies who are about to take to their lying-in are apt to fall prey to all kinds of irrational fears and . . . things. She may well feel herself to be unwell. It would hardly be a surprise.'

Of course, in that he was quite right. The movement of the womb about the body was a source of changing moods and tempers in all women, as the physicians told us. It was only as the woman came close to being delivered of her child that the womb became more stable, as I understand it. And when the child is born, the womb will migrate about the woman's body once more.

So many women were prone to suffer and many die in these terrible times for a woman. Was it any surprise that so many women were equally joyful and terrified of childbirth? For me, it was a relief as well as a sore trial that I was unable to conceive. I should have enjoyed raising a child.

This gave rise to a fresh thought – perhaps I could go and learn more from the people at the palace where the queen was taking her ease in preparation for the birth?

Saul was speaking. 'No, I cannot imagine why Sir Edmund should seek to stock arms of all types. It seems peculiar, especially the idea that he has been sending them to Kent. Why, if he wanted arms for defence, he should obviously keep them close to hand.'

'Perhaps he has enough for his household already,' I said, almost without thinking. And then I felt my eyes widen. 'If he has, then the arms must all be for others, men who are not in his household.'

'Yes. He must be selling them on.'

'Or holding them for others,' I said.

'What possible . . .' He stopped.

We looked at each other, suddenly alarmed. We were of one mind.

If Sir Edmund was building a force – and from the quantities of arms, he must be – then what could be his objective? If it were to protect the queen, he would stockpile them in London, so that he and any men he raised to his flag could go to St James's Palace and protect the queen against any rebellion. But the fact he was gathering weapons outside London meant he desired to arm others. If he were, that must mean he did not intend to support the queen. He was planning his own army.

Yes, he could have been intending to assault a neighbour in Kent to steal lands or animals, but how much more likely was it that he was intending to steal a larger swathe of territory? Could he be planning to overthrow the queen while she was unwell and incapable of joining and motivating her troops, owing to her lying-in, waiting for the birth of her heir?

He frowned thoughtfully, and I was sure that his mind was wandering, as it was wont to do after a few glasses of wine. However, I was wrong.

'This is interesting. I know that the secretary of state, John Boxall, will be interested. If I can supply information about Vanderstilt and his business, and if de Vere were engaged in business that could affect the city, it might bring my name to the attention of those who could promote it.'

PART NINE

Jack's Tale Continues . . .

SEVENTEEN

Thursday 25th August

The torturer busied himself with the whole panoply of tools at his disposal while I watched, spellbound.

You may believe this or not, but I could not make a sound. I tried, several times, to speak and plead with him for mercy, for my life and health, but when I opened my mouth, not a word would come. There was something truly hellish in that foul, noisome chamber below the ground. The light from the glowing logs as they turned to charcoal, the demonic shadows cast on the walls, the metallic clatter of pincers, shears, tongs, brands, all designed to unman me.

They succeeded.

Over time I had heard tales of the hideous experiments designed to force even the most recalcitrant to speak and stop the agony, but this was worse. Here I could see the methodical work of a master torturer. All the tools set out in the right sequence, all close to hand, just like a leatherworker at his bench, or a goldsmith at his. It was so . . . *mundane* and normal, it made me want to scream.

There was a knocking at a door, and the man glanced at me, winked, and was gone. I had barely a moment. I rattled the chains which were bound to my wrists with leather bracelets, but the chains were firm, and when I tried to pull my wrists free, all I got was a pain in both where the skin had rubbed raw and bloody. It was maddening, and at last I managed to give a whimper as I felt blood run down my forearms to my armpits. Then the whimper turned into a fully fledged wail as I realized I was still fixed in place. I would never be able to escape my doom here.

What would it mean? Would I be burned all over my body? Would the torturer use pincers to cut away the flesh from arms and breast? Would they use *peine forte et dure* to try to prise all my secrets from me before taking me out and executing me?

I sobbed at the injustice of it all. I had done nothing wrong!
I was a wronged man! All I had done was attempt to preserve
my life at a time when others sought to destroy me, for no reason
other than their own ambitions.

There were voices, and I bit my lip, struggling still more to
try to free myself, but nothing prevailed against the leather and
iron. I was as trapped as a bird on a limed branch.

The voices came closer, and one seemed surprisingly familiar.
It was that of a man I knew, I realized, although my mind was
still so petrified with terror and horror that I did not instantly
recognize it. Yet still, the familiarity started to attack my fear,
and I started to be aware of a certain calmness creeping in on
me.

It was when the two men appeared before me that I recognized
him at last: Humfrie.

He greeted me with one of his sour-looking twists of his lip.
'Let's have him down, Tom.'

The torturer walked to me, and released both of my arms from
the buckles.

'What happened to his wrists?'

My phlegmatic and mute torturer looked at my wrists and
the blood which had been smeared over both, and shook his
head.

Humfrie grunted to himself. 'Are you well, Master Blackjack?'

'I'm fine,' I said, but at that moment my eye lit upon a maul
on the table with the other tools of physical destruction. I sprang
towards it in order to beat my torturer to a pulp, but my springing
was less than effective. Rather than a light pounce, such as a cat
might achieve to land upon a favoured mouse meal, my legs
permitted only a half-step, and then refused to support my weight
any longer. With a mild wail of complaint, I found myself on
the floor, looking up at the two of them. 'Humfrie!'

A hand came down and grasped my wrist. That stung, and I
gave another yelp, adding to it a series of imprecations against
the torturer and his ancestors.

'This is a friend of mine,' Humfrie said, jerking a thumb at
the torturer. 'Tom here is happy to set you free.'

'What of my assailant?' I demanded.

'You made the mistake, coming here with weaponry enough to murder the queen and half her guards,' Tom said.

I glared at him. 'I thought you were mute!'

'Oh, no. I just find it keeps the room quieter for a while if I pretend. What, would you expect me to keep speaking to the prisoners in here? What good would that do them? It may raise their spirits, but it wouldn't help me if it did. I'd just have to use more pain to release their tongues. Better and kinder to let them be still.'

The glare did not leave my face. 'Where is my suit of clothes? My gun and sword?'

'I should ask the officer who brought you here,' Tom said. 'His name is Stephen Orbin. You'll find him out at the guard house, I daresay.'

With Humfrie at my side, I made my way back to the open air. There was a series of steps from the ghastly chamber, and these led up to a large, open quadrangle. Here, I could see several men and women walking about, taking the air.

One man in particular caught my attention. No, it was not my officer from the guardroom, it was a fairly tall, rather podgy man, stooped, with a cardinal's hat and gown.

'Come with me!' I said, and marched over the grass.

The cardinal saw us approaching, and I could see his eyes passing over both of us as if testing us to see whether we were dangerous or not.

I was not of a mood to pay attention to such feelings on his part, being still outraged and fuming that I had been knocked on the head, bound, threatened with torture and robbed of my possessions.

'Your Excellency,' I said by way of introduction. 'I have urgent news for the queen, and must give it to her without delay, but the fool on the gate threatened me, broke my head and stole my property. I must speak with the queen. She will remember me.'

'How could anyone not remember you? With your shirt all bloody and your wrists chafed from being bound,' the man said mildly. 'Do you swear you mean her no harm?'

'I have come to this pass because of my determination to warn her! Look at my injuries!' I expostulated, holding up both wrists.

A guard near the cardinal stepped nearer, as though I was likely to throw myself on him to try to beat him to death with my bare hands. I gave him a stern gaze. My stock of grim expressions was expanding by the hour.

'Who did this to you?'

'The officer, Orbin, at the gate.'

The cardinal waved a hand to another guard, instructing him to bring Orbin to us, before continuing on his slow perambulation about the quadrangle. When he glanced over his shoulder, he beckoned to us, and we fell in at his side.

This was Cardinal Pole, I learned, the famed counsellor to the queen. He was an elderly man with deep-sunk eyes in a narrow face. His eyes seemed to glitter and gleam, and perhaps it was his devotion to his religion that kept him so determined, but I did not like the look of his complexion. It had that greyness that spoke of a man who has been unwell, and that, together with the brightness of his eyes, seemed to indicate an unhealthful soul.

Of course, if I had thought of it, I would have been more concerned. This was, after all, Reginald Pole, the man who had planned with the queen to bring back the Catholic Mass to the masses. They were determined to save people their own way, no matter what. I suppose both were as enthusiastic as each other, and content to see that those who were reluctant to accept the queen's good intentions, and who remained obdurate, should witness the error of their ways by experiencing the flames of hell even as they left the world of misery and pain. Yes, they saw to it that all their victims were burned to death at the stake. I confess, I do not understand what God would think of this form of persuasion. In any case, I was only aware at that moment of the injuries done to my wrists, and how I might achieve revenge on Orbin.

There was enough time for us to march halfway around the quadrangle before Orbin appeared. He was wearing my jack and hat, and I was sure that he had my pistol concealed beneath, since he also wore my powder and shot pouches. To say I was angry would be an understatement. I was absolutely enraged.

'Give me back my coat, you thief!' I burst out as soon as he was near enough to hear me.

'Cardinal, this man is a dangerous felon. I stopped him from entering the palace, and had him apprehended and taken to the torturer. I believe him to have been making an attempt on our queen's life.'

'Is that why you took his weapons and clothing?'

'I felt he would hardly have need of them.'

'Perhaps you should return his clothing,' the Cardinal said mildly. 'Although you may keep his weapons for now.'

'Yes, Your Excellency.'

'Now, Master Blackjack, perhaps you could tell us again what it is that you think threatens the queen?'

'You do not know, perhaps,' Orbin said silkily. 'But this fellow is the suspect in a murder enquiry at the moment. He is suspected of the murder of a Dutchman for money.'

'I am innocent! I was not even near that house when he . . .'

'When he was murdered, you were about to add?'

'Yes. I was nowhere near there.'

'So you admit he is murdered.'

'Well, I . . .' I scowled. He had trapped me, you see. It was most unfair. 'He has disappeared, and I have been accused, so I use the words you use. I know nothing of where he is.'

'Yet the officers wanted to arrest you.'

'Yes, well, that was a mistake. Cardinal, I . . .'

'He was found here carrying various weapons, Cardinal.'

'I am here to speak with the queen, Cardinal,' I said, 'and this fool will keep trying to prevent me! But I believe that there is a plot to have a rebellion against the queen, and her life is in danger!'

'Cardinal, you must listen to me,' Orbin said, and as I turned to him to remonstrate more forcefully, there was a sudden dull cracking sound, and Orbin's eyes rolled up into his head. He seemed to go quite stiff, and then suddenly flopped like a marionette with its strings cut, to form a rather ungainly mess on the grass, where he squirmed a bit, moaning loudly.

Humfrie shrugged in an apologetic manner. 'He was delaying your eminence. I think Master Blackjack here should be heard.'

'Very well,' the Cardinal said, giving the body at his feet a rather disdainful glance. 'Tell me what you know and I will speak with her.'

And so I spoke at length, all about the disappearance of Vanderstilt, mentioning the injustice of my own treatment, and

then speaking of Sir Edmund's house and how it was full of
weaponry for which he had little need. I did not see the need to
mention that Vanderstilt was likely murdered on his way home
from Sir Edmund's house. That was plain enough to me, but I
didn't want any more confusion about whether or not I had been
involved in his untimely demise. However, I was keen to know
what Sir Edmund might want such an arms cache for, and my
own suspicion had been enough to bring me here, as I said.

'Sir Edmund is a loyal subject to the queen,' Pole said thoughtfully, fixing a gimlet eye on me. It was daunting.

'So he has said. But his actions betray him. I think he plans
to overcome the throne and take it for himself – or for his
companions. That is what I have been told. He will dispossess
the heir and give the throne to anyone who pays him in gold.'

There have been many things said about the Cardinal, and
many of them by me. However, he was yet an Englishman, and
devoted to the queen.

He listened to me, watching me for much of the time,
although for a short period his attention was taken by the trio
of guards who had gone to scrape up the fallen remnants of
Orbin. Humfrie had merely clobbered him over the head with
his dagger's pommel, and Orbin now looked as though he was
coming round again, although with a head worse than any
hangover. With my own sore skull, I sincerely hoped that he
would be in considerable pain for the rest of the day – or week,
if possible.

Two men had Orbin's arms about their shoulders now and
were half-dragging, half-carrying him away, the toes of his boots
scraping at the grass. Before they could go far, Humfrie retrieved
my weapons and the Cardinal had a servant hold them for me.
Orbin was well enough to throw a baleful stare at me – but then
again, it might have been the fierce concentration of a man who
could no longer focus. I hoped it was so.

That was the end of our restful discussion. The cardinal nodded
to himself, indicated that he would go and inform the queen
immediately, and ordered two men to wait with us and keep us
out in the quadrangle while he went indoors. I was confident that
he was going to speak to the queen to appraise her of the possible
threat to her safety.

'How did you know to come here today?' I asked Humfrie.

'Me? I have been following you on and off for some days. I couldn't stay with you last night, but today I followed you from the Cardinal's Hat and made sure you were safe. No one followed you.'

'But how did you get into the palace? Did you climb over the walls?' I said, only half in jest.

He looked a little shifty. 'Ah, well, I have my own business interests and they bring me here on occasion.'

I frowned at the man. 'Business interests?' Indeed! The man was my hireling, a helpful contractor who would help me with a few of my more difficult tasks – those which involved removing men who could be embarrassing to our Lady Elizabeth. 'What sort of interests do you have here?' I said, and then I gaped. Yes, my mouth fell wide.

Any who know me will confirm that I am a man of swift thought and consideration, and this was not the most difficult conclusion to reach.

He had the grace to be abashed. I knew full well that Humfrie had no trade other than his ability to end lives. He was a most professional assassin, competent, unflappable, and generally quick – and *kind*. Not the usual term for a man dedicated to ending life, I know, but he was not the sort to leave a dangling man slowly throttling, or making a stab that would end a life given an hour or two, with all the concomitant agony – no. He would cleanly murder his victims so swiftly that half must have met the angels before they truly realized they had left their corporeal bodies behind.

'You kill for the queen?'

'Only *occasionally*,' he said defensively. 'I know you work for Lady Elizabeth, but a man has to live, and your work has been dry of late. I had to seek another contractor.'

'You kill for Queen Mary?'

'Not often. More usually it's for the cardinal. He has a number of men whom he suspects of plotting against the queen or the Church, and he is good enough to make use of my services when he needs.'

'I . . .' But no words could quite express my shock and disgust. Yes, disgust. The man was supposed to be my hireling. To learn

that he had divided his loyalties between me and Cardinal Pole
was a blow. 'How much does he pay?'

'Not as much as you, Jack. That's why I'm still loyal to you.'

That was good to hear, at least. After all, if Humfrie were to
go to the queen or Pole and tell either that I was actually working
for Elizabeth, I would be keen to have Humfrie's kindly knife
end my life as quickly as possible, with as little fuss – or pain
– as he could manage. The alternative would be more time in
Tom's chamber, becoming better acquainted with all the tools of
his trade, which was not appealing.

That raised another question. 'How do you know the torturer?'

'He and I have our own special skills, and on occasion we
overlap. There are times when I need information, and you know
I dislike tormenting my victims. Then, sometimes he has need
of removing a fellow, and he does not like to end life. We have
known each other for many years.'

I sat back, musing on this. It was, I supposed, not surprising
that enterprising men of their type would work together period-
ically, and yet I was still struck with a sense of unfairness.

'I should have told you, Master Jack.'

'No. Pray don't mention it,' I said. I would have continued, but
there came the gallumphing of many boots, and suddenly we were
surrounded by a posse of sergeants and constables all keen and
eager to go and break down doors, and ideally a few heads too.

The cardinal was behind them all. His servant passed me my
gun and other weapons as he spoke.

'Here is a warrant from the queen for the arrest of Sir Edmund
de Vere. Here are your men, Master Blackjack. Take them to de
Vere's house and see what you may find. Bring him back here,
and set a guard on his house.'

This was not to my liking. I had little desire to be thrown into
a fight with Sir Edmund's men again. I could still remember the
way that his men had appeared. All were large and threatening,
to my recollection. I agreed to go with the men, because after
all, a man doesn't quibble when it's a man like Pole giving the
orders, but I was glad to recover my handgun, powder, shot, knife
and sword. I was reluctant to walk about London without the
means of protection.

The walk to Sir Edmund's house was a good mile or mile and a half from the palace, maybe more, and I felt every yard of that way. My feet grew heavier with every step. I was not just worried about the response of Sir Edmund to my appearance with a small armed guard; I was still also thinking about Humfrie and his loyalties, and how they had to be enormously divided between me and the queen's counsellor. All the way, I could not help but throw little glances at Humfrie, wondering whether even now he was planning to see me removed, because the queen would be keen to have a paid hireling of Lady Elizabeth removed from the scene. Humfrie could hardly dispute the fact that I was employed by John Blount, who was himself a servant to Sir Thomas Parry, Lady Elizabeth's most trusted lieutenant. I almost wanted to blurt out my apologies, to offer myself up to Humfrie's mercy, to beg his forgiveness for any slight I may have given him and plead for my life – but it is difficult to beseech a man when walking at some speed in the presence of a company of armed men, in the middle of a busy London street. Besides, when I looked at him, Humfrie's face betrayed no indication of malice towards me. Rather, he seemed in a relaxed mood.

It was little comfort to me.

Arriving at Sir Edmund's house, the men instantly deployed without instruction. Humfrie stayed remarkably close to me, which was unsettling, bearing in mind my concerns and suspicions, but if he intended me harm, there was little I could do about it. He might have been keeping at my side purely to defend me against the men from the queen, or from Sir Edmund's men – but that seemed far-fetched.

The three urchins were farther along the road, their hoops and stones forgotten in the excitement of seeing a band of men at arms appearing at de Vere's house. I signalled to them to be off, and they obeyed with customary promptitude – by which I mean the little scrotes ignored me.

I watched as the queen's men disposed themselves. Some hurried to the rear of the house, some to the stables, while a couple walked about the house looking for additional exits. It appeared that there were none, and soon the sergeant, a bull-shaped man with the head of an ox and a brain to match, nodded to me, and I found myself ushered to the front door.

The warrant was in my hand. I swallowed hard, raised my hand and tapped gently on the timbers.

'There is no one . . .' I began, when the sergeant thrust me aside none too gently, and beat on the door with his staff's butt, bellowing, '*OPEN IN THE NAME OF THE QUEEN!*'

I swear, he left my ears ringing, and I turned to remonstrate. But before I could, the door opened and I caught a glimpse of a familiar face – it was the man who had been ordered to take my gun from me the last time I was here. His expression now was that of a boy who has thrust his hand into a biscuit bag, only to discover it contained a snake. 'What the . . .?' he managed before the sergeant shoved him from our path and entered.

Humfrie took my wrist and pulled me in with him, while the rest of the cavalcade swept in with the force of the Thames after a heavy rain. I found myself pushed against a wall, while the men opened doors, shouting at people in their path, the sergeant demanding to know where Sir Edmund was, where were the weapons, who was in the house, and any number of other questions that washed over the sandy-haired servant.

'The weapons were in there,' I said helpfully, pointing at the door. Two men, directed by the sergeant, tried to open the door, but it was locked. They broke it open with mauls, and inside I could see the racks still in place, but almost all the weapons were gone.

'Where are they all?' I asked the servant.

'What? Who?'

He was clearly a fool. I spoke slowly and distinctly for him. 'Both. When I was here last, those racks were filled, and there were many servants all about the house. Where are they?'

'Sir Edmund has gone to his manor in Kent; to Hailward, near Bromley. His servants are gone with him,' the lad explained, and from the look of him, he was telling the truth. I was all for letting him go, and going to see whether there was any wine in the buttery, but the sergeant clearly had a different view of the correct way to proceed, and had the poor devil held by two beefy types who looked as though they would rather like to throw the poor fellow into a pit filled with ravening mastiffs. I didn't fancy the boy's chances, were that to happen.

Before I could proceed through to the armoury, there came a clash and shouting from the garden. The sergeant and his remaining men instantly took to their heels, running through the hall to the kitchen and out beyond to the garden. For my part, I thought that the preferable route was back the way we had come, because it was growing clear that there was a serious fight brewing out there, but Humfrie had me by the elbow now and I found myself running outside with him.

It was a ferocious battle. Men lay on the ground, some few with the groggy appearance of those who had been knocked on the head. After Orbin's assault on my own pate, I could empathize with them. In past years, many people have taken it into their heads to beat me about mine and, invariably, I have found the result to be a lack of coordination of my legs, a feeling of intense nausea, and a sense that all is very definitely not well in the world. God appears to have taken a short break from his usual duties, which should involve looking after the poor and injured, like me.

Not all were unconscious. There was one fellow who had set up a loud wailing, flapping an arm about the place, which had the unfortunate result of flinging blood about. He had a large gash in his forearm, and the blood sprayed liberally. Some was flung over me when he made a spectacularly emphatic gesture, and I felt it on my face and throat. It was enough almost to make me succumb to the temptation to vomit, but I wiped my features and turned away.

The sergeant was standing at a small jetty at the bottom of the garden, staring out over the river.

'What is it? What's happened?' I asked.

He looked at me as if I was somewhat less intelligent than a water rat. Then he pointed. 'He's there,' he said.

Just reaching the farther shore was a little boat. The oars were being plied enthusiastically by four men, while Sir Edmund stood in the back bit. What's it called? I could never get used to nautical terms – they seem designed just to confuse a fellow, to give sailors an opportunity to laugh at the stupidity of land-living, sensible types. Anyway, he was there, shaking his fist and looking as bitter and enraged as any schemer might on learning his plots were discovered.

That was the adventure of the garden. Sir Edmund had escaped, for now, the queen's justice, but if there had ever been any doubt

in the mind of the sergeant as to whether the knight had truly
been guilty of the offences alleged, it had clearly passed.

Pausing only to order that all of Sir Edmund's remaining men
should be bound and held under guard, he made his way to the
nearest of them and started asking where the weapons were, what
Sir Edmund's plans were, did he have a force on which he could
call, and similar questions.

The men being tied up were the remaining guards Sir Edmund
had installed in his house. They had been left, I assumed, purely
to hold the house safe from thieves – and possibly hold off any
pursuit while he made good his getaway. Merely poor soldiers
whose only purpose was to hold off his own capture. I was in
two minds about that, naturally. From one angle, it struck me
that it showed good common sense on the part of Sir Edmund,
since if I had been in the same position, I would obviously have
done the same thing. A man has a duty to protect himself, after
all.

On the other hand, being a man who had all too often been
the recipient of such behaviour, I felt more than a little disgust
for the man's cowardice in not remaining to share in his men's
punishments. The least of which would be a couple of days in
the stocks, no doubt. For others, the consequences would be
considerably worse. They may be treated to a view of that same
chamber where Tom worked his bloody magic, summoning
answers to questions from the unwilling, or given a short visit
to the Tyburn tree where they could dance along with the other
traitors, felons and unfortunates.

Soon it became clear that there was little information to be
gleaned from the men in the garden. They were soon placed
under the guard of a troop of law officers, while a magistrate
was summoned to ensure that the house was locked and protected
from ransacking by locals seeing the possibility of a quick profit.
The queen would be thoroughly disappointed to learn that some
London ne'er-do-wells had been through the place before she
could confiscate de Vere's goods, like plums through an unsus-
pecting man. It's best to eat plums in moderation, I learned after
that experience.

While Humfrie and I discovered a broached cask of wine in
the buttery, the sergeant and his men went through the rest of

the house, from attic to cellars, but there was little enough to be discovered. I had wondered whether there might be the body of Vanderstilt in the cellar or concealed in a barrel, or buried in the garden, but the men seemed perfectly competent in their searches, and could find no evidence of a body or of murder having been committed here.

Which was interesting, I thought. I had assumed that Vanderstilt would be found here. Of course, it did not mean that the man had not been slain and thrown into the Thames. Here, past the Fleet and the Walbrook, the river was full of ordure from the city, and more than one body had ended up in those filthy waters to my own certain knowledge.

It took the rest of the afternoon to see the premises thoroughly investigated, and at the end of the day the sergeant indicated to me that we should probably return to St James's Palace to report on our discoveries, such as they were. Mostly lists of names, and some notes about men in Gloucester and York, and someone up on the Northern March. It made no sense to me. Worse, the whole escapade was not to my taste, and I sought to excuse myself.

'I fear I have other matters which take my time.'

'Matters which are more important than the queen's?'

'No, of course not, but I have business which needs my urgent care.'

It was all to no avail. The sergeant was most persuasive, especially when he set two men to escort me back to the palace. I suddenly found that I could, perhaps, afford the time.

At the palace, Humfrie and I were told to wait in an antechamber, where we cooled our heels for a significant stretch of time before the sunken-eyed cardinal returned to us. He stood before me for some little while with an expression of disappointment on his face.

'I understand you failed to catch him,' he said.

'We could not help it. He was warned. Perhaps he had men keeping watch on the road,' Humfrie said mildly. 'He was already over the river when we arrived.'

That was a point which had evaded me. Sir Edmund had been clambering aboard his craft even as we broke into his house, which was remarkably fortunate for him, I thought.

'Yet the fact remains that he has spirited away the weapons,' the cardinal said. He scowled as he looked at us. 'The strain which the queen suffers is appalling, and meanwhile you have allowed rebels and felons to escape and make their way to Kent, where no doubt they will foment trouble again, just as the madman Wyatt did during his rebellion. You are responsible for this.'

'We did all we could!' I protested. 'What more could we . . .?'

But Humfrie had held up his hand to halt my flow of objections. 'What do you want us to do?'

'We need to capture him and bring him back to justice,' the cardinal said.

I felt my mouth moving, but thankfully this time I could make no comment.

Humfrie nodded pensively. 'It will not be cheap.'

'I am sure you will manage.'

'We will need help with the expense.'

'It is your civil duty to your queen.'

'I am sure Her Royal Highness would not begrudge men who perform services for her to be reimbursed.'

'You don't know much about royal finances, then,' the cardinal said heavily. He looked across at Humfrie. 'Very well, then. Reasonable expenses will be covered.'

'What of men? We have no idea the size of his household down there.'

'I will give you a company of men.'

'And transport? We shall need horses.'

'Yes, yes.'

'And . . .'

'Master, *enough*! You have enough to capture him and bring him to justice. You will aid the queen and bring him back to the queen's peace.'

You will notice that I kept silent while this discussion continued. I had my own concerns, ranging from whether I could petition the queen for a pardon for the matter of Vanderstilt's disappearance so I did not get arrested again, to what on earth I could do about my house. I would have to evict Vanderstilt's servant, of course, and try to acquire a new tenant as soon as possible, while my finances were still so low.

The cardinal left us a little while later, and shortly after he had gone, a courtier appeared in the doorway and asked us to follow him.

I don't think either of us realized what was happening. In my mind, I know, were thoughts of a meal before we were to set off, and possibly the opportunity to choose a horse. That itself was not something I looked forward to. As I have mentioned before, I am not overly fond of horses. I know others are very keen on what they consider to be sagacious beasts, but from personal experience they tend to be vicious brutes with an over-inflated opinion of themselves. They can kick, bite, throw a man from the saddle, and generally behave like wild creatures, all the while reminding a fellow of the unpleasant fact that they are many times bigger than him, and if they choose, there is little a man can do to control them.

Still, although I paid little attention, I became aware that we were not going in the direction of the stables. In fact, we were taken along many corridors and passages – some overlooking large quadrangles, one converted to a tennis court, I saw – and were taken all about until my mind was utterly confused. This palace was huge.

It was only when we entered a long corridor with a roaring fire in the hearth that I realized what was happening.

The courtier motioned to us, and I dropped immediately, bowing as low as I could without actually striking my head on the floor. I threw an anguished look at Humfrie, who appeared reluctant at first, but then he realized who this was and copied me.

Queen Mary spoke quietly. 'Master Blackjack, please approach us.'

It is an odd experience to meet a queen. I had before, when this lady was four years younger, and looked more chubby-faced and cheery. At the time, I felt sure that she would be an enthusiastic little baggage in a bed-walloping, not that I dared try my fortune. She had that sort of genial look about her, though, and I feel sure that Philip, when he married her, would have enjoyed his marital bed. Not that it had persuaded him to remain a moment longer in her kingdom than he was forced to, the greasy foreign dog.

'Come closer, sirs.'

She was lying on a seat with cushions of silk behind her, her belly considerably swollen, her legs on a stool with more cushions. About her were various ladies, some of whom I noticed giving my figure a speculative look that spoke of considerable boredom in the duties of a lady-in-waiting. I was pleasingly assured that more than one of these women would be happy for a little diversion, were I free. However, I was also aware of the unfriendly eyes of eight guards about the place, and knew that any attempt to chat with them would likely be short-lived.

She was speaking, and I quickly returned my attention to her. 'Your Royal Highness, I am glad to be of any service,' I said.

'I recall your face,' she said, peering at me. Her face was not young any longer. It was wrenched and twisted with pain, and there were deep lines at the side of her mouth, while her eyes were grown sunken, like a woman suffering from a disease rather than preparing for her lying-in and birthing bed.

She smiled, and I saw a reflection of the lady I had met. 'Master Blackjack, it seems that you always appear when I am in danger. First with Wyatt's revolt and now . . . Sir Edmund: is he a traitor, do you think?'

'I do not know, Your Highness,' I said. 'But I am sure that money and power motivates him. From what I have seen, he is driven by greed. Like a glutton, he constantly demands more.'

'I do not understand,' she said, and her sudden anger held, so it seemed, a trace of sadness. I am not sure what her parents were truly like, but I have heard that her mother was a Spaniard, and had a temper to match, while her father – well, we have all heard of King Henry VIII's manner. He was a Tudor, and was keen to let anyone know it.

She looked away from me, staring at the fire, and pulled a shawl over her shoulders a little tighter. She looked like a woman of five-and-sixty – pale, and wan, feeling the cold of a winter's day, although the afternoon was very mild. 'I have done all I may to bring peace to the country, bringing the people back to the one true religion, and yet some *dare* to attempt to overthrow my reign! I am only a weak and feeble woman, and here I am, ready to give birth to my son and heir, and yet there are some who would disrupt any moments of peace I enjoy, for their own aggrandizement! Such greed and betrayal have never been seen before! In my kingdom, I insist that all should be honourable – they should be loyal, obedient to my wishes, and accept they owe me their service!'

I felt that old squirming in my belly that spoke of real fear. After all, this woman could order my death on a whim.

She continued, 'This knight de Vere is a traitor. John Boxall has heard of his acts, and already his accomplices all about the realm are being captured. His plot will fail, and those who sought my destruction will find redemption at the end of a rope!'

All this came out in a snake's hiss. I was hopeful that she would not turn against me. Yes, I confess that, just now, listening to her, I was not convinced that I would not be grappled to the floor and carried back downstairs to Tom's chamber of horrors.

She looked at me just then, and there was an intensity and focus in her eyes that almost unmanned me. And then, God be praised! She smiled.

'I thank God that there are still men like you about me, Master Blackjack. Men upon whom I can rely, like the good Cardinal and Master John Boxall. I know that, like them, you will serve me and protect me, no matter what. You are a beacon of trust-worthiness. Do you promise to serve me and protect my son, if I am unable?'

'Of course, your Royal Highness.'

'If I die?'

I swallowed. 'But, your Royal Highness, you will not . . .'

'Enough of the oil, Blackjack,' she snapped, a touch of Henry's daughter returning. 'I am old to be a mother, and there is much pain in this. Women can die giving birth, and I feel sure that my own time may be approaching. Do you so swear?'

'I will do all I can to protect you and your son,' I said. And swallowed.

All I could think at the time was that it was a great relief that Master John Blount could not hear me.

EIGHTEEN

Friday 26th August

The manor was a large house built at the foot of a hill. A river had been diverted from its course and now swept about the place in a deep moat that had been well maintained from all that I could see. The house itself was built of ochre-coloured stone at the base, rising to recent extensions with black-painted oak and white, lime-washed daub. The chimneys told of improvements, with bricks constructed in elegant patterns rising high into the sky.

However, it was not the appearance of the buildings that took my attention; rather, it was the appearance of the men all about. There were groups of pikemen, others bearing matchlock guns, some archers, and milling all about were more men with swords and spears. There were not a hundred men, I estimated, but all were armed and ready for a fight.

I glanced at Humfrie and then at the sergeant, who appeared to be rethinking his original plan to ride to the doors of the manor and demand that Sir Edmund come out to him. The sight of all those men made our thirty seem rather paltry.

'What will you do?' the sergeant said.

This was the first time he had deferred to me and I was not appreciative.

'What do you mean, *what will I do*? I am no commander of men! I have not led a force to storm a manor like this. He even has a moat! How can we break into that?' I demanded hotly.

I have to confess, it was not only the sight of the castle that had left me tetchy and out of sorts. As you will know, my demeanour tends always to be cheerful and patient, but today, after being forced to ride for several miles, after being introduced to a horse that could only have been trained by the Devil himself – which seemed to take a particular delight in trying to uproot me from my saddle, and who clearly thought it great sport to travel under every branch that hung low in a bid to evict me from my seat – I was out of sorts. It was not helped by the thought that soon I might be forced into joining battle with Sir Edmund and his merry men.

'Where did he get all these men from?' I wondered.

'Many are farm workers. Peasants from his lands, I'd reckon,' Humfrie said. He was sitting beside me on his horse, leaning down with his elbows resting comfortably on his mount's withers. He was chewing a little dried sausage while he took in the scene. 'Mayhap a few mercenaries from Spain as well. I don't think you'll be able to storm the place with this force,' he said. 'They don't look the best trained and professional fighters, but there'll be enough who can handle a bow or spear to destroy your men. You'll not get in there by assault.'

'What, then?'

'Subterfuge,' Humfrie said succinctly.

'And how do you propose that we do that?'

'A very small group. Two or three, to go to the gate and ask for entry, and beg an audience with Sir Edmund. When inside, they can overcome the porter and open the gates, and allow more men in. If successful, the three will have overwhelmed the knight and forced him to tell his men to submit.'

'And if he doesn't?'

'The attempt will fail.'

The sergeant nodded, dolefully. 'Who would be best to try this?'

'We three,' Humfrie said, the damned fool.

'*What?*' I said.

'Master Blackjack here already knows the knight . . .'

'*Me?*' I said.

'. . . Sir Edmund will not think him a great threat. As for me, well, I hardly look dangerous. And you are a representative of the queen.'

'Wait!' I said, not that either was listening. A grizzled old warrior who was riding with us threw me an amused look. Well he might. *He* wasn't being offered a one-way trip to Purgatory, was he!

'I would suggest that as soon as we enter, I go to the gate to force it open, while you go with Master Blackjack to meet with

Sir Edmund. All you need do is overwhelm him, force any of his guards about him to surrender, and make him tell his men to submit to the queen's force.'

'And that's all?' I said.

'There is an alternative,' Humfrie said. 'We can ride straight back to the queen and tell her that we didn't dare obey her direct command.'

The sergeant prevaricated. 'We could ride to the sheriff and demand enough men to lay siege.'

'In the time it would take to gather a force, Sir Edmund could already have marched on London,' Humfrie said reasonably.

'With only a hundred men?' the sergeant said, almost scoffing, but not quite.

'A hundred here. A hundred at the next manor, a further hundred at the next . . . How many manors are there at the Kent side of the Thames? And in Surrey? And with how many others has he plotted to make this bid for the throne?' Humfrie wondered aloud.

'Oh, very well.'

'Wait,' I said, desperately racking my brain for any inspiration that could delay or halt this ludicrous idea. 'Um.'

In the years since I first met Humfrie, there have been several times when I have been inordinately grateful to know him. When I have been instructed to murder a particular person, when I have been in need of defence, and others, he has been a stable, rational second string to my bow.

Today was not one of those days. As we rode down to the gates to the fortified manor, in my mind, I was running through my store of epithets suitable for the man. Some were quite pithy, others purely obscene, but all had the merit of being heartfelt. I was betrayed by the fool, brought to this ridiculously dangerous position, entirely due to his stupidity in throwing me to the wolves, as it were.

Our road took us down the slope of the hill, through thick woodland, and here the verges had barely been cut back. There were many opportunities for my horse to dislodge me, and it was a bitter, infuriated and thoroughly unhappy Blackjack who followed the sergeant and Humfrie through the lines of men and weapons to the bridge that gave access to the castle and the yard.

I admit, reluctance and anxiety aside, it was a relief to spring down from the horse and place both feet on solid ground once more. I stood holding the reins and waiting impatiently for a groom to come and see to the horse, and when a steward appeared, a man I recognized from Sir Edmund's London home, I was curt to the point of rudeness. This is not how I tend to behave, even before staff, but on this day I was so thoroughly disgruntled that all thoughts of gentility and manners had quite fled.

That lasted quite some time. We were forced to stand waiting in the yard, while the steward disappeared to speak with his master. About us a knot of guards kept close watch, all gripping weapons in that undemonstrative way that said they knew their tools very well, had practised with them often, and were more than capable of using them again with a view to seeing how effective they would be in, say, dismembering a Jack Blackjack.

When the steward returned, the sergeant and I began to move towards the door, but the steward barred it to the sergeant. I alone, apparently, had permission to enter the house.

Of course, I would like to say that I remained calm, though angry, and that I was immediately determined to be demanding as soon as I saw the knight.

I was not.

There are some interviews which are difficult to recall because, naturally, the memory fades. Others are hard for the opposite reason. They are burned on the memory like brands, because they are embarrassing, painful or just terrifying. This meeting managed to combine all three.

'Master Blackjack, I hope I see you well?'

'Oh, well enough. I . . .'

'You have ridden far. All just to see me? And you have a sergeant with you. The same officer, no doubt, whom you brought to my London home? It was good of you to introduce him to both my houses. And now what?'

'Um?'

'What do you want to do? Is it your intention to arrest me? To hold me for questioning by the Lady Elizabeth's own investigators? Or do you plan to take my little manor here by storm?'

'The queen asks that you return to London and speak with her.'

'Why?'

That was, you know, rather difficult to answer. I could have been honest and told him, well, she wanted to introduce him to this fellow Tom, who had his own rather specialized workshop under the palace, but somehow it did not seem the right moment.

'Do you think Mary has been a good queen?' he asked.

He was standing at the table on his dais, grasping a large goblet of wine with which he gestured to emphasize his speech. Behind the table there were several of his men, three more ranged along the wall. None of them appeared to possess the bright, sunny aspect of fellows welcoming a new friend into their group. Rather, they appeared to hold as one a revulsion at the sight of me. Harsh, I know, but I was uncomfortably aware that they might have valid reasons for being distinctly dubious about me and the reasons for my presence.

It did seem unfair. I mean, it was hardly my fault I was there. It was *their* fault for trying to start an insurrection.

'The queen?' I said. 'Oh, I don't know. As a woman, I think she's . . .'

'She is a tyrant! Worse, she's incompetent! Look at the way she has ruled the realm! She rules only to gratify herself. And how good will her offspring be?'

'Her son would be . . .'

'Who can tell? Will she have a son? She might have a daughter – or nothing. For all her declarations of pregnancy in recent months, she has given birth to nothing. And now she threatens our connections with Rome and Spain! We are only a small country! We cannot afford to be separate from our religious allies. I seek to maintain the succession and her son when she is gone.'

I tried to smile accommodatingly.

'She even lost us Calais!' Sir Edmund continued. 'Though we fought for the city like lions, her actions and lack of support made all our sacrifices pointless. Her diplomacy has been hopeless, her religious beliefs have torn the country apart, and her desire for ever more blood, whether from priests or others she claims to be heretics, is insupportable. We need strong government. Honest, reliable government that will uphold the law and not seek to enrich a few at the cost of all. A leader, someone who can return to France and take back Calais and the French empire, who can stop the bickering between religions and return us to Henry's new church, and who can give the realm meaning again.'

'I see.'

'There is only one man who can do this,' he said, and leaned back against his table. 'Only one man can fight all the lies and distortions. She threatens me? *Me?* I will show how crooked her government is! I'll bring my army to London, and there we'll take over the reins of power once and for all.'

'I see,' I said again.

'And then I'll invite her husband, our king, to take control, as he should have already. And would have, were it not for the craven fools she has advising her.'

'Oh!'

'Are you with us, Blackjack?'

'Oh, well, you see, I'm in a difficult position,' I said.

As I spoke, there came a cry from outside, and then the clash of weapons.

'S'hounds!' Sir Edmund said. 'We're under attack!'

I do not mind confessing that I was all agape.

The first thing I noticed was less the noise of battle from outside, and more the expression on Sir Edmund's face. He looked like a man who has dipped his spoon into a plate of stew only to find a rat's head. *How could this happen,* he was thinking.

I was thinking rather the same. Obviously I knew that the sergeant and Humfrie were determined to hold the gate until we had forced Sir Edmund to surrender, but just at that moment, I was unsure how to proceed. After all, I was the one in a room full of Sir Edmund's supporters, men who could have destroyed me in an instant. I stepped politely away from the doorway, so as not to block their exit.

'Stop bleating! You sound like a goat,' Sir Edmund snapped. I'm not sure who he was talking to, but his eyes were on me. 'Master Blackjack, I think you had best come with me now. This is your work, isn't it?'

'Mine?'

'God's blood, but you whine like an unpaid whore,' he said, which was entirely unfair. I mean to say, he could never have left the Cardinal's Hat without paying. I would like to have seen him try!

'Come!' he said, and by the way he grabbed my arm, it was clear that he did not mean only his men-at-arms. I tried to explain that, really, I didn't wish to upset him or his companions, but it served no purpose. His hand was like a fist of iron about my bicep, and I found myself being hurtled over the paving slabs to the front door, and thence to the outer court.

It was there that I saw Humfrie and the sergeant, both of them fighting a small number of men trying to get to the gates, no doubt planning to open them and allow their comrades from outside to enter and bring justice of a sort on the three interlopers.

'Put up your weapons!' Sir Edmund bellowed, almost deafening me.

I was glad to see that his words had an immediate effect. His men all drew away from the two, and the sergeant stood panting. He had a body writhing before him, and his leg was bloody where his thigh had been stabbed. Humfrie, of course, appeared uninjured.

'You two, put down your weapons,' Sir Edmund commanded.

Humfrie and the sergeant said nothing, but kept a strong grip on their weapons.

'If you don't, you shall watch your companion here die,' Sir Edmund said and, fitting action to his words, he drew his dagger and rested the blade on my throat.

I don't know if you have heard this, but there is a distinct chill to a knife's edge when it is as sharp as a razor. On too many occasions I have been granted an opportunity to notice this. There would appear to be some form of magic that infects the sharpest, and instils in them a coldness that is worse than the touch of ice. Certainly, that is how my neck always reacts when confronted by such a weapon. It was the same today. I could feel my Adam's apple retreat from that hideous chill, until I was almost throttled, and oddly, it felt as if other parts of my anatomy were likewise attempting to crawl inside my body.

'Um!' I said.

'Shut up!'

Humfrie shook his head. 'You don't want to do that.'

'I think I do,' said Sir Edmund, with what I can only describe as a deeply unpleasant chuckle.

'You will regret it. The queen favours Master Blackjack.'

'And you think that will endear him to me?'

'No . . . but if you kill him, your death will be all the harder.'

'I will not suffer death!'

'Your rebellion is finished. You sent messages to Gloucester, to York and to the Scottish Marches. Those in the Marches wished to support you, but they will not.'

'You think so?'

'They're under attack from the thieves of Scotland. The Border Reivers wage unceasing war on them. You expect the men of the north to leave their lands, their cattle, their wives, their families to the reivers? You think they'll send their best men here to you to fight an uncertain war against the lawful queen, anointed by God? You think they'll all come here to do your bidding? They have war enough on their own lands without seeking it here.'

'What do you know of it?'

'Only what the queen told us – Boxall learned of your plotting. Your messengers to Gloucester and York have been captured and held. They told much about their instructions, all those written down, and those they were to carry by their own speech. Your collaborators are all captured. There is no supporting army being raised to help you. You, and the men of Kent here with you, are the only force you have. Do you think you can march on London with a few hundred men? The city guards will destroy you.'

The knife felt very cold indeed now. I wanted to speak, but I was quite certain that anything I said could easily cause the keenest shave I had ever experienced. Even swallowing was a hazard.

'What would you suggest?'

'Tell your men to disperse. Your officers here should ride straightway to the coast, to take a ship to France or Spain. Wherever they wish, they will find occupation enough for their talents. Here, alas, they will find no peace except in a coffin.'

'And me?' Sir Edmund said in what I can only describe as a nasty tone.

'I would have you do the same. There is nothing for you in the queen's realm.'

'You lie like a horse thief!'

'You should take what you can and flee the realm. There will be nothing for you except death if you stay. A traitor's death: quartering. Others may be granted their freedom. The queen is in an accommodating mood, since she is about to give birth to her heir, but not you. You are the instigator.'

'That is just rumour!' Sir Edmund snapped, but I could tell that his men-at-arms were listening. One of them turned to him, and it looked like he was about to add his own words of support for Humfrie's proposal, but Sir Edmund snarled something at him and he subsided.

'What else will you do, Sir Edmund?' Humfrie continued. 'March on London? You cannot without dying. March to Wales? You think you can fight the men of Surrey? Of Dorset? Of Buckinghamshire? They will all be gathered to oppose you, no matter what you intend. Your force will be destroyed. Every man hanged but for you. If you stop now, all can escape the queen's ire. Cross the Channel. Save yourselves.'

When I look back on that scene, which was not a pleasant one for me, naturally, I am still surprised by it. There was a distinct lack of enthusiasm on the part of the men all about Sir Edmund. I imagine they had a different feeling about things, learning that the mad warriors from the north as well as the forces from York and the west country were no longer going to be joining them. It is, after all, one thing to join with a charismatic leader who exudes confidence, and who promises positions of authority and the chance of making money; it is another to realize that your leader has introduced you to a one-way journey ending at Tyburn's tree, and that you have no prospects of a future in your own country. Many men were exchanging fretful glances, and shifting their weight from one foot to another. There was a lot of unhappiness in that court.

The blade felt very tight against my skin again. 'You *cowards*! You think I can't see you all? You want to run away? Leave here and make a new life in exile? How long will you last in France or Galicia? No money, no honour, what will you have to offer?'

'Our lives,' one enterprising fellow said, and I could not help but give another muted wail as the knife dug in again.

Sir Edmund swore most unpleasantly. 'Any of you who want the coward's escape, you can run! Those who honour their oaths to me, follow me!'

And so saying, he turned, shoved me in the back, and propelled me to the door to his hall.

Once more in the chamber, I peered about me with the enthusiasm of a witch seeing her own pyre. There were many footsteps behind me, and I was suddenly thrust in, stumbling and falling on the floor as I went, ending up in a scrambled mess at the foot of the wall.

When I turned, Sir Edmund had put his dagger back in its sheath, and stood with his hands on his hips, while three other men of his followed us inside. Two were dark-haired men, while the third was a blond who had the build of a giant but the vacant expression of the village idiot. He stood gazing at me as though waiting patiently for some new thought to occur to him. Meanwhile Sir Edmund stared at the doorway as if hoping for more of his men to join him. The only man to enter was Humfrie.

'Is this all?' the knight asked, not at all plaintively, but rather with a sort of wonderment. It was plainly hard for him to comprehend that all his men could have deserted him so utterly.

Humfrie peered at him in that manner I knew so well, like a coffin-maker assessing the planks he would need. 'They are all gone. So are your men from the encampment outside. You are deserted.'

'The fools think they'll be given mercy,' one of the dark-haired men said. He hawked and spat.

'And all because of *you*!' Sir Edmund said, turning to me with a snarl of sheer rage.

'It's not *my* fault!' I protested. 'I had nothing to do with it. You think I wanted to come here? All I was trying to do was find out what happened to Vanderstilt! I was accused of killing him, and I wanted to prove I was innocent!'

'That damned fool again? I told you, I had nothing to do with his death!'

'How could I know? I wanted to prove . . .'

'Your innocence, yes. But you failed, didn't you? You thought

I was involved in his death, when it was nothing to do with me! And your foolishness has ruined me!'

'There is still time for you to escape,' I said. 'Take your horse and begone! All of you! What can you hope to do? Four against the queen's army?'

'What, let you go free so that you can alert the sheriff and have us chased to the coast to be captured? Oh, no, Master Blackjack. When we go, you will come with us.'

It was clear that he had come to his own decision. He would not sit and await the queen's justice. We all knew how things ended for Wyatt after his attempt to wrest power from Mary, and Sir Edmund had no desire to emulate his example. While I protested and complained, I was bound with my hands before me, as was Humfrie, and taken outside. Our sergeant was on the ground. Apparently the wound in his leg had been fatal, and he lay amidst a pool of his own blood. He would not rise again, poor soul.

Humfrie and I were taken to our horses, which were still tethered outside the gate, and the blond giant helped me astride the brute with my bound hands before me, so I could at least grip the pommel. Much against my wishes, I soon found myself forced to follow Sir Edmund, who had a leading rein bound to my beast's bridle. Of course, I had hoped that we would follow the road up the hill, thereby passing our own little posse, but the shrewd knight had, I supposed, guessed at the location of our band, and instead he took us along the river's path, heading steadily south and east, occasionally taking us into the waters themselves – to throw any following hounds off our scent, I assume – before suddenly leaving the river and taking a road that led almost directly east.

I have no knowledge of the county of Kent. I was born in that county, but this part was not a territory I had been to before, and I have studiously attempted to avoid it since. Still, I confess that the land was pleasant. There were orchards aplenty, fields, pleasant groves and pastures, and I could see why this was a popular shire for those who kept trying to steal their own portions of it. Why Sir Edmund was so keen on taking over the whole kingdom when he had a manor here, I could not understand. Just simple greed, I supposed.

We must have travelled a good five or six miles, when it happened.

Humfrie suddenly gave a shout, spurred his horse into a gallop, and flew away, wrenching the leading rein from the hand of the dark-haired man who had been allocated to guarding him. He and the second dark-haired man took off after him in an instant, and I did have a brief thought of doing the same, but when I looked at Sir Edmund, I could see that he had my rein wrapped three times about his left hand, leaving his right free to assault me, should he wish to. I had already had my gun and edged weapons confiscated, and I was not going to try to best a knight like him without anything to hand, so I watched mournfully as Humfrie pelted away leaving a cloud of dust in his wake.

'It appears I am not the only man here with a lack of loyal servants,' Sir Edmund commented, and the blond giant laughed. It was not the sort of cheerful chuckle that a man might give, say, when seeing another slip on a patch of ice. No, this sounded considerably less pleasant.

He also sounded close. When I looked over my shoulder, he was only a foot or two away, his hand on his sword. 'Sir Edmund, we have no need of this rabbit, do we? Why not just kill him now?'

Sir Edmund glanced over at us. He said nothing, but he truly did not need to. His face wore that kind of uncaring expression which the rich use when catching sight of a beggar. Then I saw him nod.

With a shriek of terror, I moved out of the way of his sudden lunge. He had already unsheathed his weapon – a horrible, long, grey, worn sword that had seen an end to many lives, from its appearance – and it missed me by a scant three inches.

I gave another scream as the sword slashed at me, catching my left buttock, and forcing me to spring forward. Alas, two things happened. First, I lost my balance, and tumbled from the beast, rolling over his neck and falling headlong to the ground, where I lay with a sudden loss of interest in matters about me as the world darkened and brightened, darkened and brightened.

At first I thought this was the inevitable result of this latest assault on my pate, and expected to lose consciousness at any time. It was with a sort of inevitability that I accepted my doom, since there was nothing I could do about it in any case. I remember thinking, *Ah, well. That's that, then. What a poxed way to die.*

And then I realized that the sudden darkness and light were caused by two warring parties – the giant and my horse. His attempt to cut at me had struck not only my backside, but also my beast, who took a dim view of this assault, and was plunging and kicking like a trained destrier. One hoof caught the giant on the thigh, and I heard the crack of the bone snapping even as he gave a high-keening wail of anguish. Not that it stopped my brute, which kept on leaping and kicking with gusto. Rearing up, he brought both forehooves onto the giant's skull, and I heard that blow even more loudly. In truth, I see it as plainly now as I see my hand before me, and the sight and the sound still return to me in nightmares. It was not the sort of thing a man could easily forget.

The body slumped to the ground, and I saw that his sword was still in his hand. I managed to assemble my thoughts swiftly, and darted to it with all speed, running my bindings down the blade to release myself, and was almost free when I realized that another horse was trotting over to me.

Looking up, I saw Sir Edmund bearing down on me, his own sword raised high in his hand, ready to bring it down on my head.

I whimpered at the sight and dropped, somehow managing to catch hold of the giant's sword as I went, and held it up to block the blow when it came, looking away fearfully as I did so. And although there was no ringing of blades meeting, I did feel the sword judder and grate, as if it was sliding through leather and catching a thick rope or something. And it grew enormously heavy.

When I turned to look, I gave a bleat of horror and dropped the sword, for only a matter of inches from me was the face of Sir Edmund, glaring ferociously like a farmer seeing the fox in his coop. He slowly slid to the ground, and I realized that he had leaned down to stab at me, but the giant's sword was longer than his, and as I thrust it upwards to protect myself, I had inadvertently managed to stab him in the throat. My sword had plunged up into his brain. He was dead before his own blow could fall.

I climbed shakily to my feet, and stood staring at the two: one man with his forehead stoven in like a rotten apple beaten by a maul, the other with the sword I had wielded projecting from the top of his head, and a seriously surprised expression on his face.

There was a clattering of hooves, and suddenly Humfrie was with me, leading a horse. 'Nice work, master,' he said thoughtfully.

That was when I threw up – and then collapsed into my own vomit.

'That was a most professional job,' Humfrie said as we rode slowly back to the manor, leading the horses with the bodies of Sir Edmund and his companions tied over them. 'You did well.'

I still could not speak. My clothes reeked of my sickness, my head throbbed with horror and my injuries, and the fact that my arse was throbbing in time with my head did nothing to improve my overall sense of wellbeing.

'I would not have thought of a thrust like that. His own efforts to swing at you meant he had the additional momentum to help your sword penetrate his head,' Humfrie said wonderingly. He had the most curious, unpleasant fascination with death. 'Still, it is a shame.'

'What is?'

'The queen really wanted him alive,' Humfrie said. 'She wanted us to bring him back for her to question him. Ah, well. Can't be helped.'

That was enough to send my nerves all a-twitter again. Now, in addition to the memories of two men's deaths, I also had the joy of anticipating the return to the queen's presence without the one thing she had wanted: the living presence of Sir Edmund so she could enjoy seeing him dismembered. That thought brought back the memory of the sword in his head, and I would have been sick but for the fact that I had already emptied my stomach.

'He denied trying to overthrow her,' I said when I could speak clearly again. 'He said he was seeking to protect the succession.'

'He would say anything to avoid Tom's devices,' was Humfrie's opinion.

We found the rest of our posse near the manor, and Humfrie

sent a messenger to the sheriff to let him know all that had happened, and to see to it that the ports were watched for those guilty attempting to escape. A second man was sent to London to tell the queen that the insurrection was over, and that the leading protagonists were being pursued or were already dead. When all that had been arranged, I repaired to the hall with Humfrie, where we successfully discovered a store of wine. We allowed the rest of the posse to partake of a barrel or two of beer that was in the buttery, and we both sat back with jugs of wine, easing the strain of the last days of riding, and in my case, fighting.

'How did you best the two men following you?' I asked after the first jugs had been replenished.

'They were fools,' Humfrie said with some disdain. 'They tried to chase me like some felon who feared them. It took me only a short while to find myself a strong sapling on the ground, and when they came, they were inexperienced at fighting on horseback, as I suspected. So when they were close, I engaged the first, using my sapling as a spear, and knocked him from his mount, taking his sword and killing him before the other could wheel and return. When he did, I used my sword to cut his hand free and then took his life.'

'I see,' I said.

Perhaps my voice was a little high-pitched, because Humfrie threw me a sympathetic look. 'I know you dislike taking life, Master Blackjack, but on occasion it is necessary. Like today. And of course it's good that you killed Sir Edmund. He was a danger, no matter what the queen wanted.'

'I am relieved that he is no longer a threat,' I agreed. I could once more see the expression of black rage in his face as he turned his horse to ride to me and try to cut my head from my body. It was enough to make me shudder, and then I refilled my glass with shaking hands.

'Aye, and in any case, we can share, perhaps, in a little profit,' Humfrie said. 'Your master did ask me to remove him.'

'Eh?'

'Your master, John Blount. He came to me when you had been arrested and had disappeared. He was keen to find you, but also wanted to remove Sir Edmund in case he was a threat to the kingdom's peace. If I go to him and say that we took the knight's life, we can share in the reward.'

That was a surprise, but also good news. Any additional money just now would be very welcome, and the idea that I had boosted my reputation as a professional killer was no doubt going to be beneficial. If John Blount believed that I was wholly or even merely partly responsible for removing another obstacle to Lady Elizabeth, that would have a favourable effect, no doubt.

I took another gulp of wine. It was a curious thing, but I was beginning to feel an unease. All was well, as far as I could tell. Sir Edmund was gone, the tor who had followed me was gone. The queen would be glad that we had helped to prevent another rebellion, and may well reward us for saving her kingdom, and Lady Elizabeth would also be glad to know that we had removed an impediment of some form to her own future and wellbeing. Not that I understood how or why Sir Edmund formed any kind of difficulty to her.

Yet . . . there was still that feeling that something was not right. That something was unfinished, perhaps. Or that my own wellbeing was not fully satisfied by this result. At first I felt sure that it was only the miserable result of my tenant's disappearance. That was, certainly, a difficulty. But then I remembered: there was not only the knight and his collection of merry men, but also the matter of Master Perkin Bagnall and his second ambulatory mountain. I felt that I had fulfilled his mission perfectly, removing the danger to the queen and preventing an uprising, and yet I felt a curious nervousness about Bagnall. Something did not feel right about him and his approach. That first time, when he had followed me to my little excursion with Susan Appleby, and the disappearance shortly afterwards of Alice . . . And now there was the matter of de Vere's words. He had sought only to protect the queen's succession and her son, so he had said.

Suddenly I was filled less with nervousness, and more with a complete terror. I was convinced that there was something deeply suspicious about Bagnall and his interest in me. What could have caused that?

In my experience as an agent for Lady Elizabeth, nothing was too outrageous in politics. All I knew for certain was that I wanted no part of it. It was too hazardous.

NINETEEN

We left as early as our heads would allow us the next day, leaving behind ten men who were happy enough to remain away from their wives in the company of the remaining barrels of beer and casks of wine for a few days.

I mounted the sergeant's horse. My own brute had a slash in his flank still, and I wasn't going to try to ride him. He had the spirit of the Devil when he was hale and hearty. The thought of trying to control the monster when he was out of sorts did nothing for my headache or the wound in my arse.

You know the feeling. It was one of those beautiful autumnal days. The sun was bright and high, the trees just beginning to grow dark as the leaves prepared to fall, the warmth was better than the chill of a winter's morning, and my hangover meant I felt terrible. My tongue was a furred gag in my mouth, my armpits and groin were sweaty and sore, my stomach recoiled from any form of solid food, and my head . . . well, I leave that to your imagination. Let it just be said that the interior of my head contained a small army of demons who were that moment enjoying a massed assault on my skull. It thundered and reverberated from a thousand hammer-blows from their tiny but impressive weapons, and it felt as though my head must tumble from my shoulders under their onslaught.

Humfrie, to my delight, was little better than me. I believe he usually drank only London beer, and the potency of the knight's wine had caught him by surprise. This morning, he looked like a mastiff which had swallowed an apple, only to discover that it contained a wasp.

It is enough to say that the journey was, for the most part, conducted in an agreeable silence. Neither Humfrie nor I were of a mood for small talk or gossip. However, when we reached London Bridge early in the afternoon, he was sufficiently recovered to suggest that we ought to go to see the queen without delay, although both of us were fairly approving of the idea of a quiet journey to an alehouse with a view to stabilizing our bodies and ensuring that neither was unhealthy before her majesty, which would not be a good idea.

In the end, we broke our journey at the Blue Bear, where he had a quart of good ale, and I sank a pint of wine. Both of us felt better for that, and it was a moderately happy pair who completed our journey to the palace.

My friend the officer was not on the gate this time, and his minions allowed us both to pass, with a bad grace, admittedly, but we were at least recognized and permitted to enter.

It was inside that I began to get the first inkling that something was wrong.

The men and women in the palace were quiet, all hurrying about their business with haste and little chatter. That was odd. I know many large houses, and have visited several palaces in the service of Lady Elizabeth, and generally the noise of chattering and gossiping servants is deafening. This was almost like the place was in mourning. We both began to fear the worst.

We were taken to the Cardinal, who looked, if anything, more gaunt and pinched than before. He took no time to let us rest, but wanted an instant update. 'What happened?'

I allowed Humfrie to give him the main details, while I stood by with a relaxed demeanour. The Cardinal gave me an occasional suspicious look, but I don't know why. I was feeling much happier than I had for a couple of days, and could not help but smile.

'All is well enough, I suppose,' he said when Humfrie was done. 'It would have been better had you brought the fool back here to be questioned . . . but I am glad that you both achieved his end. There will be a reward, I am sure, but just now, Her Majesty is out of sorts. She will not receive visitors. However, I shall inform her of your services to her, and I am sure that she will be appreciative. You have saved her and her realm from an insurrection. Such lawlessness cannot be permitted, of course.'

'I will tell Bagnall,' I said.

'Who?'

'Perkin Bagnall. He was the man who told me that Sir Edmund had been gathering weapons to overthrow the queen.'

'Bagnall? That name is familiar to me.' He frowned. 'He is a servant of John Boxall, I believe.'

There was something in his eyes that spoke of a fresh suspicion, and when I considered, it was unsurprising. After all, why should Boxall tell his man to have me announce de Vere's treachery to the Cardinal, when Boxall could himself have done that? It would place him in a stronger position with the queen, after all.

It was clear that the same thought had occurred to the Cardinal. There was something very curious about Bagnall's tale. Bagnall, I thought, had best take care of himself. He might soon be introduced to Tom and his tools.

TWENTY

I woke in my house, and this time I could yawn, stretch, and feel moderately at ease for a while. I had no fear of officers appearing to arrest me, because I had received an assurance from the queen, via Cardinal Pole, that she would write a pardon for me and ensure that it was sent to the relevant authorities so that I would be free once more of any suspicion. The idea of renewing the acquaintance of the repellent turnkey at Aldgate was deeply unappealing, as you can imagine.

Raphe and Cecily appeared almost glad to see me return. Hector even sat at my side and placed a paw on my thigh while I ate, and although I snapped at him for form's sake, he almost swaggered away as though recognizing that this morning I was all bark and no bite.

Cecily had grown a little less harsh in her judgement of me, and she appeared to be grateful that I permitted her and Raphe to enjoy themselves. I had enough experience of the harder realities of life, after all, and the pair of them did seem suited. She had a good brain, and was organized and efficient at cooking and maintaining the house to a good standard – and he was obedient to her wishes and instructions. The two appeared to be on good terms, which lent my house a cheerful atmosphere, and I was glad of that. When I had broken my fast, Raphe was quick to clear away the dirty crocks and indicate that he had lit a fire in my small hall, and set out a jug of wine ready for me.

I did wonder briefly why they were being so obliging and considerate – it was not their usual approach to their master – but as soon as I was seated in my chair with a wine in my hand, all thoughts of them dissipated like morning fog on a river.

Perhaps I should have been interested in why Blount had been so keen that Humfrie should assassinate de Vere, but just then it was of little concern to me. Blount rarely told me why this person or that must be killed: he merely gave his orders and I passed them on to Humfrie. At least this once he had cut out the middleman. I only hoped it would not become a recurrent policy of his. Humfrie was cheaper than my retainer, after all.

It was at least reassuring to have heard that Blount had been seeking me. Mayhap he felt now that I was a useful employee, not one to be discarded lightly? I was not foolish enough to think that Blount had sought me out because he missed my company, or from any loyalty or friendship. That was too much to hope for.

But no, my mind was more firmly fixed on Bagnall and his troll. Who was this Bagnall, and why had he confronted me with his warning to the queen?

Obviously Bagnall was operating some devious scheme of his own; plainly he had some form of antipathy towards Sir Edmund, which explained why he sought to have the knight removed. So, what was his motivation? Did Bagnall consider de Vere a rival? A rival, perhaps, in politics? Bagnall was, he declared, a loyal subject of the queen, and sought only to bring Sir Edmund's betrayal to her ears. But he also worked for Boxall. What did that mean? He was determined to flout the Spaniard's desire to control the throne, from all he had said, but was there some other design behind that? I could not tell, and it was that which exercised my aching head.

After all, no man with sense would want to bring about the threat of war again. And if de Vere was keen to remove the queen's heir and replace him with a Spaniard: that did not sound well to many English minds – Blount or Lady Elizabeth, for two. It was one thing for an English-born and raised boy to ascend to the throne, but something very different to just pass it over to a Spaniard. Of course, the Spaniard was the boy's father, so should be a less appalling regent – so long as he didn't try to retain power for too long. But de Vere had a rational concern, it had seemed to me, that the Spanish, once holding the throne, would keep it for themselves, whereas Bagnall appeared to want to ensure that the boy himself took it and held it without foreign interference. Well, that made sense to me.

Of course, it depended on whether he lived long enough to get his arse on the throne. Which also depended on whether

Queen Mary gave birth to a boy at all. Going on past experience, it was quite possible that she would not.

I pulled a face. It was too much for me. I had saved the queen, apparently – and the rest of us – from a fresh civil war, and that was good to know. The realm was safe. Lady Elizabeth was safe, and that meant my own position here in London was hopefully secure, sheltered under her protection.

In my parlour again, and settling back in my seat before the fire, another thought struck me: what if Bagnall was working on his own behalf, not that of Boxall? Was he a rival for some other reason? I had considered briefly the idea that he might have perceived de Vere as a rival in love.

And suddenly it all slipped into position like a well-carved mortise and tenon. Bagnall thought of de Vere as a competitor for the affection of some woman, and decided to dispose of him so he could enjoy his lover in peace. That was possible, but unlikely. I mean to say, which young wench would think of a scrawny fellow like Bagnall, when she had a hale, hearty, wealthy suitor like de Vere as an alternative? Love is blind, or so I've heard it said, but women aren't. A large house, multiple servants, small castle in Kent, or a tatterdemalion like Bagnall? I knew which any woman would choose. It was like comparing me with Bagnall. A ridiculous comparison, obviously. I had not only the wealth, the looks, the brains and . . .

That was when my gaze focused on the fire with a sudden, searing realization. Bagnall – he knew about Alice. Did he view *me* as a competitor for *her* favours? Had this whole matter been dreamed up by him in order to destroy me? Because Alice rejected him, preferring me, naturally, had he lost his temper and, in a rage, slain her out of hand? And then he sent me to the queen's palace to see me thrown in gaol or executed . . .

No. He had the second giant with him. He would only have needed to give the order and my life would have been ended. It was foolishness. I was speculating on the impossible. It was pointless. I must put all this death and destruction behind me.

However, I did still have to discover what I could do to bring more money into my coffers. I had a small purse of gratitude from the queen for my services to her, but it was a niggardly amount, and not enough to maintain my household for long.

I had to evict Vanderstilt's servant and find a new tenant. But then it occurred to me that while Peter was there, the place was being cleaned and maintained. It meant I could keep up appearances, and as soon as there was a new tenant, I could let the place with the minimum of fuss. I could easily have the house rented, especially since the servant Peter could be offered with the building itself.

That, I was sure, was the best option for me. Keep the house looking like a place that was lived in, and as soon as a new tenant appeared, I could either throw the old man from the place, or sell him along with it. It was the perfect scenario.

I would go and make sure he agreed. Sometimes servants can be uppity and difficult, especially foreign ones, but I was certain that this man would welcome the opportunity of remaining in a comfortable house, especially since it offered the possibility of employment in the future, and especially since any new owner, I would make sure, would be an Englishman. As a Dutchman, he must be grateful to be saved from working for another Amsterdammer.

No more Dutchmen for me. As far as I knew, Vanderstilt had been murdered by a fellow countryman. These foreign fellows are often so quick to anger, and all they think of is revenge and feuds. They are not stable and cultured like we English.

Besides, I could mix a visit to my old house with a quick look in at Susan Appleby's – and ideally arrange another meeting with her.

The thought of a fresh bout with Susan was enough to put a spring in my step that morning, and I took up my favourite cane, a necessary precaution after the injury to my buttock (I wished I had made more of that injury in the service of the queen when I had seen the Cardinal; he might have seen fit to increase my reward) before setting off. I wore my sword and dagger, but for today I had left my handgun behind. That had been retrieved from de Vere's saddle bags, and it was good to wear it again on the ride back to London, but it was a heavy tool to carry when going to meet a friend like Susan, and I had enough weaponry about me without it. Besides, when it dangled from my belt, the barrel would keep striking the wound in my buttock. It hurt.

I was wearing an old, dark-green suit of clothes with red piping and matching hat and breeches, and I have to admit, I cut a fine figure as I made my way through bustling streets, damning the clumsy fools who barged into me and once, nearly, knocked me into the main street itself. A dog flew past me, striking my knee, and almost made me fall into a pile of ordure, but I recovered myself, and ignored the sniggers of some nearby onlookers including two brats of low class who stood barefoot watching the crowds.

Continuing on my way, I was aware of a heightened sense of anticipation. Obviously any man wandering through the streets of London will have a degree of concern for his safety. Usually it is a simple matter of a fellow knowing that the people about him included a number of expert dippers who would thrust a hand into a prominent purse and hoick out all the coins they may, or simply cut the purse strings and take the whole lot. Today, having seen the two urchins, I was sure that my natural instincts were warning me against their predations. I walked nearer the houses, my ears straining for the sound of bare feet on the cobbles. If I had been them, I would have had one dart past me quickly, rushing on ahead, while the other dawdled a little. Then, at an opportune moment, one or the other would cause a mild disturbance, and in the midst of the reaction, the second would snatch his pelf.

I was ready for them. I saw the first quickly move ahead of me, and it was done so smoothly and professionally, I never saw him so much as glance in my direction. Then he was past, and I had gripped my purse more firmly in my left hand, my right hand on my dagger.

It didn't take long in coming. I was only able to take six more paces before I knew the lad was there. I whirled, fast as a striking feline, and found myself not staring at the face of a short, alarmed, beggarly thief, but the belt buckle of a man. When I turned my gaze upwards, I realized it was the troll once more.

It was enough to make me groan.

Now, as you know, I had been thinking about these two – the troll and Perkin Bagnall – and had not yet reached a firm conclusion about their interest in me, nor their reasons for wanting to see Sir Edmund destroyed. However, I was perfectly certain that whatever it was they wanted, it was likely not to be to my taste.

I have a simple rule of thumb in such situations, as I had demonstrated before in the matter of being chased on the way to my renewal of affectionate relations with Susan last time, and I was no more keen today to become embroiled in Bagnall's schemes. However, the troll was impervious to discussion, and although I did think of fleeing, the pain in my buttock, not to mention my headache, meant flight would be troublesome. Rather than a gallop, all I would manage would be a rapid hobble, and I didn't think that would be adequate to escape even a brute as slow as this fellow. Meanwhile, although I carried a stick, I felt sure that it must break over his head without making any sort of impression, and that would leave me without my favourite stick, and confronted by a furious troll. I could draw my sword, but his leathery hide would probably blunt it. Or, more likely, I would strike a blow that would only serve to enrage him. Killing quickly with a sword takes more skill than I possessed.

I decided to go with him.

At least it was not a long journey.

Perkin Bagnall was sitting in a comfortable, high-backed settle by a fire in the Dog and Fox, a pleasant enough little tavern just a short distance from Cheapside, and when I saw him, I marched to him, sat at his side, took up his cup and sank half its contents. I refilled it from the blackjack on the table and turned an enquiring eye to him.

'I do not have time to spend all my days with you, Bagnall. I am a busy man, and I do not appreciate interruptions every hour. If you want me, you can send a note to me at my house, and not waylay me.'

'My apologies, Master Blackjack,' he said with an infuriatingly deferential manner. He appeared and sounded so meek, I was forced to lift my chin slightly and look down on him. It's best always to let such people know their own place in the world, and this fellow was several levels below mine.

'Well?'

'I understand you was successful stopping the knight from launching his attempt at rebellion?'

'Of course.'

'That is good. Interestin' you could do that. I 'ad to ask around about you. And I started hearing that Sir Edmund might not 'ave been your first – well, job, as it was. Of course, now there are other matters which require your attention.'

'Such as what? I doubt you have any issues that concern me!'

'Oh, but I do, sir. You see, Sir Edmund might not have been the only schemer.'

'I know. He had accomplices up and down the country.'

'Yes . . . and there might be others, an' all. Men who'd want to have the other religion foisted on the kingdom again. Old King Henry's new church.'

'Who?'

'That's the thing, you see. De Vere was trying to protect her heir and Church against other forces, and that was why he had the weapons collected. I suspect Cardinal Pole will soon realize there're others determined to bring back the Church of England. And you stopped de Vere from protecting the Catholic faith, you see. It would be grim, if he decided to bring some form of punishment down on your head.'

I stared at the poltroon and wondered how hard I would have to stab him to silence him forever. Yes, I am not a natural-born murderer, I know, but there are times when even I can be moved to violence. Still . . .

'What are you talking about? He wanted to wrest power from government. You told me so!'

'Yes,' Bagnall agreed, toying with his cup. 'But, you see, he was working for other people. These people wanted to ensure that the queen was secure in her position, and that, when she died, her full authority would be maintained by her husband and his associates. They wanted to make sure that her child was recognized as king, under a regent with the full power and authority necessary.'

'Who would that be?' I asked, trying to follow his reasoning.

'The King, of course.'

I shrugged. 'That is what De Vere told me, but you said that he was seeking the throne to sell it.'

'But you killed him,' Bagnall said.

There was an unsettling look of admiration on his face. I didn't like that.

He continued, 'Yes. The boy will be his son, and the birth of the young king may well mean the end of the queen's life, but that would not prevent his inheriting his throne. And with his father protecting him, he would be secure. Secure as any Spanish *bastard*!'

'But . . .' I could feel a huge lump of ice forming in my belly at this news.

'Yes, my apologies. I may have midguided you,' he said with a movement of his lips that was more a sneer than a smile.

'You mean . . . you say that I killed the man who was protecting the queen's legacy? He was raising an army to *protect* her son? With the help of the Spanish? I thought he was trying to overthrow her!'

'Please, keep your voice down, Master Blackjack. We don't want others to take an interest in us, do we?' he said with a sly little smile.

'But you mean I've . . .' I stopped. I was too appalled to be able to express myself.

'Yes,' he said thoughtfully, finishing the last of the wine. 'You're in a troublesome situation, master. Of course, you can protect yourself. Perhaps I can help. I work for those who'd prefer not to have a Spanish prince rule our country, whether he be called *king* or *regent*. Titles ain't my concern. What me and my friends want is the future of the realm. Like you.'

'Your friends like Master John Boxall, I suppose?' I said, and was rewarded with a nod of admiration.

'So, you've been learning about me, too.'

'I have good reason to know who you are,' I said. My mind was wandering along several deeply unpleasant pot-holed paths just now, and all of them appeared to end up in Tom's undercroft with a burning brazier and collection of pincers and brands and hammers. 'What does Boxall want?'

'Perhaps the same as the queen. If she has an heir, it is possible she will need a regent to protect the boy. But the queen has shown signs of motherhood and giving birth before, of course.'

'She has been unlucky,' I said loyally.

'Either that, or God 'as marked her for 'er sins,' this worthy stated. And now his eyes took on a hard edge and he leaned forward to me, his voice low and hard. 'But the country needs a strong man to rule. Not a Spaniard, an *Englishman*, someone who can control the barons and keep the population under control. A man who can take back Calais and the empire for the English crown.'

'Who?' I said, bewildered. 'If the queen does die, surely her sister would take the crown?'

'Ah, well, of course, it'd be better if Lady Elizabeth was not in the way.'

'Yes, I suppose,' I said, and then gaped as his words and his tone struck home. 'You mean you want someone to kill my Lady Elizabeth?'

'Your voice, master. Keep it down. That would certainly be a task o' great service, yes. And not a difficult one for a man so experienced in such affairs,' he added with a sly little smirk. 'You've murdered Sir Edmund, after all. But yes. I'm a devoted supporter of the queen and her heir. We don't want Spaniards coming and running our kingdom. But Elizabeth, she's a constant threat to the queen's line. Just like Lady Jane Grey was. She has to be taken off the board so she doesn't threaten our queen any more.'

I could have stabbed him there and then. But the fact is, I would still have to contend with his troll, and I did not feel able to fight against him as well.

'You know,' he said thoughtfully as he rose to his feet. 'I thought at first you was just a pipsqueak of a pocket-dipper. I was going to blackmail you to keep your past secret. And then I realized you was a bit more valu'ble. That's how you got your money and your big houses. So now, you see, I think we can come to a decent arrangement, like.'

It was a deeply pensive Jack who walked from the tavern some little while later, and all the way, uppermost in my mind was the fact that I had to leave London. I could not think of harming Lady Elizabeth or anyone, and the idea that I should be considered suitable assassin material by yet another man was appalling. How could I escape?

Like an old mare who has lost her rider, I allowed my feet to take me where they wanted without thinking, and it was only when I stood outside my old house, opposite the Applebys' dwelling, that I realized I had walked in the wrong direction.

I did not wish to sit down with the steward of Vanderstilt and discuss the options I had set out for him. No, better by far to leave those talks for another time. However, it was still possible that I might have an opportunity to speak with Susan and, just then, a supportive feminine ear was what I craved. Someone who could listen to me without the encumbrance of political interest or other irrelevancies. And perhaps offer some physical condolences after all my trials.

When I knocked at her door, it was a while before I could hear the steward's steps in the hallway. He was ever lackadaisical when I knocked, and I wondered whether it was his reaction to me alone, or whether it was his usual inept effort. He was a most incompetent servant, in my opinion. I would have dispensed with his services – but then again, I still suffered under the inefficient and laggardly Raphe, so perhaps I was no better than Susan and Saul.

'Master,' he said, without mentioning my name. He was that sort of insulting churl who enjoyed limiting his politeness, as if my name was beneath his contempt. I knew why, of course. He was one of those types who always feels jealousy in the presence of a man like me, who possesses money, status, and the ability to impress women.

'Where is your mistress?'

'Out.'

Not even a vestige of politeness. Just a slight twitch at the corner of his mouth as though giving me as little information as possible was the highlight of his day. 'Ah, then I can enter and wait,' I said.

'No, master. It would be a poor servant who would allow strangers into his master's hall. Without Master Appleby's permission, I cannot let you in.'

'Don't be ridiculous! You know me well enough!'

'Aye, I know you very well, Jack Blackjack!' he said, and this time there was a snarl in his voice that quite shook me.

I retreated a pace or two. Not, of course, from any fear of being struck, but because it would be unseemly for a gentleman to engage in a brawl with a vagabond like him in the street. I gave him a haughty frown, mentioned that I would be sure to discuss his rudeness with his mistress and master, and was somewhat disappointed to see that he gave an even more disdainful grimace and advised me to do so.

'I know what you have been doing with the mistress,' he said.

Now, often when I have heard words of that nature, I have been inclined to treat them with the scorn that they deserve. However, it was true that, first, I had been enjoying the companionship of his mistress at various inns about the city; second, that I had been suspected of that before, by Saul, her husband; and third, that the previous time I had been threatened with death and other very dire and potentially painful punishments as a direct result of Saul's discovering and paying two henchmen to bring condign justice upon me. I had, by dint of hard effort and quick talking, managed to persuade him that he was entirely mistaken, and indeed deluded in considering me to be so disgraceful in my behaviour, and in thinking his wife so faithless and disloyal. My words had worked their magic on him, and he had ended by apologizing profusely, but that did not mean that all his suspicions had been eradicated. I knew all too well that a man's doubts, once established, can all too often be rekindled.

That being so, I attempted to mollify this miserable excuse for a man.

'Come, now, I have done nothing but enjoy the company of an intelligent and witty woman. You are fortunate to have such a kind, understanding mistress.'

'Oh, aye. I know how kind she is to *you!*'

Now this was the point at which my concern grew into a definite, focused alarm. Yes, of course I had valid reason to be worried. If Saul were to discover that I had indeed been playing sheath the dagger with his wife, he would be justifiably annoyed. And a small amount of annoyance in the mind of a wealthy London fellow like him could all too easily translate into copious quantities of money paid out to lowly churls who would be more than happy to spend their time investigating the inner workings of a Blackjack body.

'I don't know what you mean!' I said hotly. 'But were you to tell such untruths to your master, it would not benefit you. I would ensure that your lady's good name was defended properly, and such lies and calumnies denied!'

'I know all about you, Master Blackjack,' he said with that

same, nasty tone. I was willing to bet he had no idea what my professional occupation was, but that was by the by. 'You are a foul womanizer, swiving my mistress, cuckolding my master, and all the while seeking out other female prey. Oh, yes, I know all about the wench up near the gate. And when I tell my mistress, do you think she'll want to have more to do with you?'

It was plain to me that he was talking about poor Alice. 'I have no idea what you mean, fellow! What woman, what prey?'

'A maid. You know whom I mean, I'll warrant! The poor maid who died only a few days past, and who . . .' He gave a nasty smile. 'Oh, yes. I know about the poor maid who was killed. And no one has been caught for her execution yet. But one man had been swiving her regular, hadn't he? *You!*'

'How did you come to . . . to think this? It is untrue, and a terrible slander on my nature! You must have been told this – who told you such an invention? Who could have persuaded you that I was such a man?'

'Your secret is not so secret! I was told by a man who knew you, and I was happy to give him your new address,' the fellow said.

'Then he must have been the murderer!' I exclaimed. 'Why would I slaughter a maid I was enjoying!'

A fleeting uncertainty crossed his face. A passing thought had assailed him – surely a rare and inconvenient occurrence for the miserable peasant – and another had come to me.

'Who was this man? What did he look like?'

Really, I dislike demeaning people, or putting them down, but this was a different matter. This man had risked my life, and was prepared to do so again. My life, my home – everything could be at risk. It was insupportable. 'Who told you?' I said again.

He gave another of his slyly contemptuous little smiles, and this time I had endured, I felt, more than enough.

I pulled out my sword and set the point on his throat. Even as his eyes widened in quick terror, I pushed my way inside the house.

I was not of a mood for lengthy inquisition. I kicked him hard on the shin, and he squeaked and fell backwards in pain as I slammed the door behind me. 'Speak, and speak quickly!' I commanded with the authority vested in me by virtue of the two and a half feet of steel held unwavering at his throat.

It has often been said that I have a masterful nature about me, but rarely have I had such a speedy response. In my own time I have had moments of – well, not fear, of course, but of needful reflection, when others have held knives or swords at my throat. It is a time for careful consideration, I have always felt.

He fell back, his horror all too evident. There was a soggy sort of sound, and from a glance at his hosen, I could see that he had successfully emptied his bladder. I held the blade to his nose, and he was transfixed by the sight of the blue-grey steel. A faint gibbering sound came from him.

'I will say this once again. Your mistress is an honourable woman, and I am too. No, I'm a decent man, I mean! Stop your caterwauling and tell me, who said to you that I was having an affair with her or with Alice?'

'It was the man. He came here to ask me about you.'

'I thank you for that. So you were happy to send a murderer to destroy me!' I said, and I confess that when I spoke my face must have betrayed my anger, for his registered sheer panic. He was convinced I was about to push my weapon into him – and in truth, I am not sure I wouldn't.

It is not a lack of gentlemanly reserve that drove me to such an extreme, but simply the anger that he had put me in danger. That kind of behaviour is unforgivable. My life could have been ended, and this dreg from a filthy privy must have known that.

'*Who was it?*' I hissed from between my teeth, and he began to talk, exceedingly swiftly.

I listened dumbfounded, for there was no doubt who he was describing. A slight man, with two enormous guards behind him – it had to be Perkin Bagnall and his (then) two trolls. If they had meant me harm, I could have died. And this useless imitation of a steward would have been responsible. I swear, it is good fortune that I was not holding my pistol, because in my anger I could have pulled the trigger there and then by accident. As it was, I was tempted to thrust with my sword.

But my good sense and better manners came to his rescue.

'You should be grateful that I am a gentleman,' I said, and I think my chilly tone was cutting. He cowered back once more. 'I will let you live, for now! But if I hear of any insinuations or . . . or other things you've been saying about your mistress – or me – I will be back. I will find you, and you will not escape my vengeance again. *Do you understand me?*'

'Yes, master.'

'Good!' I said, and carefully removed the blade from his throat, thrusting it home into the scabbard with a flourish. 'I shall be gone now, but remember, I know *everyone* in this street. I will hear if any rumours or gossip are being spread about me and my business.'

'Yes, master.'

I walked from the house and into the street. About to return homewards, I stopped. On a whim, I crossed the way and knocked on my own door. There was a period during which I began to swear about the laziness of the modern class of servant, no matter how successful the master of the house. It was definitely not a day for knocking on doors even here, in this moderately exclusive street. First the fool at Susan's home, and now my own old doorway was closed and barred to me. All because of bone-idle servants.

At last the bottler, Peter, appeared in the doorway, and now he stood gazing at me blankly, as though he had never seen me before.

I pushed past him, and walked into my small parlour, where I took my seat and beckoned him to follow me. He cast an apparently worried look towards the kitchen, but then he obediently followed me inside. 'Sir?'

'There is still no sign of your master?'

'No, master,' he said with obvious anxiety. Well, any servant losing a master must be fearful, knowing he might be evicted at any moment.

'Don't worry. I am come to offer you a home here for as long as necessary. I will pay you,' I added. This fellow was a foreigner, after all, and they're always glad of some good, English coin. 'In return, you will keep this house clean and tidy, understand? While you do that, you may continue to live here.'

Well, I was rather expecting effusive gratitude, but in that I was to be disappointed. Still, I suppose since he was a Hollander, it was only to be expected. The magnificence of my offer, since he must know I could throw him from my door at a moment's notice, clearly bowled him over. He was thrilled to be allowed to remain, I suppose. In any case, he merely nodded at me, his gaunt, greying features betraying nothing except the sort of under-standable nervousness before an important man like me.

'That is settled, then. Good. Now, if you do a good job, when the new tenant arrives, I shall recommend you to him. So, you see, you have every incentive to keep the house clean and tidy. Yes?'

He nodded again, and I was left with the thought that this fellow was actually quite a fool. Maybe he had suffered from a blow to his head as a child, or maybe he was just the village's son whom they were most glad to be rid of. For whatever the reason, he continued to stare at me as if overwhelmed.

'Well, if that is agreeable, get to your task,' I said. His clothing, I noted, was still shabby, and the dirt remained on his hosen. 'But have your clothing cleaned, too. You should clean your hosen after gardening. You look a mess. Do you have fresh clothing? Have those things washed and change into something else. Appearances matter, you know.'

I was left with the firm conviction that I had made a good choice.

The man did seem to be several sticks short of a bundle, but that was all one to me, provided that he kept up his side of our agreement. So long as he was assiduous and kept the place tidy, that was the important thing. And, of course, I had made a good bargain, bearing in mind I had made no firm commitment to the sum of money on offer to him. That was something I could argue about later, if he dared bring it up. We had no contract, there was no sum of money on which we had shaken hands – and if he tried to sue me, what would he achieve? I was a London gentleman, and he was a mere penniless foreigner.

It was easy to see whom the magistrate would trust.

Yes, I felt good, and demanded a jug of wine. That way I could consider more about Bagnall and the danger he posed to me. The more I considered him, the more I became convinced that I must warn Blount about him. If John Blount was to learn that Bagnall was threatening Lady Elizabeth, he would likely ensure that such a danger was removed.

The only issue I could see was that he would likely order me to be the engine of removal.

I had just reached this unhappy conclusion when I decided to leave. There was little for me to do, I felt, other than at least warn Blount, and then see whether it would be possible to enlist the services of Humfrie once more.

With that determination I left the house and made my way up the road towards Blount's house.

Or I would have done, but for the blow that struck my pate.

I have the dubious honour of having experienced, on several occasions, a blow to the head. There are many different types, I would say, from the simple collapse into darkness without any noticeable transition from being fully compos mentis, which invariably hurts even more than the worst hangover after ale and brandy, to the lighter-feeling blows that merely stun and leave me realizing that I am suddenly on my knees and no longer upright.

All of them leave a fellow feeling considerably the worse for wear, and all are to be associated with a dull pain in the head, nausea, some wobbliness in the legs, and generally a deep confusion about what is, has, or is about to happen.

This was, happily, unlike those past events.

Today I was not torn with confusion or a need to vomit. Instead, I was aware that something had knocked away both legs, and the darkness was not the experience of falling into a deep well or pit, but rather just that the sun was blocked by the appearance of a vast excrescence. It could have been a mountain . . . but it was not. The cause of this latest misfortune? Two men, built along the lines of – well, imagine St Paul's Cathedral and Westminster Abbey standing side by side, and you get the general idea. They had faces rather like those of the gargoyles set about church roofs to scare away evil. I don't know if they would work for devils, but they certainly succeeded in scaring *me*.

'Er . . . Hello?' I said.

I was, of course, in a recumbent posture, staring up at these two, and while I gazed up at them, wondering why on earth I had been stupid enough to leave my gun behind, a third face appeared. It was that of Master Loughgren. He peered down at me with mingled disdain and disgust. Since my nostrils were picking up the distinct odour of the street, by which I mean the ordure from humans and beasts, I could understand his expression. I would have sprung up with urgency, but the two grim-faced fellows were still there and glowering, and remaining seated seemed safer.

'You are a sore nuisance,' Loughgren said.

'Eh?'

'Get up. You're lying in shit.'

I obeyed. He was not entirely accurate. I was six inches from proof of someone's earlier voiding, and managed to rise without falling into it. He glared at me. I stood with a nervous grin on my face. 'Ah, Master Loughgren!'

'Come with me. And *you*!' he added, pointing at the lesser of the two gargoyles, 'I said to *ask* him to come with us, not try to break his God's-arse *neck*!'

'Sorry, master,' the fellow muttered in a voice like gravel being crushed.

'I am sorry about that,' Loughgren said, and invited me to join him in a pot of wine. After all the excitement of the morning, I was keen to accept the offer of wine, although since my meeting with Bagnall, and his associated demand, and then Susan Appleby's steward, I was not of a mood for the company of a man like Loughgren. However, when faced with two brutes like his henchmen, I was even less keen on the idea of trying to escape. Especially since my arse was giving me grief again after falling.

We were soon ensconced in a private room at an inn, and I sipped cautiously at a fresh cup of wine with Loughgren. It was quite a small chamber, made dark by the hulking shape of one of the bodyguards standing in the doorway and preventing any other men – or light – from entering.

'I wanted to speak with you about Alice,' Loughgren began.

'I had nothing to do with it!' I said.

'You weren't her lover?'

'I . . . I had nothing to do with her death.'

'No. I doubt you did,' he said, peering at me in the darkness. A small fire in the grate gave the room an unpleasant orange glow, now my eyes had acclimatized, and lent a devilish appearance to his features. 'But she was murdered, I think, because of you.'

'What? Why would someone murder her because of me?'

'I was expecting you to tell me that,' he said. His eyes were quite unblinking. It made me think of a reptile. 'Then again, I have heard that Sir Edmund de Vere has also recently died, and a certain Dutchman is missing. The girl, my maid, was known to you, the Dutchman was your tenant, and the knight was an associate of the Dutchman. That all leads many to suspect you of being involved, since you are the one link between them all.'

'I had nothing . . .'

'However,' he continued, as though I had not spoken, 'the fact is that the three had one unifying element when it comes to you: you had no reason to harm any of them, not that I can see. Tell me, Master Blackjack: to whom are you loyal?'

'The queen,' I said quickly (because any other response could be dangerous).

'Ah!' He did not look reassured. 'Perhaps I was wrong to think you were unconnected with events.'

'I don't know what you mean!'

'Pray, do not wail. We do not wish others to take an interest in our discussion.'

'I can tell you about Sir Edmund's death,' I said quickly. The idea that Loughgren's two lackeys might take it into their heads that I was unimportant, or irrelevant, was highly undesirable. I could see no reason why they might decide, for example, to learn how much effort it would take to pull off one of my arms and beat me about the head with it, but I had no wish to give them reason to do so. 'I was there.'

'Speak!'

I told him about the arms, about de Vere's collection, his departure from London, and his death in Kent. 'Now I believe he planned to bring Spanish rule back to the throne, perhaps with a regent in place.'

'And you think his plan has been disrupted?'

'Yes, I believe so.' I explained about the arms from Holland through my tenant, the collection of them and Sir Edmund's intention to supply them to his own rebels.

'When would he have done this?'

'I think he plotted to protect the throne for the queen's heir,' I said. 'He meant to control government and do what he wanted.

The Spanish king could come over whenever he wished to take the crown for himself.'

'I see. And then they would keep their religion and the kingdom under thrall to the Spaniards,' he said.

'Yes.'

'Why? Surely it would be better for him to serve his queen and her heir to wait? His place was to protect her.'

I had thought through that, of course. 'But the queen is confined for the birth. Her advisors and generals are thinking of her and the succession. What better time for de Vere to launch a rebellion to protect the queen's inheritance? And perhaps he did still support her, and wanted to protect her from others who might seek to take the crown for themselves? He gathered his army with a view to protecting her, and her heir, until the Spanish could arrive and take over the realm.'

'Possibly. What does this have to do with my maid and your tenant?' he asked.

'I don't know,' I confessed.

'She had spoken about a lover,' he continued. 'She said he was a vain fellow, well-dressed and wealthy enough, with an appealing look to him, according to our other maid, Marge.' He looked at me with a certain amount of doubt, it seemed to me. I could not tell why.

It was tempting to mention Bagnall at this point, but I was reluctant to bring up any other names. However, one thing did make me frown.

'What is it?'

'I was just thinking: Alice was murdered a little after I saw her last. Surely someone must have seen the man who killed her.'

It had occurred to me, you see, that no matter what Bagnall said, he was surely the man who knew me, who had been following me, and who might have seen Alice and decided to punish me by killing her.

'I have heard that a man was seen after her. Marge said she saw a man.'

I caught my breath. It took little time for me to describe Bagnall and his two walking rocks. 'Was that the fellow?'

He blinked in momentary confusion, and racked his brains.

'No, I don't think so. You say this fellow was in his twenties? Marge described an elderly man, gaunt and haggard. And alone.'

'She must have been mistaken.'

'Perhaps,' he said, but he did not sound convinced.

The interview was over, apparently, and Loughgren rose from the table. 'I doubt we shall meet again, Master Blackjack. I am sorry for your loss, but I suspect you will soon find a woman to replace poor Alice. In the meantime, keep safe and restrict your-self to your usual business. I think you are not ready to be involved in matters of state.'

The sarcastic bastard left the room, his two henchmen with him, leaving me seething. He had no knowledge of me, my capabilities or my skills. To warn me in that manner was an insult. I was so angry, I polished off the rest of the wine he had bought, before demanding another. It was almost mid-afternoon by the time I flounced from the room and straight into a wall.

There are very few occasions when I would have felt that running into a wall would have been preferable to hitting a man, but this was different. I had run into the grim-featured troll who accom-panied Master Perkin Bagnall. As I looked up, his face cracked to show a few teeth. I realized he was smiling.

A fist the size of a – I won't say a hog's ham, because it seemed a great deal larger than that. Let's say it was about the size of an ox's thigh. That was certainly how it appeared to me. Anyway, it took hold of my jack, and while I squeaked in conster-nation, I found myself grasped, and so tightly that I was unable to flee as I would have liked. That was a relief, since from the look of the troll, considerations such as the correct way to grab and hold a man upright would have involved a great deal of brain power. In retrospect, I believe my continued existence was almost entirely due to the fact that he held my jack, and it was more a matter of good fortune than design that he did so and didn't take a handful of my throat instead.

I frantically beamed a welcome at him.

'He's unhappy with you,' Bagnall said. 'So am I.'

I jumped. The voice had come from just behind my left ear,

and it was so unexpected, it was a miracle I didn't leap straight over the head of his henchman and on to the roof of the nearest building. Well, if I hadn't been held there, anyway. Without the fist at my jack, I could have managed it in one bound, I assure you.

'Master Bagnall! I am glad to see you,' I managed at last. 'Um . . .'

'I doubt that. Why were you talking with Master Loughgren?'

'Oh, *him*! Ah, well, he sort of found me,' I said.

'Of course.' There was an underlying lack of conviction in his voice that I could not miss. I smiled again, trying to show that everything was satisfactory, and that there was no need for any animosity between us.

He didn't smile. Instead he leaned his head towards the man mountain. 'You haven't asked why he's unhappy. That's rude.'

'Oh, er . . . I didn't mean to be . . .' I said.

'Stop yammering. It's the thing about you that's most irritating,' he snapped. 'Do you know why he's unhappy?'

I was tempted to say that a brain with little to occupy it, especially one which could not contend with more than two thoughts a day, must inevitably find life more than a little confusing, but I managed to contain my wit. 'Um. No.'

'He's lonely. Since his brother has disappeared, he's been very lonely.'

'Oh?' I said, trying to inject a tone of surprised sympathy.

'And the odd thing is, it was when his brother was following you that he disappeared. Curious that, ain't it?'

'Ah, well, accidents will often happen,' I said. 'You only have to look at the amount of traffic on the roads here in London, and then there's all the trash and garbage thrown into the streets – it's all too easy to stumble or trip. The scavengers are so slow to come and clean up the . . .'

'I don't think he fell over. Do you? He was quite a large man. Do you think he would disappear?'

It was impossible not to look up at the granite features holding me fixed there. Nothing short of a charge of cavalry could make something like that disappear, I thought, but again managed to stop the comment from reaching my lips. It was safer that way.

Shortly afterwards I had been hustled from the inn's doors

into the road, my arms gripped in a giant fist behind me, and we were heading down my old street towards the house where Vanderstilt had lived.

'It is the sort of problem that happens in London. Only a little while ago, my tenant disappeared. In the house just down there,' I added, pointing with my chin, adding verisimilitude to my statement.

'Yes. Perhaps it is time that you disappeared too,' Bagnall said. 'I don't think I can trust you, can I?'

I would have answered, but as he spoke his tor threw a fist into my flank, and as I gasped in surprise, he lifted my arms behind my back, and I had to wail in pain.

I am told that there comes a time in every man's life when his whole existence flashes before him. It is something that I have come to recognize with a sort of reluctant acceptance. It is the time when the fellow's life is about to end.

There's not much else to do, when you are presented with a mountain who possesses fists the size of cannon balls, who desires to turn a fellow into a thin gravy over the cobbles of the road. The last time it happened, I think, was when I was held by miners on Dartmoor, or when I was held by the Gubbinses towards Lydford – or was it that time when I found myself on a ship bound for France to be enslaved? In any case, it was a common enough experience, and while I certainly did not welcome the reminders of some of the more memorable and unpleasant experiences of my life, at least they were quickly passed over.

Which brought me back to the present. I was swiftly dragged from the tavern and bundled along my street back to my old house. I have to confess, this seemed to me to be a serious intrusion. I mean to say, it is one thing to set upon a man while out in the streets, and it is one thing to assault him when a villain has broken into his house, but to assail me and then drag me to my own house, that was a step too far, in my opinion, and I started to give vent to my dissatisfaction. At least, I did until the troll clapped a hand over my mouth. I wasn't sure where that hand had been, but let me say that it reminded me of when I was on Dartmoor, and saw all the sheep, and fell into some of their excrement. The odour of the troll's hand made me think that perhaps a flock had found him asleep and defecated on him. It seemed possible.

At my house, the obnoxious Bagnall battered on my door, and soon it was opened by the scrawny wretch of a bottler, who let us all in with every indication of servile politeness.

'What is happening?' I demanded as Bagnall's man pushed me into my own parlour. 'Who do you think you are?' Because, after all, I am a man of property and thus a fellow of some importance in our great city and owed a degree of respect.

'Stop your whining,' Bagnall snapped, which was a travesty. I do not whine.

'What is happening? What do you want?' I said. 'I have nothing here. This is all Vanderstilt's stuff. I have no money here, nothing of value, so if you were planning to . . .'

I found myself suddenly sitting in a seat which the tor had thrust at me from behind. As I sat, he lashed a rope about my upper body, then arms and legs, until I was trussed as effectively as a prisoner in a gibbet. I could not move.

'Now, master,' Bagnall said, and there was a deeply unpleasant look on his face. 'We know who you work for, and we know what you do. So when you decided to kill Vanderstilt . . .'

'What? *No!* I have a pardon for that, and I didn't do it anyway!' I protested. A hand slapped my cheek, and almost knocked my head from my shoulders, I swear. It is fortunate that I have a robust frame.

'Shut up. We know what you did. Killing him, then my other servant. And murdering the girl as well – I suppose her death was understandable, if unnecessary.'

'Which girl? Wait! You mean little Alice? I had nothing to do with that! I thought *you* killed her!'

'Don't be ridiculous! Why'd I kill her?'

'I don't know, but Loughgren told me she was seen with another man that evening.'

'What else did you discuss with him?'

'Who? Loughgren? He told me to keep out of politics, and I have to admit, I—'

'What did he say about me?'

'You? Nothing. Why should he?'

'Are you truly so dim? Have I not told you that I am a loyal subject of the queen, and all I do is to protect her and her heirs?'

'Yes.'

'And Loughgren works for her sister.'

I opened my mouth to speak, but then hesitated with my mouth wide. This was, as they say, a conundrum. Suddenly some of Loughgren's words made rather more sense. He was keen to see Sir Edmund and his plots defeated, and he had been interested in talking to me until I stated that I was loyal to the queen. So Loughgren was also involved, I assumed, in working with Lady Elizabeth.

'He works for the queen's sister?' I said, more by way of saving myself further questioning while I absorbed this news.

'We know much. We're determined to protect the queen and her servants, and you are an agent of her enemies. We know all this.'

'*Eh?*'

'We know because Loughgren is an enemy. You were with him. You had been seen about his house before, and used his maid as the excuse for visiting Loughgren, didn't you? You will tell us all you know. We want to know who your confederates are, where they are, and what they planned?'

I heard a strange, high-pitched noise which I did not recognize at first. Then I realized it was me making the sound. Why? Because the door had opened and, as he spoke, the torturer from Queen Mary's palace at St James's entered. He gave me a sort of welcoming, but apologetic, smile, ducked his head, and began setting out tools on the hearthstone while I gibbered.

I spoke quickly and at length about my innocence of Vanderstilt's and Alice's deaths, and tried to explain that the troll had died while chasing me, a death of which I was entirely innocent, but it had no impact. Tom continued laying out his devices, humming to himself like a tailor working with his needle and thread. I have met many tailors who will sit cross-legged on their tables, working at their massive sheets of cloth, and they always hum like that. It drives me to distraction.

Today, I was already distracted enough.

It didn't help when Bagnall chuckled. 'You are good. I admit, if I didn't know better, I would think you were innocent. But you see, others ain't so easy to fool. You see Tom here? He's here to make sure you don't hold anything back. He'll make sure you tell us all you know.'

'But I've done *nothing*! I *know* nothing!'

'I have to admit, I didn't believe the stories about you. Some said you were an agent for the queen's enemies, and I didn't think you were clever enough. But then Vanderstilt died – the man who was informing us about everything to do with Sir Edmund, and we learned he lived here, in your house; then we learned that Alice, the housemaid to George Loughgren, met you regularly. Things began to hang together. As you will with your confederates.'

'It wasn't a plot! I adored Alice!' I blurted.

It was not the right thing to say. His face hardened, and he leaned forward in a thoroughly unpleasant manner. 'You were keen to harm anyone who supported the queen, weren't you? Just as you did Vanderstilt.'

'What reason would I have for murdering my tenant!' I wailed. Yes, I wailed. There comes a time when a man cannot continue to be rational in the face of such wilful stupidity, especially when a fellow like Tom is pensively setting out the tools of his trade. 'I didn't want to hurt Vanderstilt!'

'That's a shame,' he said. He glanced over his shoulder at Tom beside the hearth, where he was using bellows to make the coals gleam like the Devil's own furnaces. 'Well, we shall soon learn the truth.'

PART TEN

John Blount's Chronicle

TWENTY-ONE

Sunday 28th August

Since the Thursday, when I had visited the woman living opposite Jack's old house, I had enjoyed little success in my search for Jack Blackjack. I proceeded along those thoroughfares which I was aware he frequented, even travelling down the stews in the noisome district of the Bishop of Winchester where the whores congregated, but all was to no avail.

It eventually became obvious that the fellow was concealing himself deliberately. I knew full well that when Jack decided to take advantage of his own nondescript appearance, he could all but evaporate and disappear as quickly as morning mist over the Thames. Thus it was that I resorted to placing certain watchers over both his houses, and returned to my own home and paperwork.

It was not until the Saturday that I began to wonder whether there might be more to the matter. Accordingly, I set my papers aside and exercised my intellect to consider the facts.

First, I had heard of the flight of de Vere, and I suspected that there would soon be news of his complicity in a plot against the Crown. Meanwhile, the Dutchman renting Jack's house had disappeared: this could be the result of a mere waylaying, his own realization of the danger into which he had fallen by supplying weapons to de Vere, leading to his own flight, or it could be that there was some aspect of matters which he had discovered which related to the third issue: the maid of Loughgren's. It was at least certain in her case that she had been murdered.

I reflected on these matters all day, and it was Sunday morning, as I awoke, that I decided to take action.

First, I made my way to Jack's houses. Cutpurse had been installed at the first, in a doorway from where he had a good view of both Jack's old property and the door of Saul and Susan Appleby's home. Sam Cutpurse could tell me that Jack had not appeared. The only man to visit the house was a merchant-looking type, who had knocked on the door the day before, and spoken hurriedly with the ragged bottler in the doorway. He had tried to get closer to listen to their conversation, but the language was unknown to him. From that I deduced that the two were, like Peter, Hollanders.

My mind turned to Lewan de Beaulieu. There were not so very many Dutch in London, and from Cutpurse's description, it could well have been him. What would he have wanted with the house from where Jack's tenant had disappeared?

It also led me to wondering about the other man who was involved with de Beaulieu: Loughgren. All appeared to me as enmeshed circles, like a good chain, in which the various links represented the people. There was Loughgren and de Beaulieu; there was de Vere and Geoffrey Vanderstilt. But then there was Peter, who was somehow connected, so it appeared, with de Beaulieu, while Alice was maid to Loughgren. And about all these six was Jack, who was somehow tilting at them all, while denying any responsibility.

All this was in my mind as I walked to his new house, where I enquired about movements, and to my surprise, I learned that Jack had been there, and had only recently departed. It was enough to make me curse, but as my intelligencer pointed out, he had sent an urchin to fetch me when he saw Jack, and it was hardly his fault if I was not at home when the boy arrived.

Bitter, I left him with instructions to fetch me as soon as Jack was to appear again, and on a whim I strode up to Loughgren's house. It was already past noon, and my stomach was rumbling, which only served to add to my already failing temper.

It was plain enough that the family was attending Mass. A maidservant opened the door to me, a scared little chit who gazed at me with eyes so wide, I feared they must spring free if she were to sneeze.

'Which church does your master attend?'

She indicated the great block of stone with a spire reaching to the sky, and I made my way there, standing outside it with the chains of people still rattling through my brain.

* * *

I soon saw Loughgren up at the front, and I stood in the doorway as the service was conducted, watching the congregants make their way to the altar rail, take the crumb of bread and sip of wine, and thence return to their pews.

Loughgren did not rise immediately as the service ended, but sat thoughtfully in his pew, boxed in from the others all about. He had a pleasant seat nearest the altar, surely a proof of his wealth, and his family sat with him, while two henchmen occupied stools at either end of the pew.

Eventually, when the majority of the congregation had left, he deigned to rise. The nearer servant opened the door to the pew for him, and he stepped out, closely followed by his wife, two sons of some fifteen and seventeen summers, and a daughter. He led the way to me, where I stood by the door.

His eyes met mine, and I saw a flicker of resentment as I stepped forward. 'Master Loughgren? May I speak with you for a moment?'

'I do not conduct business on a Sunday,' he said firmly.

'I am not here to discuss trade,' I said.

There was steel in my voice, I gauge, because he gave me a disdainful glance, but then nodded. He sent his family on their way with one henchman, but retained the other.

'Well? Is this about Alice again? I am sorry she is gone, but why the interest in my maid?'

'I have the pleasure of working with the queen's officials in some matters,' I said. 'I understand you lost your maid only a short while after taking delivery of weapons from Master Lewan de Beaulieu.'

'Yes, that is true. It was a sorry loss,' he said. 'She was a good worker, and a personable young woman. I hope the queen's officers will soon find the man responsible.'

'These weapons: it would seem a large consignment that you have been collecting,' I said, and watched him closely.

'What of it?' he said coolly. There was no indication that he found the question alarming.

'There are some who might wonder why a man in your position would require so many?'

'That is easy. Some few are for the defence of my properties here in the city. This is not a safe place for a man, any more than it was for poor Alice. Then again, I am a merchant, and I achieved a good price based on purchasing a larger quantity than I need. I intend to sell the rest to others who are concerned about their security. You should consider some for your own protection.'

'Why should I need protecting, I wonder?' I said. This sounded very much like a threat.

'At times of danger, all may consider that self-preservation is of concern. There are many footpads in a city like London.'

'You know of many such attacks?'

He gave a sneer. 'I have heard that many asking too many questions can find themselves at risk. Especially near the docks.'

It was tempting to punch him in the face. The man who tried to waylay me had said a man called 'Luffrin', or something similar, had ordered the two men to attack me. 'How well do you know Lewan de Beaulieu?' I asked after a moment.

'Why should I help you?'

'I am working with the authority of the Crown,' I said sharply. It was not strictly true, but he was not to know that. In any case, it worked.

He chewed at his lips for a while, glaring at me, and then reluctantly said, 'He is a well-respected merchant. I have worked with him several times on similar trades.'

'Another merchant in the city has gone missing – had you heard? A fellow named Vanderstilt. He too was importing weapons.'

'For whom?'

'Sir Edmund de Vere. He had planned to use them against the queen, but his plans have been sent awry.'

'Have they, indeed? That will be reassuring to many,' he said. He sucked at his teeth for a moment. 'If you know of Sir Edmund, there is a little information you may not be aware of: this Vanderstilt was planning two further, larger shipments to Sir Edmund and his confederates. I believe this might have precip-itated *unfortunate* consequences for the queen and others.'

'Naturally you told the queen's officers about this.'

He smiled cynically. 'I informed those I considered most able to thwart de Vere's plans. Sir Thomas Parry and others in posi-tions of authority.'

That was when I found myself paying close attention. 'Sir Thomas, you say?'

'Aye.'

PART ELEVEN

Susan Appleby's Testimony

TWENTY-TWO

Sunday 28th August

Yes, I saw them. I had been at home some little while, when my groom called me to the door. There, I soon saw two men: one a vast slab of a man, the other more like a small greyhound, but without the elegance. He was a lanky, wiry, rather emaciated-looking fellow. I took one look at him and could hardly avoid curling my lip. He was not the sort of man who would impress any woman with a heartbeat.

As I watched, I saw the big man punch Jack, then lift his arms behind his back, and poor Jack cried out, just before he was pushed violently to his own door, and thrust inside.

It was enough: I could hardly leave a neighbour to be beaten and abused by two knaves in the street! I hurried to instruct my steward to go and bring the grooms and others. We had a fair-sized complement in the house, and we could muster five others, and soon we had them all, some armed with clubs, the cook and his boy with knives, and that was when I went to Jack's door and told my steward to knock.

I heard an unearthly scream as he struck the timbers. At that sound, I knew that Jack was in mortal danger. I told the cook's boy to give his knife to a groom, and to run as swiftly as his legs would carry him to Aldgate and raise the hue and cry.

Even as he was pelting away up the road, the door opened just a little, and as it did, my steward thrust it wide, and we were inside, pushing the servant away from the door and back towards the kitchen.

In the parlour, where Jack had entertained me so lavishly on past occasions, I saw the enormous man holding Jack by the shoulders. It was Jack who had screamed, and even as I looked, I saw that a little fellow with a mild smile on his face was standing at Jack's feet with a red-hot iron in his hands. Another man, the skinny fellow I had seen in the road, was just behind him, gaping at our sudden appearance.

There was, just for a moment, a distinct pause while the two groups of men stood staring at each other. Then, with a gurgle, the man with the iron in his hand suddenly dropped the hot metal. His eyebrows rose in a sort of inverted V over his nose, and he clutched at his cods, where the toe of Jack's boot had just met his softer parts. There was a subtle intake of breath from three of my own men, and my steward winced at the sight, and then the fighting started.

Jack and I were spectators, of course. He was bound to a chair, enveloped in cords that held his arms and breast to the chair, while I, of course, as a mere woman, could do little. My men streamed into the room, two to the whippet, three to the giant, and they hammered and beat at them until the giant was on the floor, a perplexed frown on his face, and the other man was snoring from the cudgel blow to his brow. He would have a lump the size of a goose's egg there before long, I judged.

When he too was bound, I entered, and inflicted my own kick to the torturer on the ground. He gave a protesting whine, which only made me kick him again, but harder.

While the trio were held, I called to the steward and demanded wine, and then went to untie the bonds holding poor Jack. He was in a terrible state, bruised, with a mark on his forearm where the vile little man had burned him, but fortunately that was the total of his injuries just then. It would have gone badly for the torturer had there been more. As it was, I administered a fresh kick to those parts already injured by Jack, and left the torturer squirming.

'Jack, my darling,' I whispered, and he would have kissed me, I think, but for my warning finger on his lips. After all, I did have all my servants about me, and there are limits to how much I trust any of them, let alone a group like that. 'Your poor arm!'

'Yes,' he said. There were tears of gratitude in his eyes, I saw, and I was pleased to think that I had saved him from a terrible death. The look I cast at the others in that room, those who had captured and tormented my Jack, was not friendly. It also occurred to me that Jack would enjoy expressing his gratitude to me later, when we were alone.

I called for the steward again, but there was no answering call nor sign of his approach. Jack, now standing, rubbing at his wrists, took another kick at his tormentor, and then stood glowering furiously at him.

'So, Master Blackjack, what now?' the other wretch said. He said it in a sly, nasty tone that made me want to kick him instead. His head looked sorely battered, it should be admitted, but the man could speak levelly and calmly. Just now he had eyes only for Jack. 'You know for whom I work – the queen's chief secretary, Master John Boxall. Release me now, in the name of the queen, and submit.'

Jack curled his lip. He looked quite in command of himself and the situation, even as his poor scalded arm must have been agony. 'I had nothing to do with harming Alice. I have an alibi for the day she died, which I can confirm for you with a witness,' he said. His tone made me shiver slightly – I hoped he was not going to mention my name, for that could lead to a great deal of embarrassment for me with my husband, but I need not have been concerned. He continued, 'I was with a companion, Piers, who can confirm I was with him at the Cardinal's Hat all that day and evening.'

'Where is the man?' I said, after shouting again for the steward.

'I know where the wine is stored,' Jack said. 'I will fetch it.'

I went into the hallway with him, and when he passed through into the kitchen, I accompanied him, leaving my servants to monitor the three accomplices. The constable should soon arrive and take charge of them, but I confess that the excitement had left me feeling distinctly stirred, and as Jack went to the cellar door, I grabbed him by his jack's open lapels, and forced my lips upon his. We had little time, and we quickly hurried down the dark staircase into the cellar, where I prepared myself, and he pulled aside his codpiece.

It was not the most satisfactory of couplings, but neither of us wanted to delay. Although as we rutted there, my back to the rather damp wall, I heard a sudden loud thunder – someone was striking the door with a club, or some similar weapon.

'Jack, *Jack*!' I cried, but to no avail. He continued in his urgent strivings, and I confess that I was about to succumb again myself, when I grew aware of an unpleasant odour.

You often find such smells in dank cellars in London. No

doubt, I thought, there was a cesspit near the house's foundations, or perhaps a rat had died and was adding its own noxious fumes to the atmosphere in there, but the simple truth was that rather than enjoying rattling his cods, I became discomforted. I mentioned this to my lover, but he seemed impervious to my increasingly agitated attempts to persuade him to cease, until I slapped his face. Twice. That succeeded at diminishing his ardour, and he held his cheek with a hurt expression while I extricated myself from his clutches and allowed my skirts to fall to a more decorous position.

'What did you do that for?'

'Someone is at the door,' I said by way of explanation. 'And what is that stink?'

'I don't know! Why'd you hit me?'

I persuaded him, by degrees, to adjust his codpiece and go to seek a candle. Something, I felt sure, was not right, and the sooner we had drawn off a jug or two of wine and could leave this foul chamber, the better.

Upstairs, there was mayhem.

PART TWELVE

John Blount's Chronicle Continues . . .

TWENTY-THREE

A s soon as the door was opened, I thrust it hard, and Cutpurse and two of my men barged their way in.

I had stopped at Jack's new house to collect Raphe and others, and now had hurried back to Jack's old house to fetch the last intelligencer. He had been able to tell me that Jack was once more in attendance. He had arrived with two others, and shortly thereafter his neighbour had entered with a party of other men.

Now I was to see how many had invaded his home and threatened to harm my servant. The steward of Mistress Appleby glowered at me when I marched in, but I had little time for his better feelings. Instead I went to Bagnall and stood over him. He was bound hand and foot like his accomplices.

'I fear you are in serious trouble, master,' I said. 'This city takes house-breaking very seriously.'

'I didn't break in! Jack Blackjack owns this place, and he invited us.'

The steward from over the way sneered at him then. 'When we came in, he –' he pointed to the oldest man, who lay beside the fire, clutching at his cods – 'he was torturing Blackjack. I doubt he invited them here so that they might assault him.'

'I was only acting on the command of my fellows here,' the old man whined. His voice was high and taut with conviction – or pain.

'Where is Jack now?' I demanded.

That was when we all heard the unearthly scream. The steward burst out, 'My *lady*!' and ran to the kitchen, and I told my men to wait for me as I hurried after him.

PART THIRTEEN

Susan Appleby's Testimony Continues . . .

TWENTY-FOUR

Of course, when Jack saw it and realized that it was a hand protruding from the soil of the floor, the shock was enough to make him give a cry of horror. It was immediately clear what caused the odour. It was Jack's tenant. Soon the scent of death had that of vomit added to the horrible chamber.

First my steward, then Master Blount appeared in the doorway at the top of the stairs, my steward hurrying down the treads to me, pushing Jack away in defence of my poor, failed chastity. Jack responded by again heaving, and depositing a portion of his breakfast on my man's boots. He gave a sound expressive of disgust, and would have soundly beaten Jack, had I not gripped his fist and remonstrated with him.

Meanwhile Master Blount was kneeling at the side of the body. 'You!' he said to my steward. 'Fetch two men with spades, then the coroner and the constable. This fellow needs to be exhumed and inquest held before he must be taken to church and have the last rites read over him, poor soul.'

To assist in the command, I pushed at the fellow, but not unkindly. His devotion to me deserved better treatment, no matter what he thought of Jack, and I was, it is true, impressed that he had thrown himself to me as soon as he'd heard the sound of Jack's horror.

I took Jack upstairs and placed him in a seat in the kitchen to recover from his puking, then told my men what we had discovered down in the cellar.

It was Bagnall who was first to speak. 'Here? Vanderstilt is here? How could Blackjack have brought him here?'

I held my temper under a tight rein. This man considered himself intelligent and quick-witted, and yet here he was with all the evidence placed before him, and still he could not move his mind from the road on which it had embarked. I despair of men.

'Could Jack have been responsible for a man here? No. He could not. What, do you think he entered, carrying the dead man over his shoulder? Would that be easy? No. Do you think he opened the doors here with his own keys, and managed to do so with such surreptitious care that his entry went unnoticed? I doubt that too. Would he be able to carry the body here, walking the streets, without anyone seeing him? Unlikely. And how would he know that his tenant was leaving the house that day, where he was going, and what time the man would return, so that Jack could tell what would be the best time for him to come and launch his attack?'

'He might have met the Dutchman by chance.'

'Late in the evening? Jack happened on the fellow up near the Tower and decided to execute him? Or came here and chose to murder his tenant? Why should he do so? What benefit would he attain from such an act?'

Bagnall had the grace not to continue to promote his confused and frankly risible assumption of Jack's guilt after I said that.

'Who did kill him, then?'

'Who could have installed him in the cellar of this house? Who would have known where his money lay? Who would have had the opportunity? Who would have been trusted by him?'

I could see that my groom was considerably brighter than the man Bagnall. He had an expression of great understanding, and I began to think that, were Jack to disappear one day, this fellow might be a suitable replacement. He had the sort of elegant good looks that I enjoy, and his intellect was plainly of a similar level to my own.

'Do you truly not comprehend yet?' I said.

Bagnall was still frowning.

'His own servant! The man who has demonstrated his guilt by fleeing even now! Who else?' I said, with great restraint.

'Him?' Bagnall looked shocked. 'Petty treason? But the man was his servant!'

'You have never known a servant to prove faithless before?'

That was when the fresh knock came at the door, and soon the house was filled with constables and members of the other houses in the street, all come to gawp and enjoy the sights of other men's misfortune.

I left them to it and went back to the kitchen.

Jack was seated at the table. His face still bore the look of horror that had dawned at the sight of his tenant in his shallow grave, and remained a green hue. I tried to entice him to think of something else, but soon, I confess, I gave up, and my mind turned to reflections of the build and appearance of the groom. What was his name? I would have to find out. Not that it was a safe venture to risk my reputation with a servant of my own household – but it was an appealing daydream.

'He was here all along,' Jack said. 'Peter killed him!'

There was a clattering of shovels and a muffled expletive from the cellar, mingled with shouting and blows from my parlour as the constable and his men took Bagnall and his confederates and carried them off to gaol. I was glad when the door slammed behind them all.

'Yes, he was plainly not sure what to do with the body,' I said. 'I would think that he would find it difficult to retrieve his master's corpse and carry it through the streets to conceal it somewhere else.'

Jack nodded. 'It's not so easy to move a dead body,' he said. He added, 'Or so I've heard.'

'I don't suppose it is,' I said. He was gradually regaining a little colour in his face. That disappeared as the three men from the cellar appeared in the doorway, bearing a sheet on which Jack's tenant was lying. As they left the cellar door, they had to turn to go to the hall, and as they did, the body slumped and fell from the sheet. The stench of decay was appalling, and I could see that the hand had been nibbled by rats.

Jack took one look, and was promptly sick once more.

PART FOURTEEN

Jack's Tale Continues . . .

TWENTY-FIVE

Sunday 28th August

That afternoon was not one I was likely to forget in a hurry. After the interview with Loughgren, to then be grabbed and once again threatened with torture by the hideous Tom, I was already exhausted, without having discovered the body in my cellar. But then, to see the proof of Vanderstilt's servant's crime, was horrible. It made me think what I would have looked like, had Tom been able to spend more time with me.

Thank the Lord for Susan!

I was careful, after we had discovered the body, to try to keep poor Susan from seeing Vanderstilt's corpse. The sight must have been distressing to an innocent woman like her, and I managed, I think, to shield her from the sight, until the clumsy trio of labourers brought Vanderstilt up from the chamber below. Naturally, I was resilient, being a sensible, experienced fellow, but the scene must have been difficult for a frail woman like Susan.

And yes, it was a gruesome sight, with proof of rat attacks at fingers and stomach. A fellow may see such things occasionally, when a body is found in a street or alleyway, and such things may well be still worse, if a passing hog or sow has decided to break their fast on a corpse in passing, but this was somehow much worse.

John Blount was organizing men, deploying guards to take Bagnall away with his unpleasant companions, arranging for the coroner to come and view Vanderstilt's corpse, and generally getting in everyone's way. He was a thoroughly officious fellow in this mood.

I hastened to take Susan from the house as the three servants deployed to bring Vanderstilt back up began arguing over who was responsible for dropping him, and laughing at my reaction when I berated them for offending the lady. They appeared to assume that I was feeling queasy, but of course it was nothing more than simple disgust at their language in front of a lady.

No, I will not likely remove the events of that afternoon quickly from my mind. Especially later, when I had deposited Susan at her home and could begin to make my way homewards. It was not a long walk, but I confess that I felt considerably the worse for my experiences. My arm was throbbing, as if the Devil himself had touched me there, and I was sure that I would have a dreadful scar. As it was, whenever I passed a horse trough, I dunked my poor arm into it to try to dull the pain a little. It worked – momentarily – but as soon as I moved off, the pain returned with full force.

I returned to St Helen's, and was glad to see that the dog was not inside. I could hear Hector barking outside, and when I entered, slamming the door behind me, I was glad to be able to lean against the door with my eyes closed for some moments. Yes, my arm was burning still, and my head ached, and I had a strange nausea in my belly that was disconcerting, but at least here I could relax – and my nightmares were over. The plot of Sir Edmund had been thwarted, and I had received the gratitude of the queen for that. The danger of Perkin Bagnall had been averted, so far as I could tell. Loughgren must soon know that I was in fact on his side in the matter of politics, since Master Blount promised to advise him of my role in the service of Lady Elizabeth. Yes, all things considered, I felt my problems were soon to be over.

I sighed with relief, opened my eyes and began to walk to my parlour, but I had taken little more than a single step into the room when I saw a rather curious sight. There, sitting in my chair, was Raphe. Naturally, I was about to berate the young fool for his overweening pride and foolishness in stealing my chair, when I realized there was something wrong – it lay in the warning look in his eyes, in the apparent bindings holding his wrists to the arms of my chair, and finally in the crunching sensation at the back of my head as something struck it with full force.

I think it is fair to say that I did not sink to my knees in a delicate or sophisticated manner. Rather, it felt as though I dived headfirst into an enormous pit that opened before me.

* * *

Yes, I have had experience of waking from blows to the head. Yes, they have invariably been unpleasant awakenings, and yes, recovering from this blow was bad enough without the leering expression of the old servant peering down at me. It was Peter, the haggard old sinner, who was never an appealing sight, but never was a sight less welcome than when recovering from a strike like that, and the fact is more especially true when recovering consciousness only to learn that my hands had been bound together, my ankles also, and that the fellow responsible was now standing over me with a hammer in his fist.

Raphe was still in my chair, but there was a rasping sound from behind me, and when I strained my head, painfully, to peer in that direction, I was taken by the sight of Lewan de Beaulieu.

He grinned, shaking his head. 'You have cost me much, master!'

'Me? What have *I* done?'

'What have you *not* done?'

'You were selling arms to Loughgren so he could raise an army and threaten the queen, weren't you? And then, no doubt, you would have insisted on a position of power in the government, where you could make more and more money, and then . . .'

'You really are a poor fool, when it comes to matters requiring thought, aren't you, Master Blackjack? Peter, I think you should go. There is no need for you to remain.'

The old servant nodded grimly and dropped his hammer. It accidentally landed on my shin, which was painful, but I was able to stifle any signs of pain. A fellow has to keep up appearances.

'Do stop the whining. I am sure he didn't mean to hit you again,' de Beaulieu said. 'And by the time everyone can come and find you here, he will have left the country.'

'He was working for you!' I managed, bravely concealing the agony in my shin.

'Of course. I was happy to assist young Vanderstilt at first. After all, he was the son of a friend of mine, but I fear he grew too greedy – for his own good, as well as everyone else's.'

'I don't understand,' I said, I think reasonably.

'It is very simple. I am a merchant who depends on trade with your country. In the past, I have happily worked with your merchants and brought wealth to the city as well as my own pockets. But I fear Vanderstilt decided to take more than was justified. He worked with those who sought to sell your country to the Spanish, and that I could not allow.'

'How did . . .?'

'How did I know? I installed Peter as his steward and bottler when he first came here to London. It seemed an ideal scheme to ensure that Vanderstilt had an experienced fellow to help run his affairs. And of course it allowed me to keep an eye on his business. Fortunately, as it turned out, because Peter was able to warn me of dealings that Vanderstilt had.'

'So you could see that his ships were held up in Holland,' I said cuttingly.

He chuckled. 'I fear, not. That was all at the request of your Secretary of State, Boxall. He heard that de Vere was plotting to raise forces, and he saw to it that the ships were delayed while he laid his own plans to foil the rebellion. I was happy to help.'

'Why?'

'My friend, I am no Catholic. The Spanish killed my father during their wars to suppress the free peoples of Amsterdam and the low countries. You think I would happily assist those who sought to give the throne of England to the Spanish king? No. It became clear that de Vere was a danger to all – to those who trade, those who wish to live free, and all others.'

'So you had Peter kill Vanderstilt?'

'No. I would not do this. But he overheard conversations, and he learned that Vanderstilt meant to help the Spaniards. He told me, and at the same time I learned from a friend in Amsterdam, that he had been recruiting mercenaries. De Vere was hoping to bring a force from Holland, and Vanderstilt was aiding him. That was why I decided to inform certain men; men of power, who work for those who do not whole-heartedly embrace the Catholic Church. I believe one of these paid Peter to commit the deed. I had no part in this, but I am happy to have supported those who are on the side of righteousness and the true religion.'

My head was swimming, and not only from the blow inflicted by Peter. 'But . . . what of Alice? The maid working for Loughgren? Did he kill her too?'

'No. She was an unfortunate victim. I understand Master Boxall had been concerned that you could have been involved in the rebellion, and he had her followed and questioned.'

'So, who killed her?'

He looked at me very straight. 'You should ask your master that question. It was not me or my man. It was Boxall's men.'

PART FIFTEEN

Jack's Tale Ends

TWENTY-SIX

Friday 2nd September

My wounds were not severe. Five days later, I was sitting comfortably on my bed, recovering from my exertions, when the door was opened. I had thought that it might be Susan, who had threatened to come and ease my sufferings, but soon, when I heard the loud voices, and then the clumping of steps on my staircase, I knew I was not to receive her careful ministrations. A pity, because I felt that a quick mattress-walloping would do me the power of good.

'Still abed?' Master John Blount sneered as he entered.

'I have been grievously injured,' I said piteously, holding up my sore and bandaged arm as evidence. I had paid good money for the attendance of a competent physician, and although he had made me faint when he drew blood, at least he had confirmed that I had many wounds and deserved to rest and recuperate.

'You look well,' George Loughgren said, entering behind my master.

'Better than my nephew,' Blount said drily.

'What will happen to me?' I asked. This was, after all, the thought uppermost in my mind.

'You? Nothing. The queen has heard from Boxall that you have saved her from sedition and rebellion at the hands of Sir Edmund; Lady Elizabeth has heard that you saved *her* from the attempts of Bagnall to depose her as heir to the throne; you have been pardoned for the murder of Vanderstilt and the maid – so your life can continue as before,' Blount said.

'But Bagnall – he can speak his tale to the queen and make things difficult.'

'Ah,' Blount said. He looked thoughtful.

'What?'

Loughgren peered at me. 'He is no threat to you. Sadly, he failed to escape your house.'

'He died at the hands of Peter, Vanderstilt's servant,' Blount said firmly.

'No, he was alive when I left the place,' I said. 'Peter had already left.'

'I think if you test your memory, you will discover that you are mistaken,' Loughgren said, equally firmly. He was quite right. Suddenly I was quite convinced that Bagnall *had* died there.

'Besides,' Loughgren said, and now his face was quite blank, devoid of all emotion, if you understand me. 'He is not to be missed. It is clear that it was he who captured poor Alice and murdered her. He thought she might be able to tell him about my shipments of arms. As it was, he learned nothing.'

'How can you be so sure?' I said bitterly. Because, yes, I was bitter. Her death was a shameful, miserable crime. She was pure happiness, and did not deserve such an end.

'We have Tom's word on it,' Blount said.

That thought made me shiver. I suddenly did not want to know more.

However, there was more for me to hear. Such as, Loughgren's role as an intelligencer for Lady Elizabeth. He had been working for Sir Thomas Parry, collecting weapons for the lady to supply to her men, and to ensure that, should there be a dispute about the succession, she would have the means to defend her rights. Loughgren was one of those men whom Sir Thomas had made use of, and as always, he had not told others about his man. John Blount and Loughgren had discovered each other's part in Parry's scheming.

They departed soon after that. It was, I suppose, the reason for their visit. They had come to advise me that I was safe, that the story across London was that the servant – a known, evil lunatic, who had slain his master, slaughtered an innocent maid, and then, when accosted by Master Bagnall, had cut his throat as well – had died trying to flee to Holland.

It was all too easy to believe. I mean, who would doubt that a killer who has once enjoyed the pleasure of murder would not wish to experience that thrill again? And this man had taken three lives – or so the story stated. Except I was convinced that the foul old man was even now enjoying a comfortable retirement in Amsterdam at de Beaulieu's expense.

I was angry at first. After all, it meant that the death of little Alice was relegated to that of a poor wench who was merely incidental. She had been such a vibrant, sweet-natured little thing, that ending the story of her life in this mean-spirited manner seemed a disgrace. It was a foul way to end things for her.

But a moment's reflection made me reconsider. For one thing, it clearly ended Bagnall in a happy manner. If he had been allowed to live, the likelihood was, my life would have remained in danger. Perhaps he might have discovered who my real mistress was. He might have accused me, baselessly of course, of being an enemy to the queen. His death was, obviously, most convenient. Not only for me, but for Lady Elizabeth as well.

And there, of course, matters ended. Except stories do not end so completely and smoothly, of course. For soon the realm was to suffer fresh conniptions. First, the queen's long-anticipated birthing never occurred. The poor woman, having yet again suffered all the grief and pain of pregnancy, was forced once more to endure the anguish of discovering that there was no child to bring peace to her unhappy soul. And shortly thereafter, she succumbed to a disease that brought an end to her reign.

And that meant that my life was to turn topsy-turvy once more.

But that story must wait for my next chronicle.

PART SIXTEEN

John Blount's Chronicle Ends

TWENTY-SEVEN

Thursday 17th November

I t was with a sense of trepidation that I heard the news of the death of the queen.

Obviously, for a man like me, this heralded a period of reorganization. With Mary in her coffin, Elizabeth would return to her rightful place as the monarch in waiting, and that must mean elevation for many of my colleagues who had worked so long and hard for this long-desired outcome. My own master, Sir Thomas Parry, would no doubt find himself in an advantageous position, and I could hope that he would take me along with him.

Jack Blackjack had been enormously useful in the years immediately before the coronation of our princess. He had smoothed the way for many of our lady's enemies to be removed from her path. He was, I knew, a most competent operative.

And yet . . . there was a curious niggling doubt in my mind as I made my way to church that morning. There would be ructions, were the princess not to be conciliatory and gracious. It was always possible that a fresh grouping might seek to remove Elizabeth from her throne. There were many who feared a fresh female monarch. All those who supported the Holy Roman Church, all those who had invested their souls in Spanish politics, and all those who sought to enrich themselves, all had their own reasons, potentially, to seek the abdication or removal of Queen Elizabeth, and replace her with a man, someone who could lead the country through the troublesome shoals that beckoned.

We would have need of Jack Blackjack in the coming years.

It was curious to think it, but it was not so very long ago that I had wondered about his value. I had thought, perhaps, he was less able than I had first assumed. I had wondered whether he was truly a dedicated assassin, or whether I had been misled. Of course, he was clever to put on a show of anxiety and concern, but at bottom, he was a cool, level-headed killer.

I was sure of that.